enjoy it!

Roy Siegel

Goodie One Shoes

An Emily's Place Mystery

ROZ SIEGEL

HILLIARD HARRIS

P.O. Box 275
Boonsboro, Maryland 21713-0275

This novel is a work of fiction. Names, characters, places and incidents either are the product of the author's imagination or are used fictitiously. Any resemblance to actual persons, living or dead, events, or locales is entirely coincidental.

Goodie One Shoes Copyright © 2010
By Roz Siegel

All rights reserved. No part of this book may be reproduced or transmitted in any form or by any means, electronic or mechanical, including photocopying, recording, or by any information storage and retrieval system, without the written permission of the Publisher, except where permitted by law.

First Edition—2010
ISBN 1-59133-311-3
978-1-59133-311-1

Book Design: S. A. Reilly
Cover Illustration © S. A. Reilly
Manufactured/Printed in the United States of America
2010

To my grandchildren: Hallie, Evan, Willa, Josh, and Eli—
May you always remember that the first step in trying out for anything
is simply showing up.

Acknowledgements

Where does inspiration come from? A casual comment; an intimate revelation; a sudden recollection; a neighborhood's vibes and vitality. To all who aided in the genesis of this book, consciously or accidently, I say Thanks! Thanks! Thanks!

Special thanks to: The love-of-my-life, my husband Lloyd, without whom my experiences on the Upper West Side would have been entirely different; my ever-observant son Randy and daughter-in-law Maren who often asserted, "An Upper West Side woman is like no one else on the planet"; my always supportive daughter Janine and son-in-law Larry who loved the stories I wrote for their children and continued to encourage me to write others; my dear friend Sue Cohen whose father did, in fact, own a shoe store; Emily Putterman-Handler, whose awesome shoe-making classes have become a living legend; Maryanne Eccles, former Editor of the Mystery Book Club, who taught me the pleasure of a good mystery; Miranda DeKay whose bird may one day write his own memoir; Al Zuckerman, my agent, who took a shaggy dog and not only gave him a haircut and a collar, but found him a home as well; my editor and publisher, Stephanie Reilly, for all her hard work and enthusiasm for this work; and last, but certainly not least, Theodore Dreiser, whose steak-seduction scene in SISTER CARRIE should never be underestimated.

Chapter 1

<small>Wooden platform shoes called Chopines were reputedly invented by Venetian husbands to keep their wives from straying. The style was endorsed by the Catholic Church because it inhibited other sinful behavior like dancing.</small>

A Jimmy Choo Sandal. A Manolo Blahnik mule; a Sergio Rossi slide, a Prada sliver-heeled boot. As magic as Cinderella's glass slipper. Even when they don't fit, they can determine your life—or end it.

You can tell a lot about a person from their shoes. You can see right off if a woman is spending more on her shoes than groceries. If she is careful about life and shines her shoes, or has a scattery, slipshod character and wears her cream-colored high heels in the rain. You can tell if she is daring, from the shade of hot pink on her feet—or shy and simpering, sloshing around in misshapen flats. If a lady of a certain age, as I like to describe myself, wants to try on a pair of Jimmy Choo three inch heels, I would bet she either just got divorced or became a widow. Either way, she is looking for a new man.

I know these things because I own a shoe store on Broadway and 98th Street in Manhattan. I didn't always have the store; it's a second career. But selling shoes is in my blood. My father had a shoe store on Franklin Avenue in Brooklyn for twenty-five years. He had higher hopes for me.

I tried. Even went to graduate school and got a Ph.D in English. Taught part-time at Hunter College for years, twenty to be exact, all the years I was married. Married the "right guy" too. A lawyer who made his living arguing. And he was good at it. So good at it, he was the District Attorney for the Bronx for ten years.

After Larry and I split, I found that Henry James and Geoffrey Chaucer didn't generate enough revenue to live on. Not unless you were lucky enough to get tenure and that didn't seem to come my way.

Anyway, to make a long story short, after I found out about Larry and the Russian girl I decided I wasn't cut out for marriage either. My father and mother were dead, so there wasn't anyone left to disappoint.

I moved out of our fancy co-op on Central Park West—Larry went nuts when he realized that I had thrown all his hand-carved chess pieces one by one out the window of our 15th floor apartment—and disappeared with no forwarding address. I found a little ground floor—some might call it basement—apartment in a Brownstone on West 92nd Street. It was only two rooms but I had a share of the garden and a neighbor who invited me for lasagna every Thursday night. It felt good to be free. The truth was I didn't want anything more from Larry—especially money. I wanted to try life on my own.

So I was walking back from leading a "reader's group" for a bunch of wealthy women over on the East Side and trying to figure out how to pay the rent without meeting the fate of Lily Bart or Sister Carrie, when I passed a For Rent sign on a small shoe store on Broadway, just a few blocks from my new apartment.

The walls had peeling flower wallpaper and the carpet looked like an old horse blanket—kind of dirty brown with lots of worn spots. But the thing that made me fall in love was the smell—a musty smell that could only come from years of slowly seeping water damage mixed with the sweat of first generation immigrants trying to eke out a living. All of it valiantly half-smoothed in some pine-smelling deodorant that I had last encountered when I visited my grandma at the nursing home. The door creaked—there was actually a bell that clanged when I pushed it open—and all the shoes I could make out on display were shoes my mother would have worn. Tom Wolfe said you can't go home again, but I could sure try.

I may be a sentimentalist but I'm not entirely stupid. I could immediately see the possibilities in the large, but smudgy window on Broadway.

Suddenly, I knew I could do this. I knew all about shoes. Everyone I knew loved shoes. And everyone wore shoes. Even vegans who refused to wear leather. If ever there was a product that would always be a necessity, it was shoes.

And I could make it unique. I knew the Upper West Side. It's true that a creeping gentility had made inroads above 96th Street. But a couple of expensive, hi-rise condos do not a neighborhood make and the long time rent controlled, rent stabilized and rent subsidized population—from the barely employed musicians, artists, writers, actors and waiters, to the retired teachers, nurses and postmen, to the welfare mothers, assorted stragglers and *"luftmenchen,"* who somehow made a living as handymen, messengers, dish-washers, numbers runners, confidence men, seller's of second-hand anything, lap-dancers, escorts, and ladies of the night—the neighborhood hung on tightly to its seedy past.

I knew what women in the city still wanted. A place to try on shoes they could discuss with another woman. A place that smelled of comfort and hot coffee, where tears and laughter were equally acceptable, even welcomed.

I envisioned something like a Starbucks for shoe lovers. Why not?

I'll spare you the depressing details of negotiating for a lease and renovating the store to my vision.

So maybe it's not quite a Starbucks for Shoes. But Emily's Place began to attract neighborhood attention just the same.

Every shoe was discounted. I bought discontinued shoes, odd sizes, peculiar colors, samples, seconds, damaged, failed designs, just plain mistakes, shoes "that fell off the truck." I started a vintage shoe department, plus a shoe exchange that only cost ten dollars a month for membership.

The customers loved it.

Pretty soon I had a Shoe Supermarket. There was something for everyone—From Jimmy Choo to Keds. Four inch heels to ballet flats. Gold sequins to scuffed brown leather. Eight hundred dollars to $9.95. We had shoes for the wealthy women on Central Park West and the new condos on Upper Broadway, to the welfare mothers who filled the old tenements on the side streets. Customers began coming from The East Side across the Park. They even came from Brooklyn.

And of course, I got a certain amount of street traffic. Just women passing by who were attracted to my window display.

Did I mention that I always have a really special window display?

Saks and Bendel hire specialists to set up their windows and yet shoe stores always just have a few boots and shoes in the windows. So I asked one of my neighbors, Harold Shapiro, gay decorator to the stars, to give me a hand and he turned out to have lots of ideas. I admit his taste runs to zebra skin rugs and lots of rhinestones, but so what? This is Broadway honey, not Fifth Avenue.

We went with two full figure manikins wearing boots and feathers and not too much more. Depending on the season they might be wearing three inch silver sandals or leopard skin boots and some really smashing outfit like a backless red satin evening gown or a funky vintage fur with platform shoes.

I've been doing this now for three years and I can't say I'm rich, but I pay the rent and I have some fun. I found a whole new side of myself.

Don't get me wrong. I still love books. You can learn a lot from Isabel Archer and The Wife of Bath. But all those women are dead. You can't help realizing after a while that the conversation is rather one-sided.

And so with a little of this and a little of that, women found Emily's Place was somewhere they wanted to go. A respectable hangout where they could exchange books, shoes and most of all, wisdom. They knew which apartments were still rent-controlled; which cleaner always overcharged; who did the best hair-coloring in the neighborhood. And other, more intimate things like how to drive a man wild in bed—with and without shoes.

So much advice was exchanged in Emily's Place that I even started a blog.

So here I am thinking about the erotic possibilities of shoes and it occurs to me that I have no idea what-so-ever of the kind of shoes that Daisy Miller wore. Or Sister Carrie, or Emma or, for that matter, even Madam Bovary.

I mean there are plenty of food scenes in great literature—roast goose in Dickens; steak in Dreiser. Whole books have been written about famous eating scenes. But where are the shoes in all this?

So I'm happily imagining the kind of practical laced up boot with a small stacked heel that Jane Austen's Elizabeth Bennet might have worn when the phone rang.

"Hi!" Chirpy voice, I glanced at my watch—even as my stomach lurched—ten minutes before 11:00pm. My little sister Shana possibly in trouble again. Despite my best efforts, I feel a familiar ache in my gut. Shana means pretty in Yiddish and it says a lot about my sister. She lives in an Ashram in the Berkshires where she plays with crystals, focuses "chi," analyzes auras, utters strange chants and practices what she calls "holistic medicine" with an assortment of losers.

"So how is everything?" Shana asked me in her bubbly voice.

"Fine. Fine," I told her. "How are you?"

A slight pause as she cleared her throat. "Actually, I have a small problem."

Shana's problems are never small. That is, they may be small for Shana but not for everyone else. I felt my stomach lurch again.

"There's been an accident."

I sat down heavily on the chair near the phone. I pictured my beautiful little sister, blonde hair matted with blood. My hand griped the phone so tightly my knuckles turned white. "Are you all right?" I gasped.

"Yes, Yes. I'm fine. But the car is totaled."

I breathed a sigh of relief. "Oh, what happened?"

"Deepek hit a tree. It was just bad Karma."

"Deepek?"

"It's an Indian name. He's from India. I only need five thousand. There's a great little red convertible, only has seventy-five thousand miles, top doesn't work, but so what, Joe's Garage is holding it for me."

"Five thousand?" I say. "What about the insurance? You must have had insurance."

"Of course, I had insurance. It's the law. Problem is that Deepek was driving and he doesn't have a license."

"He doesn't have a license?"

"Well, actually he does have a license but he left it in India."

"Left it in India?"

"What is this, some kind of an echo chamber? Are you going to help me or what? I know you don't have a lot of money. I called Larry first but he hung up on me."

"You called Larry?" I was repeating again. I couldn't help it. Shana took my breath away. Before my Mom died she made me promise to take care of her. I've been trying my best ever since. "You asked him for money?"

"Of course I did," She laughed. "Just because you're too stupid to ask him for money doesn't mean I should suffer. He's still my brother-in-law."

"Shana. Shana. What are you doing with your life?" The words seemed to come from nowhere. I looked up at the ceiling. I was channeling our mother.

"I refuse to have this conversation with you. My life is perfectly fine. It was just bad Karma."

Some people have bad hair days. Shana has bad Karma days. I tried to get a grip on my emotions. I loved my sister, bad Karma or not.

"Are you sure you're all right?" I asked her.

She sighed. "I just have a broken arm. You'll send the money? You can't go anywhere in the Berkshires without a car."

I promised to send the money and hung up the phone.

And then, while I sat there, I heard the outside door knob rattle and turn. I sat motionless in my chair, hoping whoever it was would go away. My nerves were already frayed by my conversation with Shana. I felt edgy, scared. 11:00pm by the clock on the wall. Much too late for respectable visitors.

And then the door rattled once more, the mail slot in the door creaked and something came through and fell to the floor. It was a crumpled up brown paper bag with something stuffed inside. I stared at it for a few minutes, scared to touch it—scared to see what might be inside. A snake? An explosive dropped by a suicide bomber? A turd left by the shoe store across the street?

Whatever it was, it wasn't moving and it wasn't ticking so I figured it couldn't hurt me. But just to make sure, I went to the back closet and grabbed my umbrella. I gave the bag a few pokes with the umbrella. Nothing happened. Not even a rattle from the paper bag.

At this point I must admit I was getting tired and hungry so I held the umbrella in one hand and opened the bag with my foot.

Inside the bag was one red, high heeled shoe.

At first I was afraid to pick it up so I kicked it this way and that for a minute or two—just in case there was a scorpion stuffed in the toe. When I finally picked it up, I saw that the size was rubbed off but I'm pretty good at estimating size. It looked like a size eight Jimmy Choo. A slide with a three-inch spike heel. This season. Very chic. About eight hundred and fifty buckeroos if memory serves.

The toe was scuffed but the heel showed very little wear. The inside of the shoe was warm as if someone had just taken it off.

At that point, my curiosity got the best of me—mixed with a cup full of annoyance at the wanton waste of separating a pair of almost new Jimmy Choo shoes, rendering each shoe completely useless. I thought of Barbara Wisman who would kill for a pair of shoes like this. And, I must admit, I thought of the money I would lose because I would not be able to sell it to her.

I brandished the umbrella over my head like a weapon, and unlocked the door. There was no one there. The street was quiet. There was a full moon over-head.

I put the shoe back in the bag and stashed it in the storeroom closet. Not much you can do with just one shoe. I took a deep breath, turned off the lights, locked up the shop and headed for home.

When I came home that night, the first thing I did—doesn't every woman—was to kick off my shoes—comfortable as they might be—and feel around under my bed for my old L.L. Bean slippers, lined in real fleece. I mean, really. If my customers knew, it would be a scandal in the neighborhood.

I padded about, on my way to the refrigerator hoping there would be something I had stashed away there to eat, so I wouldn't have to go out again to shop. Then I heard the unmistakable ring-a-ling-a-ling of my cell phone somewhere in the apartment. One of the things about being a woman of a certain age is that I can never remember where I've put my cell phone.

I started running through my apartment shaking various purses and jackets trying to follow the sound. Of course, when I finally found the thing in the pocket of the raincoat I wore yesterday, I had missed the call. But technology has now enabled me to see whom I've missed—Larry! Between you and me, if I never spoke to him again, it would be too soon.

But, surprise! There's another missed call, this one from Kim. The thought of Kim makes me smile. Beautiful, serene, Kim, whose porcelain skin and satin-shiny hair seems to cast a cloak of contentment over everyone who enters Emily's Place.

What a contrast to Louise the Loser. I actually caught Louise's hand in the till. I should have known when I hired her she was too good to be true. Modest, down-cast eyes. As neatly dressed as a seminary student just let out of school. As soon as she started three days a week I noticed some shoes had disappeared. Size ten. Always size ten. Then some money disappeared.

I came in early one day and surprised her at the cash register. She had a fist-full of bills and the store was empty. She told me she was making change.

"For who," I asked her, "Your boyfriend?" I mean who else would wear a size ten?

"I don't have a boyfriend," she told me.

I fired her on the spot. Escorted her to the door—some might say roughly—by the hair and pushed her out. She had the nerve to call a couple of months ago and ask for a reference for another job. "Sure, "I told her. "I can heartily recommend your skill in burglary, disloyalty and duplicity."

"What's duplicity?" She said.

I told her not to worry about it. She had that one covered.

I don't often feel sorry for myself. Sorry that Larry and I never had any children—and surely Shana is enough for me to care for, but when Kim came into the shop two years ago—a week after I had fired Louise—a skinny, shivering, frightened little thing, my heart almost dissolved in sadness. One look at her scuffed, worn-out

Chinatown shoes—from which her big toe was almost protruding—told me she had always needed help and had never found it.

I've got to admit to white-lady ignorance because I still can't tell the difference between Asian girls, whether they are Japanese, Korean, Chinese or something else entirely.

So as soon as she sat down, I pointed to myself, and said in my loudest voice, "Me will help you."

And then she raised these eyes—deep, round, and glowing with tears just about to roll down her cheeks—and said in perfect, British accented English, "Do you have any shoes on sale in a size six?"

Turns out the poor thing was one of those abandoned girl-babies in China who was adopted by missionaries, learned English well enough to get a job as a guide and managed to jump ship in New York where she had been hanging out in Chinatown doing odd jobs.

I poured her a cup of tea—we always have a pot of something going in the back room—and gave her a few crackers I keep around. She wolfed them down like she hadn't had a good meal in days.

To make a long story short, I kind of fell in love with her. Merissa the store manager did as well, and before I knew it, I had offered her a job—part time as a sales and stock girl. She's been with us for more than two years. I found out she had a talent for drawing, as well as languages, and helped her enroll at The New School where she takes courses in both—a little gal who never went past eighth grade!

Since Kim has no relatives here and I'm down to one and a half—one of them living in the Berkshires and the "half", my estranged husband, probably camping out in a turnip patch with his Cossack Cutie—Kim and I spend most of our free time together.

In my fantasies, I imagine Kim as my own daughter, but I'm careful to give her lots of space. Kim has her own apartment—actually a room—in Chinatown, in a shared apartment with some elderly people. She seems happy enough. She has had a cold the last few days so I told her to stay home yesterday instead of spreading the germs to the rest of us. I had called her a couple of times during the day but didn't get an answer. I figured she had shut off her phone and was sleeping.

I skipped over Larry's message. Nothing he has to say is of much interest to me.

I scrolled down to the next message and pressed the play button. All I heard was noise—the sound of furniture scraping along a wood floor, the slam of a door, a muffled voice I couldn't make out, a thud of some kind, as if something fell on the floor—various sounds of traffic and then nothing.

I looked at the time the call had come in—about noon. I called her cell but no answer.

I looked at my watch—11:30pm. I knew Kim had a class this evening. I wondered if she was feeling sicker and had tried to call me.

I stared at my shoes by the side of the bed. My sister Shana always told me I worried about everything. I guess she was right. I hesitated. It would probably be a wild goose chase. Kim either hit the call button of her phone accidently—I knew I was programmed into it, or she was moving some furniture around while she waited for me to answer. Lots of times she just hung up when I didn't answer and didn't leave a message. Most likely, she was fast asleep and I would be trudging down to Chinatown and disturbing her for nothing. And it was raining.

I looked over my bed at the portrait Kim had drawn of me, a sketch in pastels for my birthday. There were only a few quick curves and strokes but she had captured my expression, part-way between concern and amusement, that struck me as right-on.

I walked back to the bed, put on my shoes, grabbed my coat and umbrella and set out for the downtown subway. 11:30pm wasn't very late for the city that never sleeps.

It was still raining when I got out of the subway and made my way down Pell Street toward her apartment building. The subway had been filled with people, coming home from Broadway shows, setting out for nightclubs and parties, getting ready to work the night shift at jobs all over the city. And the streets were still crowded in Chinatown.

The streets are always crowded in Chinatown, especially in the last few years when it seemed more and more Chinese came here, legally or not. Chinatown has now eaten up Little Italy with the successful Italians moving up to Westchester, acquiring their bit of the American dream.

But even with the usual hustle and bustle, it struck me that the crowd further down the street was much heavier than usual. Then I saw the police lights blinking and the wooden saw-horses set up to keep back the crowd and my heart began to beat very fast.

The closer I came to the end of the street where Kim lived the denser the crowd got and the harder I had to push through. I was clutched with fear that something terrible had happened and that it had happened to Kim. My Kim.

And then at last I was right in front of Kim's tenement, with its lop-sided door and cracked window-frames. Police-tape was crisscrossed every which way around the front. I was flat up against the wooden saw-horse and saw a white sheet on the wet ground covering what I knew had to be a dead body.

No one understood any English and I couldn't get anyone to tell me anything. I got a little crazy and started yelling at the very large, red-faced policeman who blocked my way, to let me through.

"Shut-up or I'll have to take you downtown," He yelled back.

"We are downtown, you stupid cop!"

Either I pushed him or he pushed me because I started yelling "I'm not afraid of you. I marched on Washington to stop the war in Vietnam and they had dogs as well as billy-clubs!"

At that point, some guy wearing ordinary clothes came over and flashed a badge at me and said in a fairly calm voice, "I'll take care of this, Michael." He moved the wooden horse and brought me inside the police ring around Kim's tenement.

"I have to see my friend. She lives upstairs, Apt. 3G."

"What's your friend's name?" he asked me.

"Kim Chang." I looked at his face—pale, cool and expressionless. He cocked his head toward a body under a sheet on the wet sidewalk. I knew as he did, that the person lying there was Kim Chang. I guess I must have seemed pretty wobbly at that point because he took my arm and kind of held me up.

"I've got to see her," I tried to pull away.

"We already got an ID on her," the detective said. "Old lady in the apartment with her." He held me back. "Are you a relative?"

"Sure, first cousin."

"You told me you were a friend."

"I am her friend. She works in my store."

"So now you're her employer?"

"Yes." I told him. "Yes. Yes. Yes. I'm everything to her. She doesn't have anyone else."

"If you're not a blood relative, I can't let you through."

He put his face closer to mine. Even though I was completely distraught, I couldn't help noticing the blue of his eyes.

"I don't think you're a blood relative," he said. "Friend—maybe."

At that point, I put my hand over my face asked him to tell me what happened.

"Can't say much right now," he told me, not unkindly. "Except that someone murdered her."

I guess I collapsed completely because he had to call someone to get me a chair and when I came around, he was squatting down to meet me at eye level and asked, "Know anyone who would want to do her in?"

All I could do was to shake my head no, while the tears rolled down my face. "My sweet Kim," I said, "everyone loved her."

After that things are pretty much of a blur. I had a vague memory of the detective guy asking for my name and address, shoving his business card into the pocket of my raincoat and someone bringing me home in a police car.

When I woke up the next morning. It had stopped raining.

Chapter 2

In 19th Century China, carefully embroidered, ornate under soles of shoes were conspicuous signs of a woman's wealth, symbolizing her many hours spent reclining at leisure.

The next morning, the sun shone brightly and I tried to tell myself Kim's murder was just a bad dream. One look at my soggy raincoat draped over the kitchen chair told me it was all too real.

Kim. My sweet, serene little Kim. Gone forever. How was it possible that the sun could shine again as if nothing at all had happened?

I pictured Kim lying on that cold sidewalk. Then I pictured her lying in a cold, damp grave. What would happen to her body—lost so far from home?

She had no one else. Just me. I had to claim the body. I had to see that she was properly buried in this foreign land. And I had to find out who had killed her.

After I had a good cry, and a morning cup of coffee, I searched around in the pocket of my raincoat and found the card of the detective who had saved me from assault and battery charges—had I just pushed that other cop or kicked him?—and had kindly seen that I got home.

Paul Murphy, Special Detective, Homicide.

Never much liked cops, I had to admit. But he did have the bluest eyes.

I called the number on the card and heard his voice mumble "Leave a message"

Then I called Merissa on her cell.

After I opened Emily's Place and people actually began coming in, I realized pretty early on that I needed someone to help sell the shoes.

This was a delicate matter because if I was going to spend as much time with this person as I used to spend with my estranged husband, Larry, I had to really like her. Of course, it had to be a woman—a woman who really understood what other women wanted in a shoe.

So, when Merissa first walked into the store wearing deep purple Prada calf-skin boots with silver studs looking for a job, I knew I had found the woman of my dreams.

Merissa is about five feet ten or eleven inches in her bare feet and over six foot when she wears her high heels. And wear them she does, day in and day out.

Did I mention that Merissa is drop-dead gorgeous? Well, perhaps not gorgeous in the conventional way of a movie star. She is ebony dark with luminous brown eyes and the slim, slinky body that draws looks from across the room. Her voice is soft and husky and her speech is peppered with French phrases. She seems to know how to connect with everyone who comes into the store. And sooner or later they all find their way to Emily's Place—the widows, the wanderers, the Wall Street financiers; the loners, the housewives, the divorcees, the call girls, the immigrants, the refuges, the radicals, the actresses, the artists and the activists. And sprinkled liberally throughout; the homosexuals, the transsexuals, the transvestites, the alcoholics, the addicts, the angry, the players, the panderers, and the pretenders. They kneel and worship at the altar of The Shoe, here at Emily's Place, where fantasy coexists with the reality of the Upper West Side.

Merissa is Haitian and Indian and also Canadian somewhere far back. Every pair of shoes she wore to work became an instant best-seller.

After that there was Kim. Kim, Kim the wonderful. My spiritual almost surrogate daughter, who drifted into Emily's Place as a despised and perfect poster child of Chinese misery rescued by the western world, who we made our part-time assistant.

The short history of our previous assistant, Louisa the Loser made the arrival of Kim that much sweeter.

Merissa and I cried a little over the phone and then she told me she would meet me at the shop in an hour.

"Check out page three in the Metro Section," José said as he handed me the paper, already folded to that page and section.

José Ramos had come from Puerto Rico more than fifty years ago and started delivering papers for his uncle all over the city. When his uncle died, his aunt took over the business and José never rose very far. There was a wife somewhere along the line—or maybe a girl friend or a couple of each—José told his story several different ways depending on his mood—but whoever she or they were, they left him for—pick one—a bus driver with a union contract, a bar tender with a little brain or a car salesman who trafficked in stolen parts. None of them had the *"cojones"* that he had—to stay and work in a boring, low-paying job because of loyalty to the family.

I know all these things because, like so many others who were drawn to Emily's place, José found he could get a cup of coffee, a smile and a lot of free advice just by showing up.

José paid me back for these privileges by staring in a very complimentary way at my breasts, and reading my paper for me before he arrived. That way, he assured me, he could edit out the articles that would be sure to bore me, like Mircosoft's latest dot.com acquisition, and point my attention to the articles on murder and mayhem.

The truth is, I'm often up really early and sitting alone with my thoughts in the back room made me welcome any company that came along.

Today he brought Charles, the mailman, with him. I didn't know much about Charles. Unlike José, he doesn't talk much. He's tall and heavy-set with rimless glasses and a kind of colorless face that matches the gray of his uniform.

Even though José had presumably read this article in the paper, he obviously hadn't made the connection to our Kim.

"They found a shoe stuck right in her head," José related happily. "Reminded me of your windows as soon as I read about it."

I burst into tears.

"What?" José asked me, "What?" He jiggled the newspaper.

"It's Kim," I managed to get out between sobs. "The murdered girl is Kim."

That stopped him in his tracks. He grabbed the newspaper back and started reading the article again. José had only met Kim a few times but he seemed to like her.

"Kim," the mailman repeated. "She was that Chinese girl who sometimes opened the store. I never delivered any mail to her."

"She didn't live in the neighborhood," José explained. "She was from Chinatown."

In the neighborhood or out of it—the most ghastly thing to me was to learn that Kim had been killed with a shoe! Was it Oscar Wilde who said *'life imitates art'*?

Harold and I had named our two manikins. The dark-haired one was "Sadie" because she reminded me of my great aunt who lived in the Bronx. I had gotten her at a discount because her hair had lost its curl and hung down—and sometimes up—in bunches at odd angles on her head, neck and collar. The other was "Mary" because, if Sadie was Jewish, Mary needed to be gentile so we couldn't be accused of playing favorites. Besides, Mary was blonde with pert little breasts and hair that hugged her face like a helmet. Just one look at her told you that she could be depended upon to stand up straight and not fall down the way Sadie was prone to do.

Since most of the clothes we dressed Mary and Sadie in came from the Salvation Army, their looks, at any time, were more than a tad "creative." But this time Harold had glued one red boot on top of Sadie's head. That was strange enough, but when you looked at it from a certain angle, it looked as if it were embedded in her scalp.

"Wait a minute!" I had cried out, "That looks a bit creepy to me."

Harold had sneered and put his hands on his hips."Emily, Emily. You've got to start thinking out of the box. I mean, think of Marie Antoinette. She wore a bird's nest on her head and started a whole new trend in fashion."

"Yes," I replied, "And she also lost her head for transgressions against good taste."

Harold had insisted on "artistic license" and the red boot remained stuck on Sadie's head. I had tossed its mate into the closet.

Suddenly I pictured a different red shoe, dropping through the mail chute. It landed softly, innocently on my carpet. Still warm from the sole of someone's foot.

I grabbed the paper back from José and took it closer to the window where the light was better.

Could someone really kill a person with a shoe?

I looked quickly at the page. There was no photo but there was a description of the murdered woman—small, slight, Asian and her name, Kim Chang. My eyes started filling up with tears but I forced myself to read on.

Sure enough the article mentioned that the murder weapon was a shoe. The woman, in fact, was found with only the one shoe. It was believed that the murderer took the other one with him as a souvenir. She was dressed only in a bra and garter belt.

A garter-belt? My little Kim? I didn't know much about her sex life. I never asked her and she never said anything. I suppose she had fancy underwear like most young people today.

Now the tears came. The shoe, the underwear, she must have been sexually molested.

I wiped away my tears and I glanced at the window display. Sadie and Mary looked happy, oblivious to the shoes resting on their respective heads.

I couldn't bear the thought that our store windows had given some murderer an idea.

"It doesn't say the shoe was "in her head" I pointed out, shaking the paper at José. "It could have been stuck in her neck."

"Or in her belly," José suggested. "Or maybe in her..."

I could see where this conversation was going. I never gave José much credit for brains but I thought he'd have a little more sensitivity. If I wasn't feeling so depressed I'd have shoved him out the door.

"Look, "I interrupted him angrily pointing to a rack of shoes, "it would also depend on what kind of shoe we were talking about. A blow to the knees with one of those heavy platform shoes could have caused her to fall over, hit her head on a rock and drop dead. Whereas, a stiletto heel would have to be used in an entirely different way." A stiletto heel was as sharp as an icepick.

I read the article again. In truth, there were a lot of details missing. Also, the page three placement seemed to indicate that even the police were not particularly interested in this murder or its victim.

Just a routine case in the Big Apple. I shook my head. I had blamed myself for missing her phone call. Now I blamed myself for the manikins in the window of my store. I couldn't help feeling it was all my fault. Even the newspaper coverage. Poor Kim couldn't get proper attention even when she was murdered.

José finally said goodbye and went about his business—whatever that was after the papers were all delivered.

Charles sipped his coffee and lingered. He looked out over the showroom, and then turned his head to me. He hardly knew Kim. Since she wasn't on his mail delivery list, he didn't seem to have much interest in who she was or how she died. "You must have a lot of shoes," Charles said.

I was happy to change the subject. I saw him sneak a look at my shoes. Flats. Always flats in the store. After all, I'm on my feet all day. Today it is ballet slippers. Stuart Weitzman. Black ballet slippers with two little silver balls hanging from the tie in the front. Ballet slippers are very fashionable this season. And comfortable. Nevertheless, I felt I had disappointed him. I guess he thought I would wear something fancy and exotic, having the pick of everything at Emily's Place.

"I have some real beauties at home," I told him, apologetically. "These are my work shoes." After all, I have a reputation to protect.

He nodded. Being on your feet all day is something he understood. He took one more sip of his coffee, tipped his hat, picked up his bag of mail and said goodbye.

I had hoped to have a little time to reread the newspaper article more carefully but the little bell over the door tinkled almost as soon as Charles walked out and Merissa and her niece Fifi walked in.

As soon as I made eye content with Merissa, I burst into tears all over again and so did she. Then Fifi started crying and for a minute or two we all just held each other and wept.

Merissa adored Kim and probably would have been even closer to her if so much of her time hadn't been taken up with caring for Fifi. Fifi was Merissa's cross-to-bear. Fifi was Merissa's oldest sister's child. Merissa had told me that her sister died of TB in some small town in Quebec. Fifi had been born—in Merissa's words— "unfinished," or, as we would say, premature, with a few unfortunate problems. She was completely deaf, couldn't utter a word, and had been born with a club foot.

Another "unfinished" area of Fifi's body seemed to be her brain. Although Fifi understood much of what was said to her—Merissa had taught her to read lips—and even to read and write, there was something about her that wasn't quite "there." The expression on her face was usually blissful, and her head would nod from side to side as though she were listening to music only she could hear.

Neatly dressed, her brown hair falling in gentle curls around her face, large, dark eyes framed by incredibly long lashes, Fifi had the appearance of a beautiful, but not quite real doll.

Since the corners of her mouth almost always turned upward, this was the first time I had ever seen Fifi upset. Certainly I had never seen her cry. As she held on to me, as we held on to each other, I could feel her body shake with completely silent moans.

"*Alors! Mon petite*! I sure don't know one person in this whole wide world would kill *cette belle Kim*. Even Fifi, she loved Kim. Never seen Fifi cry like this before. *Mon dieu!*"

Merissa took a tissue from her purse and wiped Fifi's eyes.

"How this happen, Madame Emily? How this can be?"

I shook my head. "I should have taken her to live with me. I thought about it, but I didn't do it."

"Now, Madame Emily, not your place, take care of Chinese girl. She had her own people, down there where she lived. Can't make her into white woman *comme vous*. She needed her roots. *Bien sur,* you gave her love. You gave her a job. You done right by *cette petite bebe*."

I couldn't bring myself to tell Merissa that I had missed Kim's call for help. Got down there too late to help anyone.

I locked the front door of the store and sat down on one of the seats in the showroom. Merissa took a seat next to me, while Fifi walked slowly around fingering the shoes, the expression on her face blissful once more.

I couldn't help but marvel at the great job Ciceri & Son had done on the custom-made shoe they had manufactured to hide her club foot. From the front it was a perfect match to her Ferangamo pumps. It was only from the back that you could see the sole had been built up in a way to accommodate some special orthopedic hardware inside.

Merissa had managed to get enough money together to have her foot operated on a couple of times and I had contacted this old world Italian firm who used to do work for my dad, to do the shoe. Now Fifi's limp was noticeable only when she was really tired out.

How I wished I could restore my own spirits as easily as Fifi seemed to restore hers.

"What the police going to do with the body, Madame Emily?" Merissa asked me. "You the only kin she had."

I sighed. "I tried to tell that to the cop but he wasn't buying it. Decided my eyes weren't the right shape to be a blood relative."

Merissa grunted. "What them cops know? They don't know *merde*. You and me. We go downtown, bring *cette petite bebe* home."

I went to the phone and dialed detective Murphy again. Still only a recorded message.

"I don't suppose they are going to give the body to anyone just yet," I told Merissa, "I guess they will want to do some tests and look for evidence—torn threads in her fingernails, check out various body parts." The thought of people cutting up my Kim and looking into all her organs was enough to make me feel sick to my stomach.

Someone rattled the door knob, and pressed her face against the window. Merissa and I looked at each other.

"I can't do it." I said to Merissa. "I can't work today as if everything is the same. I can't answer people's questions when they ask me "Where's Kim? I can't do it."

"*Alors! C'es'la*. We close today. Merissa will put up the article right on the door. *Quelque persone* want to know about Kim, they can read for their own selves."

She put her arm around me and led me to the door. "Madame Emily, you go on home now and take a nap. Today is shoe holiday.

Shoe princess resting today." Then she unlocked the door and led me out to the sidewalk.

I dragged myself back home, pulled the blinds shut in the bedroom and tried to get back to sleep—but I could not escape from sadness so easily. Every time I closed my eyes I pictured Kim, dissected like a frog, lying on a cold slab at the morgue. Who could have done such a thing?

Kim was so sweet and hard-working. It wasn't her way to raise her voice or even to get angry about anything. She just seemed so innocent and happy to be in this country. To have work, a chance to go to school and a few people who cared about her.

Did she have a boyfriend? If she had sexy underwear she must have had a boyfriend, yet I never heard her mention a soul. Did she have girl friends? Again, I never heard her mention anyone.

I sat up in bed. Was it possible I was the naive one, not Kim? Believing that Merissa, me and Auntie Ma, as we called the old lady who lived in one of the rooms in Kim's flat, made up her whole world?

Yes, I knew she went to the New School at night. I knew she must have had classmates, but so far as I knew, between school and work, there wasn't much time for socializing. She might have had a whole life I didn't know about, with friends, and yes, possibly, with enemies.

I got out of bed and opened the blinds. The sun was still shining.

And then there was the question of the shoe. Was it merely a coincidence that Kim worked at a shoe store and she was murdered with a shoe? An act of violence that might have been suggested by my own manikins?

And what of the red shoe that was deposited so strangely through my mail chute the very night Kim was killed?

Not just any red shoe, but a Jimmy Choo red high-heeled shoe that sold for eight hundred and fifty dollars in a size eight.

I knew that Kim did not own any designer shoes. And besides, she wore a size six.

The red shoe seemed like a red herring to me. I couldn't see how it was connected to the murder. Since Emily's Place was pretty well known as a grand super-market of shoes, and I was—what did Merissa call me?—the 'Princess of shoes"—someone finding an expensive shoe somewhere might slip it through the mail chute, as if Emily's Place was a grand Lost and Find for shoe-related things for the entire city of New York.

In the past I had received a dirty sock, one rhinestone buckle, and a book on the history of shoes the same way.

I walked over to the phone and started to dial Murphy's number again. And then I stopped. Either he was incompetent or just didn't give a damn. Almost an entire day had gone by and he hadn't made any attempt to question me. He might not care much about one more dead girl in the city, but I surely did.

I put on my shoes, a comfortable pair of Arche cushioned for walking, grabbed my jacket and keys and walked out the door.

An hour later I was making my way down Pell Street, stepping between bushels of ice holding fish I'd never even known existed, sun glittering off their scales, heaps of vegetables from purple to red to every shade of green, and maneuvering past elderly Asians carrying vinyl shopping bags half as large again as they were themselves.

I have to admit I had no clear plan of action. I just felt that I had to get out of my apartment and try to make sense out of the events of the past few hours. I wanted in some way to make up to the dead Kim the mistakes I had made while she was alive. In the pocket of my jacket I carried my cell phone. Never again would I leave it at home.

When I finally found myself in front of Kim's tenement, I breathed a sigh of relief. The police tape was gone. That meant that they had let people back into the building. Hopefully, I could finally get into Kim's apartment.

I rang Aunty Ma's buzzer and she buzzed back. Aunty Ma doesn't speak a word of English. Most of the people in the building don't, and whether or not they had any understanding of how the buzzer system worked is anybody's guess.

At any rate, I gripped the door knob, pushed it open and groped my way towards the staircase.

The glare of the sun outside made it difficult for me to see in the dingy light inside the aging building, and the next thing I knew, I tripped on the staircase, dropped my purse and my change was rolling down the stairwell.

Falling up the stairs is a good deal easier on the body that falling down the stairs and fortunately, I had nothing worse than one bruised knee.

Hello! What was this? As I bent to retrieve some of my loose coins and a lipstick that have fallen out of the bag, my hand came in contact with a cell phone that had been hiding in a crevice between the step and the wall under the hand railing. As soon as I picked it up I knew it was Kim's. The very phone she had used to call me the night she was murdered.

I flipped it open. It still had its charge. The screen blinked "New Message." And a telephone number appeared. Did I dare to call it?

I pressed the button. I heard the phone ring. It rang several times but there was no answer and no message machine. I looked again at the phone. There were a couple of messages noted. I pressed a few more buttons. A voice asked for my code to retrieve voice mail. I didn't have one.

I put the phone in my purse and continued to pick up my change. Then I rang the bell of Apt 3A. No one answered the door and after waiting another minute or two, I used my key to get in. Kim had given me a duplicate key months ago so if I arrived early for one of our weekend jaunts together, I could wait comfortably inside—either in the communal hallway where I lingered now, or inside her room.

I locked the door behind me and looked around. The smell of steamed vegetables filled the hallway.

Kim's apartment building was one of those old tenements where the apartments had long ago been cut up into single room occupancies. You weren't allowed to cook, but for obvious reasons, no one paid any attention to that law. This wasn't the kind of neighborhood that was regularly visited by housing inspectors.

Kim had lived here since she first jumped ship and I guess she was attached to the place because she didn't want to move, even when I offered to pay most of her rent.

There were five doors in the hallway, but the only person I ever met was Aunty Ma who lived way down the hall. Today her door remained firmly closed, although I was sure the aroma of steamed vegetables was coming from that direction.

Kim's door, however, was still wrapped round with police tape. Would I attempt to enter anyway? Probably, but I was stopped in my tracks by a large padlock—obviously put there by the police—the key to which I did not have.

As I stood looking at the door to Kim's little room, as changed and defiled by strangers as her poor body now was, the door knob behind me to the hallway rattled and a key was inserted in the door.

I stepped quickly aside, and walked down toward Aunty Ma's door, half expecting a policeman to emerge. Instead, a rather well-dressed, tweedy-looking white gentleman in his fifties opened the door, took no notice of me and headed straight for Kim's room.

As soon as he saw the police tape and padlock, he stopped short, much as I had and put his key back into his pocket. A man with the key to Kim's room? This was not an opportunity I would allow to go to waste.

"Hello,' I said, emerging from the shadows down the hall. "Are you looking for Kim?"

The tweedy guy jumped back as if I had given him an electric shock and said, "Kim? I don't know any Kim. I'm looking for Louie Chan, a friend I play chess with from time to time."

"Oh, I think you have the wrong apartment—or at least the wrong door."

Tweedy Guy kept his head down and did his best not to make eye contact with me. But that was okay, I saw his shoes, Italian, custom-made, shoes I would never forget, and I knew in an instant that he didn't live in Chinatown. Tweedy Guy backed quickly out the door and practically ran down the stairs.

I waited a minute or two and then took off after him. I was dimly aware that this man might actually be a killer, but for some reason, perhaps because it was day time and I was so full of hate, I felt no fear whatsoever. On the contrary, I felt rejuvenated, fueled by righteous energy, almost invulnerable.

Besides, I was wearing my shoes with sponge soles that are absolutely silent and I was stalking him, not the other way around.

One of the advantages of being a woman of a certain age is that most people, especially men, really don't look at you very carefully. Would he have noticed that I had green eyes and a gray streak in my salt and pepper hair? Would he remember I was wearing a black jacket? I am willing to bet Tweedy Guy wouldn't know me in the street if I walked right up to him and spit in his face.

Nevertheless, I followed him at a good distance. Fortunately, he decided to go wherever he was headed by subway and not taxi because following a cab in this neighborhood—getting a cab in this neighborhood would really be a challenge.

At any rate, Tweedy Guy walked fast, like he was really in a hurry to leave Chinatown behind. He was not searching for his imaginary Asian chess partner. He almost collided with a bent-over Chinese peddler selling little tin cars that seemed to go all by themselves. He never looked behind him.

I followed him into the train station and we took the uptown train to the East Side. It was about noon and the trains were not crowded.

Tweedy Man sat down and I sat down as well, at the far end of the car.

We both got out at 79th Street and Lexington Ave. We walked past the nannies wheeling strollers, the blonde woman walking her poodle; a group of teenagers wearing blazers from the St. Mathews School down the block.

Tweedy Man walked up Lexington and turned onto 85th Street, heading towards Madison. About half way down the block, he stopped and entered a building. I followed. He said something to the doorman, who clearly seemed to know him and stepped inside the building.

I stopped outside the building and took out my little note pad and wrote down the address—1089 East 85th Street. Now what? I stared upwards. 1089 East 85th Street was an old, dignified building of the kind that wealthy people have lived in since the 1920's when most of them were built. The stone walls were a pale yellow; there were horizontal art deco cornices carved in the shape of leaping gazelles that led the eye around the facade of the building. I counted sixteen floors in all.

I gazed at the graceful figures, the smooth, solid walls. A fortress of respectability. No crooked windows here, unhinged doors or broken locks, pock-marked marble ornaments eaten away by the elements.

As if divided by a vast, uncharted jungle, the two sides of Central Park are ringed with sentinels of stone. The elegant buildings of Fifth Avenue on the East and their aspiring sisters, the queens of Shabby Chic, on Central Park West on the West. And yet, outward differences mask interior similarities. Unhappiness can hide on either side of the city.

Clearly, I needed a name to go with an address if I was ever going to learn who this man, and possible murderer was. How to get by the doorman? I paused for a minute and then I got an inspiration.

I messed up my hair and unbuttoned my coat. I started to breathe heavily. Another advantage to being a woman of a certain age. If you act a little strangely, people just chalk it up to senility. I huffed and puffed and tried to push the heavy door open even through the doorman was clearly opening it for me.

I put my hand on my heart.

"Oh my!" I uttered, between gasps." That gentleman who just went inside. He dropped something on the street and I called out to him but he didn't hear me, and I really need to give it back to him.

It's not very expensive but it might have sentimental value. I ran all the way..."

The doorman, a Hispanic gentleman who looked to be about my age, offered me a chair. His uniform was dark blue with polished brass buttons and he looked like the captain of a ship.

"Oh, no," I said, lifting my hand to my head. "I'll be fine in a moment. He was walking so fast. What apartment is he in?"

"Oh," he said, "15-B. I'll ring him up. Who should I say is calling?"

I rubbed my hand over my chest, and gulped for breath. "I might take a seat for a few minutes, if you don't mind."

He helped me to a chair.

The lobby was lined in gray marble like a vault, with a burgundy and blue oriental rug down the center. There was a large vase filled with fresh flowers and the scent of Lilacs permeated the area.

After what I considered the proper time to catch my breath, I said, "On second thought, I think I'll just write him a note and perhaps you can return this silver key chain to him for me."

I reached into my purse and took out a silver key chain with a little enameled high-heeled shoe hanging from it. One of my customers had given it to me a couple of years ago as a Christmas present. I was sort of sorry to part with it, but I figured it was for a good cause. If Tweedy Man had anything to do with Kim's murder he would have a heart-attack when he got it.

I took out my pen and my little pad of paper.

"Oh," I asked, "What is his name?" I held my pen aloft.

"Mr. Quinn," he said, "his first name is Phillip."

I quickly scribbled a note to "Phillip" and signed it "Your friend." Then I handed the note and the key chain to the doorman. I straightened my hair with my hand.

"I feel so much better now," I said. "Thanks."

Smiling my most charming smile at the doorman, I walked out into the street and took the bus back to the Upper West Side and my apartment.

I lounged around for a while, longing for darkness and a good excuse to block out reality with sleep. But long after night fell, I laid awake in bed, staring into space, asking myself questions about Phillip Quinn. Who was he? How did he get a key to Kim's Room? The more I thought about him, the more I was sure he was involved with Kim's murder.

I had finally fallen asleep, when the phone rang. I glanced at my watch. It was a little after midnight. A phone call after midnight is never a good thing.

"Ommmmm."

"Shana? Are you all right?" A small giggle reassured me.

"Why do you always call so late?" I couldn't keep the annoyance out of my voice.

"It depends on how you look at it, my dear sister. For some people this is early. Besides, I know you'll be home."

I'm not sure if this was meant as an insult or not, so I ignored it altogether.

"Did you get the money?"

"Bless you Emily. I did. How are you?" I held the telephone closer to my ear. "How are you? How is your arm?"

She laughed. "My arm is healing. My belly-button is another story."

"Your belly-button?" I asked her, "You injured your belly button in the car crash?"

She laughed again. "Of course not, I just have a small infection where my piercing was done. The ring I put through got caught on my underpants and..."

"You pierced your belly button?" I pictured my beautiful little sister with blood spurting out of her belly button.

"Not my belly-button. Near my belly-button. You can't pierce a belly-button."

"Oh," I said, "Did the piercer person have a license?"

"Very funny," she answered. "I'll have you know that women have been adorning their bodies in this way since the beginning of time. You should get another hole in your ear. The ear has been a focus of eroticism for centuries. You'd see an immediate improvement in your sex life."

I listened patiently. Who knew? Maybe she was right.

"Have you been to a doctor?" I asked her

She grunted. "I am a doctor, remember?" I've been treating the infection with aloe."

I covered my face with my free hand. "I think an antibiotic might be faster. Do you need any more money?"

She sighed. "It could help."

A pause and then she said, "Are you sure you're all right? "

No. I was not all right. I was terrible. But I was not sure I wanted to confess those things to my sister Shana.

I had not yet told Shana about Kim's murder. The truth is, Shana was not entirely sympathetic towards Kim. I thought she was a little jealous that I had found someone else to fuss over and take care of.

I might have mentioned that Larry and I never had any kids. Maybe things would have been different if we did, but there's no point spending energy on that picture.

Truth is we tried when we were first married but he was in law school and I was in graduate school studying The Great American Novel and it never seemed to be the right time. But I suppose not having children of my own accounted for the interest I took in Kim.

"I had a dream..." Shana continued, "waves of black crashing against a jagged, rocky cliff." My sister Shana has lots of dreams. Like the Delphic oracle, with whom she feels she has a strong connection. Never mind that she is Jewish and was born in Brooklyn. Her spirit travels internationally, as well as back and forth in time.

"What does it mean?" I asked her, not wanting to know.

"Tears. Noise. Violence. Death. I woke up in a sweat."

"Could be early menopause," I told her, but I burst into tears. "Kim has been murdered," I blurted out. "My little Kim has been killed." I sniffled for a minute or two into the phone while my sister made little cooing sounds on the other end, in an attempt to console me.

"Oh my God." She said at last. "How did it happen?"

"No one knows yet. She was murdered with a shoe."

"Oh my God." Shana said again.

I'm not at all sure what God she was appealing to—Shana had a number of favorites—but it really didn't matter.

"Do you want me to come?" Shana said. "I think you could use some company."

"No, I'll be fine. Besides, you never liked her."

"That's not true," Shana protested. "I just didn't fall in love, the way you did. She was certainly a lot better than Louise the Loser. I could feel her chi was not very strong. I knew she'd be vulnerable to anything bad that would come her way. I have a Holistic Health Conference in New York next week. I could come a little early."

"Thanks," I told her. "But I'm sure I can manage."

A part of me felt touched by Shana's concern. Most of our lives it had been me taking care of her. On the other hand, the idea of having to share my space with Shana for any length of time was not inviting, especially now. I would just have another thing to worry about. And Shana, while far more intelligent than Fifi, was her equal in naiveté.

No. To have Shana loose in New York City while a shoe murderer roamed around was not a good thing. She was much better off in the Berkshires where the biggest threat were ineffectual aging hippies and a couple of confused Buddhists. But now I was stuck all alone with pictures of Phillip Quinn, growing larger and larger in my mind's eye until he grew into a colossal golem, hovering over the rooftops of Manhattan. And with that final image in my mind, I climbed back into bed and fell asleep at last as the first light of dawn seeped under my window blinds.

Chapter 3

The English word "boot" was derived from the French "bote" about 1325, but it was Coco Chanel in 1958 who made calf-height boots a high fashion item in the modern world.

The morning after my encounter with Philip Quinn, I came to work as usual. I knew I'd have to wait until the Police finished their preliminary investigation before I could claim the body, or gain access to Kim's room. I was beginning to make peace with her passing. I couldn't bring her back but I could help the police find her killer.

I fingered Kim's phone in the side pocket of my purse. I checked the name and address of the man I had followed. I felt up to waiting on customers, to answering questions, to accepting condolences.

Merissa had taped the newspaper article about Kim's death up on the wall next to the door of Emily's Place so if any of the regulars asked "Where's Kim today?" we could just point them in the direction of the article. We hoped it would answer their questions but all it really did was raise more questions for all of us. Who could have done such a thing? For what possible reason?

For my part, when anyone made comments, I just shook my head and said I'd rather not talk about it. That, at least, seemed to shut them up, and helped me establish a business-as-usual atmosphere even though I knew business would never be as usual again.

I was finally succeeding in focusing on style numbers and shoe colors, and not thinking about Kim when a man walked into the shop. When any man entered the shop alone, there was an instant shuffling, a kind of subterranean rustling that occured as everyone in the store repositioned their thighs in a way that signaled their awareness of "the other."

Often times the "other" was one of the transvestites who frequent Emily's Place, particularly around any of the holidays, searching for a size ten pump. Merissa had formed a very friendly relationship with several who became regulars. She grabbed all the size tens that came in and put them away for her special customers.

And yet, when this man walked into the shop, it was clear to everyone that he was not one of those. Hence the swishing of skirts and thighs as an aroma of true male sexuality descended over the interior like the scent of a lion on the tundra.

Although Merissa circled him, it was with me he made eye-contact.

"Can I help you?" Merissa purred as she tried to lead him to a seat. At least two inches taller than Merissa, he raised an eyebrow and threw me a glance over the top of her head that clearly called out *Help me!*

"Bonjour! Is the shoe for yourself or a friend?" Merissa cooed "Size ten, I presume?"

"You would presume wrong. That would be a nine if we were talking about shoes, but I came for something else."

"And what might that be?" I managed to wedge myself between Merissa and the guy.

"Ah," he smiled. "The lady of the house? Err—Place?"

Merissa retreated with an annoyed look on her face and I extended my hand.

"I'm Emily," I said, looking directly into the blue eyes of Murphy, the special detective I had met in front of Kim's tenement. His hair was silver gray and a shock of it fell across his forehead.

"Paul Murphy," His hands were large and calloused. He wore a pair of chinos and a light weight wind-breaker. L.L. Bean all the way—except for his shoes. English. Probably made by Church. Sturdy with a wide toe and in need of a shine.

His eyes wandered across the room where Esmeralda Velazquez was trying on a Chanel sandal in bronze leather, almost the exact color of her skin. He watched as she wound the straps up around her calf.

"Nice place, you have here, Emily," he said. He reached into his pocket and took out an identity card with the letters NYPD prominently displayed. "Is there someplace we can go to be alone?"

The woman in me thought immediately of my apartment. Too bad he was a cop. A cop who took two days to return my phone call. Even though I am a woman of a certain age, it doesn't mean I've given up on sex and romance. Trouble is, I don't like Cops. I guess you might say it comes with the territory.

Like so many other people who live on the Upper West Side, I grew up in one of the poorer, outer boroughs—Brooklyn to be exact—a first generation American-born kid of immigrants who grew up everywhere else. The outer boroughs were, and still are, a kind of secondary Ellis Island. Home to the waves of refugees from Germany, Hungry, Poland, Russia and the rest of Eastern Europe who once fled Hitler's wars and those fleeing more contempory "ethnic cleansing," the Serbs, Croats, survivors of Rwanda. Refugees escaping crazy political leaders like Stalin; right-wing dictatorships like Argentina, left-wing dictatorships like Cuba, changes in governments like Iran and nutty religious fanatics like those in Afghanistan. Refugees from famines in Africa, India and Bangladesh, near-starvation in Mexico. Refugees refusing to honor the ban on having more than one child in China. Refugee stories without ending that colored the thinking of their off-spring who finally made it to the Upper West Side.

Add to this list, the wanderers and dreamers and misfits from the West-Coast, the mid-West, and the deep-south, African-Americans whose ancestors were born into slavery, innocents and has-beens from every state in the union, including Puerto Rico, all coming to New York City for a better life, and you have an idea of the thick fears, suspicions and thorny wisdom dragged across continents that form the attitudes on the Upper West Side.

So why don't we like cops? For starters, they have traditionally been on the wrong side of whatever it was our parents and grandparents wanted to do. They represent the State, the Czar, the King; the Ruling Party. In short, they represent Authority. And it was to escape the existing authority that our parents and grandparents came to this country. Cops arrested vagrants, Hippies, Communists, spies and terrorists which meant you could be next. They were always issuing fines for half-understood transgressions, requiring licenses and documents for every action and scaring the day-lights out of people who had learned from harsh experience to avoid any uniform as much as possible.

For me personally, it was like this—I got two tickets for parking my car on the wrong side of the street. *Word of honor*, I was five minutes late because my watch was slow, and when I protested, the cop told me to shut my mouth or I would be arrested. So maybe it's what Jung would consider a cultural memory, but people on the Upper West Side do not trust cops. Nevertheless, I led the way to the back of the store, where the coffee machine gave out a welcoming gurgle.

"How do you take it?" I asked, and he told me light, with two sugars. I fiddled with the coffee pot and poured him a cup.

"Thanks for seeing that I got home the other night. I was pretty upset. When can I claim the body?" I asked him.

"Not yet" he waved his hand as if to dismiss this question entirely. "How well did you know the dead girl?"

"Very well. She worked here part-time for two and one half years. We spent most weekends together. I helped her with her school work and paid her tuition at The New School where she was enrolled in a degree program," I answered back.

"Where are her parents? Where are her relatives? How did she get here?"

"She had no relatives. She was abandoned as a baby in China. Some missionaries found her and taught her English."

Murphy's face remained expressionless. "How did she get here?" he asked me again.

I shrugged. There are some things best left unsaid to the police.

"Did you know she stole-away on a freighter and jumped ship when they got to New York?"

I shrugged again. "I never asked her." The truth as far as it goes. She told me without asking.

"You should have asked. She was here illegally. Do you know it is against the law to hire an illegal alien?"

I looked up at him. "As Dickens said in Oliver Twist, if the law says that, the law is an ass."

Murphy scowled. "Dickens was an anti-Semite whose conception of Fagin was one of the worst pictures of a Jew since Shakespeare wrote about Shylock. I don't think he was an authority on anything, except maybe human misery."

A cop who knew Dickens? Murphy was beginning to make an impression on me.

He allowed himself to smile. He brushed the hair back from his face.

I decided to change the subject. I reached into my pocket and brought out Kim's cell phone. "I went back to Kim's apartment the next day. Found her phone on the stairs." I held it out proudly in front of me.

Murphy looked down at the phone in my hand. "That's evidence." He said, "Too bad you picked it up and smeared any prints that might have been there."

I felt myself getting angry. "Your guys missed it. It was lying there for two days."

"Maybe, maybe not." Murphy replied, "Someone might have

planted it later." He held out his hand for the phone.

"There was something else," I told him, "while I was in the hallway, a guy let himself into the apartment with his own key. When he saw me, he almost flew down the stairs."

Now, it seems, I finally captured his interest. He reached into his pocket and took out a small pad and pencil. "What did he look like?"

"Hard to say. He kept his face averted and ran off as soon as he saw me. He was all dolled up in tweeds, even had suede patches on his elbows. His shoes were Italian. Probably two years old, hand crafted leather, size eleven. Probably made in Tuscany."

Murphy lifted an eye-brow. "Did he say anything to you?"

"Not much. Said he had come to visit a chess partner and probably made a mistake in the floor. But he didn't go to another floor. He went straight home."

Murphy shut his little book and fixed me with a stare. "And how do you know that?"

"Because I followed him," I said triumphantly, "all the way home."

Murphy shook his head back and forth. "You followed the guy? He could have been a murderer."

I shrugged. "I was hoping he was."

Murphy's eyebrow rose again. If he were a poker player, this would be his "tell" for anything surprising. He opened his little book. "Where does he live?"

"His name is Philip Quinn and he lives at 1089 East 85th Street, off Madison."

Now Murphy snapped his little notebook shut and scowled. He clearly wasn't happy that I had learned more about his case than he had.

"Can you think of any reason this Quinn would have had a key to Kim's room?"

I shook my head. "The only thing I could think of was that he had stolen it, or borrowed it somehow and made a duplicate without her knowing."

Murphy grunted. "Did it ever occur to you that Kim might have had a boy friend? Perhaps several 'boyfriends? That perhaps she was earning some extra money with extra-curricular activities?"

That was really going too far. I jumped up from my seat, spilling my coffee on my sweater. "How dare you!" I challenged him.

That's what I mean about cops. One minute you think they are your friend, and then the worm turns. He reached over for a napkin and handed it to me.

"There was no forced entry—probably means Kim knew her murderer. That and she was found in fancy underwear. She was killed in her room and dragged into the alley."

I sat back down in my chair. "Most single women own fancy underwear. She could have had a boyfriend I didn't know about. But the other thing you hint at is completely impossible."

Murphy fiddled with his cup. It seemed we had reached some kind of a stale-mate. "We'll check out the phone and we'll check out this Quinn fellow," Murphy said. "In the meantime, do us all a favor and stay away from Kim's apartment house."

I was about to say something nasty but I held my tongue.

Murphy put down his coffee and stood up. "If you know so much about shoes, maybe you can get me the name of someone in the city who has a shoe fetish—particularly someone who is turned on by a woman wearing only one shoe."

I smiled. "Finding a man with a shoe fetish in New York would be like finding a man who likes hamburgers. Finding a one-shoe kind of guy may be easier. What kind of shoe are we looking for" I asked him, "What kind of shoe killed Kim?"

Murphy looked away. "We'll talk about that later. Right now it's enough for you to know that all we found was one shoe. Does that ring any bells?"

I played with my spoon. Damn! One of the things about being a woman of a certain age is that my memory is not as sharp as it once was. I remembered hearing something about a one-shoe kind of guy but where did I hear it? It could have been anyone from Anita the Puerto Rican transvestite to Harold Shapiro. And then it came to me. "There is someone, someone wrote about it on my blog." I closed my eyes and tried to remember, "It was someone, somewhere, who liked to have sex with a woman wearing only one shoe."

"Names?" he asked.

I shook my head. "My blog is all anonymous. People make up names, "Big-foot, Sole-kisser, Leather-stocking. I don't know who any of them are."

"Yeah you do. You know Leather-Stocking."

I looked at Murphy more closely. Surely he was more than your usual dumb cop.

"James Fenimore Cooper made him up," he said, "and don't test me."

It was nice to meet a cop who knew something about literature.

"I'd really like to help you, but I don't think even this one-shoe guy is special."

"It's a start," Murphy said. "Get me the on-line name of the person who talked about the single shoe guy."

I walked Murphy to the door.

"Tomorrow, I'll be back tomorrow afternoon."

I walked out after him and watched him amble off down the block. He looked as good from the back as from the front. Maybe it was time to re-evaluate my attitude toward the New York Police Force.

Chapter 4

The mule, a kind of backless slipper, trimmed in Marabou and made popular by Marilyn Monroe, is the kind of shoe that suggests a half-dressed woman in a negligee. Add a high heel, placing the back of the foot on a pedestal, and Voila! Instant erotica!

What do you do when you can't seem to get something out of your mind? The rest of the day all I could think of was that one red shoe, where it had been, and what it had done. Or, rather what its mate had done. There was still no reason to connect it with Kim's murder, it was the wrong size and maker, but I was beginning to have a bad feeling about it.

As soon as the last customer left, I locked the front door, tuned off the lights in the showroom and retreated to the back of the store. Then I rummaged in the back of the closet where I had tossed the shoe.

Nothing.

There was no light in the closet and I didn't have a flash so I just felt around for about five minutes.

I found my umbrella, an old pair of rubber boots, one yellow sandal, one red high heeled boot—both orphans from my window display that I couldn't bear to throw away—and one glove.

How was this possible?

The only other person who had access to this closet was Merissa.

But why would she take it? What would she possibly do with one shoe? Suddenly I pictured what was not pictured in the newspaper article. A red shoe with one very high, spiked heel embedded in the head of my sweet Kim.

Yes, one could think of uses for one shoe. On the other hand, there were perfectly innocent uses for a single shoe. Didn't we use single shoes in our display windows? I suppose you could use it as a candy dish; a centerpiece for a Halloween party, a model for a still-life water-color class, or for a hop-scotch contest. Even I had trouble fooling myself with that one. The truth was there really weren't many uses for just one shoe. So why would she take it? Did she have a customer who liked his ladies to wear one shoe? Or maybe she had taken it to prevent anyone from connecting its mate with Emily's Place.

But the police had already made the connection. Kim had worked here. Murphy was already on the trail of someone who had contacted me. And that meant that someone connected to Emily's Place might be a murderer!

That sudden revelation sent me reeling against the closet door. I held tight to the door knob and threw all the stuff back inside. Then I brushed myself off and sat down at the computer. I needed to get a grip on my imagination. I still had no reason to connect a fancy, expensive designer shoe with Kim's murder. It was the wrong size and the wrong maker.

Just out of curiosity, I called up my sales data for all the sales I had made last year. The screen in front of me glowed with names, style numbers and addresses. I typed in Jimmy Choo and another full screen appeared. I didn't realize I had been so successful! At least at selling shoes.

Shasa Belinsky had bought six pairs! Maria Flores had bought three! Beverly Kleinholtz had bought eight! There were several screens more—all filled with names and numbers. There were more than four hundred entries. The names and numbers danced before my eyes. All the joy I have brought to so many women! And then I remembered why I was checking my data base.

One woman surely was not enjoying her Jimy Choo shoes—or shoe. I studied the style numbers. I remembered ordering about ten different styles. There was a gorgeous black satin pump that sold out immediately. I clicked a button on the computer. I could organize the data by style number, but I did not know which number belonged to which shoe. I had no way of knowing the style number of the high-heeled red shoe that had been shoved through my mail chute.

The only way I could find out was to call the manufacturer—and it was surely too late for that this evening.

I sighed. Even if I knew each person's name who had bought that shoe, there would be no way to know if my customer's shoe was the one I had stashed in the closet. There were hundreds of stores in the tri-state area selling Jimmy Choo shoes. So if I knew who the original buyer was, I still wouldn't know if their shoe had anything to do with the murder. No. It would be a far better use of my time to try to track down the one-shoe guy.

Who had mentioned the guy who liked his ladies to wear only one shoe? I reeled through the last two weeks of messages. I did not know if the blogger was a man or a woman. Suddenly, the screen flashed. A new message was coming in.

"Cinderella had a shoe. Her foot was so small she didn't know what to do. Until she found the single shoe. Boo Hoo." The sender's tag was "Goodie One Shoes."

For a couple of minutes I just stared at the screen. I tried to count my breaths the way my yoga teacher had taught me, but the pounding of my heart was too distracting. I flexed my fingers a few times, took a deep breath and typed back, "Why did she only need one shoe?"

"One is hot, two is not." Came the instant reply.

I tried to think how pleased Murphy the cop would be when I relayed this information. Somehow it did not give me much comfort. But I was into it now and I needed to continue. For my own sake and for the sake of any other poor potential victim.

"Are you Cinderella?" I typed back.

"Are you the old lady who lived in a shoe who is looking for a clue?"

Before I was scared; now I was getting mad. I may be a woman of a certain age, but I am not old. "Not old, but true and looking for a clue to who loves only one shoe."

"Then you're barking up the right tree; it is me, tee hee." Came the quick response.

I snarled at the screen. If Goodie One Shoes wanted to play a game, I would give him a game. I had lived in New York too long to be intimidated by a message on a computer.

"But are you a he or are you a she?" I wrote.

"What difference does it make? Remember the snake. Too much knowledge is a big mistake."

I could enjoy this under different circumstances. I typed "What do you do with the other shoe?"

"Up your kazoo, my pretty little titie."

I hesitated. Maybe what I was doing was not a good idea. Encouraging some pervert who might be dangerous.

"Why did you write to me? I use this blog to give advice you see."

"Gone is my sister, my best friend. You need to make amends. Soon life ends."

Now I was getting frightened again. I looked over my shoulder to be sure no one was there—even though I knew I had locked the door. What did he mean by "You need to make amends?" What did he think I did to his sister?

"What have I done to make you mad? What can I do to make you glad?"

The reply came back quickly.

"There is no way to even the score, There is life and death and nothing more."

My fingers froze above the computer keys as I stared at the screen. Outside an ambulance siren blared, a bad omen for sure. I covered my mouth with my hand so I would not scream out and frighten my next door neighbor, Angelina.

This is surely much more than I bargained for. I didn't know if Goodie One Shoes was Kim's killer—but what he wrote certainly seemed full of veiled threats directed at me.

Suddenly I felt very much alone. I pressed the "Save" button on the computer, then the "Print" key and logged off my computer as quickly as possible. I know it was silly, but I ran into the kitchen and got a dish towel and threw it over the monitor. I was not taking any chances.

There was something so weird about Goodie One Shoes that I almost expected him to come riding into my living room on an electronic wave. Goodie One Shoes was right about one thing. Too much knowledge was not a good thing. But now that I knew what I knew, it was impossible to forget it.

"I'm here!" Shana announced happily. "Open the door."

I rubbed my eyes and looked at the clock. 3:00am.

"Where are you?" I asked incredulously.

"I'm standing right outside your door. I didn't need to ring the buzzer and wake you up because the outside door was open. "

Right.

We thought our security system was real clever. Everyone in the building had a code—a number that did not match their apartment. The idea was that if someone had a delivery for, say, Angelina Grosso, my next door neighbor in Apt. 1 A, that person needed to know her code, which was 401. If he just pressed 1A, no one would answer. Theoretically this would prevent thieves, rapists, and other no-goods from just reading a name on the apartment directory, and ringing the buzzer next to the name, claiming he had a special delivery for her and getting in.

The only problem with this system was that it mostly did not work. That was because many people in the building, like the gal in 3A, were sleeping most of the day, had forgotten their code or did not bother to tell it to the delivery boy. Even George Washington Green, our resident superintendent was too drunk one evening last week to remember the code to his own apartment and I had to knock on his door to wake up his wife who really didn't feel like letting him in anyhow—but that's another story altogether. Also, there was a tendency for the tenants not to slam the door behind them, which made it quite easy for anyone to enter the building, code or no code.

I grabbed my robe and opened the door. Sure enough, there she was, my baby sister, blue eyes shining, golden hair streaked by the sun, broken arm and all.

I looked once into the hallway to be sure she was not followed in then I pulled her inside and double-locked the door.

For a moment, I just hugged her. It had been a while since I was this close to anyone. I didn't realize how much I missed it.

"Are you all right?" I asked her, "Your arm? Everything?"

Shana smiled and slid off her back-pack. She yawned. "Got anything to eat in this place? I couldn't stop on the road."

"You got the convertible?"

"Not exactly," she said, "I hitched a ride in. Several rides, in fact. It took a while."

"You hitched rides? In the middle of the night? With strangers?"

She sat down on my couch and shook her head. "Emily, Emily. There you go again. Thinking negative thoughts. Negativity attracts bad Karma. It's like a self-fulfilling prophesy. That's why you're having so much trouble."

I pretended that I had not heard this last remark, and I opened the refrigerator door. I took out the remainder of roast chicken parts from the Chirping Chicken Restaurant next door and placed a couple of plates and utensils on the kitchen table. I poured us both a cold glass of seltzer.

I heard Shana moving around behind me. She opened the bedroom door and glanced in. Then she sat next to me at the kitchen table. When she reached for a piece of chicken, I saw that her nails were cracked and dirty.

"Would you like to wash up?" I asked her gently. I pointed toward the bathroom door.

"Later." She said, filling her plate with chicken.

For a while I sipped my seltzer and watched her wolf down her food. I wondered what Deepek did with the five thousand I sent her.

At last, she leaned back in the chair and smiled at me. "Thought I'd stop off here for a few days before my conference to say hello."

I smiled back." Hello!" I greeted her again and gave her a hug.

She pushed me away and looked into my eyes. "I kept getting bad vibes," she said. "I felt them all the way up in the mountains of the Berkshires. I couldn't sleep."

I didn't want her to come but I was glad she did. I stood over her and put my arms around her shoulders.

"You're really lucky that I came along. I can see you need my help. First off, you should go back to Larry and get rid of this dump." She looked at the entrance to the bedroom. "The accommodations were much better when you were living with him. One of us ought to be smart enough to get a decent place to live. Besides, he needs you. I can feel it…"

"All the way up into the mountains of the Berkshires." I finished her sentence for her.

She laughed and squeezed my hand.

"There's one thing about this visit that is not a laughing matter, "I told her. "There's a murderer running loose in this city who just killed Kim. Promise me you will not wander around in the middle of the night by yourself.

"Of course not," she told me. "I'll be sure to find a really cute guy to accompany me."

Somehow, I was not reassured, but I realized, yet again, that my sister is forty-two years old and I cannot tell her what to do. Rather, I can continue to tell her what to do but I can no longer make her do it.

We stood side by side and did the dishes. It felt good. The next morning I give Shana a key to the outside door and my apartment. When I was ready to leave for work, Shana was sitting in front of the television wearing a red tee shirt featuring a hand painted portrait of the evil eye, and jeans.

"Nice shirt," I said, rolling my eyes.

"It's the evil eye. It keeps the bad spirits away, and attracts good Karma."

"Hope it works," I told her.

She stretched and yawned. "It's working so far. Deepek is selling them in all colors."

"Deepek." I repeated lamely.

"They're made of bamboo. It's better for the planet."

I nodded. If the welfare of the planet rested with Shana and Deepek it was in more trouble than I had imagined.

"What will you do today?" I asked her.

She shrugged and waved her hand. "Something. I am waiting for inspiration."

I looked up at the tin ceiling of my apartment. As if on cue, we heard a click of the lock and the doorknob turned. I would like to say it was a sign from one of the Gods worshipped by my sister that good fortune awaited us, but it was only Bonita, my cleaning lady. Bonita and Shana had met before and seemed to like each other because now they fell into each other's arms like best friends.

"Shana!"

"Bonita!"

Was I jealous that Shana's relationships with others seemed so fresh and uncomplicated? A little. But basically I was glad she would have some company.

"You look so beautiful! Your hair. It is longer!" Bonita gushed.

"And yours. It is more blonde!" Shana commented as they admired each other.

Bonita had come from Guatamala with the clothes on her back and had dyed her hair blonde with her first American dollars. She might be poor but she is happy as a clam. She sings "La Cucaracha" while she cleans and brings me fried plantains to eat.

"And you are so beautiful in rojo" Bonita exclaimed pointing to Shana's red tee shirt.

"And you in blanco!" Shana returned.

"Let's switch," Shana suggested, laughing, and in minutes she and Bonita had exchanged tees.

Bonita was rounder—her breasts pulled against the flimsy material expanding the scope of the evil eye—but both were wearing jeans and were roughly the same height and same age.

What would become of them in this harsh world? Bonita had so little in her life and Shana, comparatively speaking, so much—and yet-here they both were, with similar tastes and sunny personalities.

I thought of Kim, her glowing cheeks, her gentle nature—crushed, bashed, hideously destroyed. I shivered. Was there some magic incantation that could keep the Devil away from this household? Even though I did not believe in the Devil, sometimes, it seemed, I did.

I took a deep breath and shook myself to drive away my thoughts. I took some cash out of my purse and gave a few bills to each of them. Then I headed out for a day's work at Emily's Place.

Chapter 5

Aphrodite, the Greek Goddess of love, often appears in paintings and statues naked except for a pair of sandals.

"Oh my, Yes! Yes! Yes! Who would believe...the cutest thing I've ever seen!" Cheryl gushed, grabbing on to my arm.

The scene that greeted my arrival at Emily's Place a couple of days later was dramatic enough to sweep thoughts of my poor Kim and her horrible murder to the corner of my mind. It was Merissa's turn to open up and I had just come in with Shana.

All the customers were on their feet and staring upwards. Silver-haired Evelyn Rabinowitz had her hand on her heart and was hyperventilating, while Harriet Moskowitz, Tiffany bracelets jingling, gasped, "Be careful, Be careful!"

Ida Esposito was pushing her way to the front of the group for a better view, Inez Veracruz was chewing on her fingernails, and Wilhelmina Simpson had thrust her rosary out in front of her as if trying to keep werewolves at bay.

Sitting on top of my central display case about ten feet high on the back wall of the showroom was Fifi, feet dangling, head nodding, and a smile as big as Canada on her face. And closest to the case, staring up at her with worship in her eyes was the six foot 2 inch transvestite, Cheryl.

"I just asked her to fetch me down that gold beauty on the top shelf—kind of a joke I thought it was—and then she jumped up and pulled herself up the side of the cabinet as if she were taking a walk in the park!"

Merissa was standing next to Cheryl, her hands on her hips and a scowl on her face.

"*Sacre Coeur*! Mademoiselle! You know Fifi don't know any better than a child. She always doing damn silly tricks like that. One day, goin fall down, kill herself dead right here in Emily's Place. How you goin' feel then?"

It was clear to me that Cheryl felt nothing but glee at the whole scene and could hardly contain herself. Her large boned frame was bent almost double with laughter. She only stopped long enough to give Shana a long, admiring look. "Who is this little sweetheart?" she asked. Rhinestone glasses with hair clip to match gleaming in the light streaming into the shop, "Great shirt!" she called out.

"My little sister," I replied.

Shana had been with me three days at this point—her conference was starting next week—and most of the time I found her sprawled out in front of the T.V.

I was happy to have her company—especially at night when pictures of poor Kim's cold, violated body surrounded me like a damp fog—but her lazy passivity was beginning to irritate me. I had suggested she come with me this morning, just to get her out of the house.

"Sisters are special," Cheryl pronounced. "Love your hair!" she tossed over her shoulder

"Don't worry my little doll baby," Cheryl called out to Fifi, "Cheryl will save you. You can jump right into these arms!" And she rolled up her sleeve to display a very hairy, muscular arm with a tattoo of an anchor on the forearm.

"*Mon Dieu! C'est ne pas possible!*" Merissa yelled upward, waving her arms. It seemed to me that even Merissa had forgotten than Fifi was deaf, and all this yelling and waving of arms was probably just causing her more confusion than usual.

I had gotten used to having Fifi stop by from time to time and sit quietly in her corner seat, listening to the silent tunes in her head and smiling at everyone who passed by. For a while she had taken no notice at all of the shoes and the customers, just seemed content, wrapped up in her own thoughts, however confused they might be. But then, one day, when we had set out the sale table, she seemed to suddenly come alive. Perhaps it was the profusion of colors and shapes, all jumbled up together that worked her up—a sensory overload that pierced her self-imposed alienation from the rest of us. Whatever it was, her face lit up like a moon that had been eclipsed by the sun, slowly emerging from the dark side of the heavens.

The longer she stared, the brighter she seemed to become, until it seemed to me she almost glowed with pleasure. Then she walked over to the table, squirmed in besides Henrietta Kaufman and Maya Thompson, and emerged a few minutes later holding a neon-green shoe with a silver buckle.

It was just a sale shoe with a tarnished buckle but it surely spoke to something deep inside Fifi. When I slipped it on her good foot she was transported instantly to another realm. She was a perfect size 8 and we smiled at each other in a moment of pure sisterhood. Naturally I gave her the shoe as a present. I gave her both shoes even though the left one wouldn't fit her.

A small price to pay for that kind of pleasure and someone's undying love. Or so I believed at that moment. Although I hated to admit it, even to myself, there was something almost dog-like about Fifi's big, liquid eyes and patient demeanor—the way she followed my movements around the store after that, almost panting with expectation of another treat. The way she sometimes curled up in the chair, head resting on her arm but eyes now always alert.

I had tried to think of some job she might be able to do, some productive work she could find to fill her day, but Merissa didn't seem to like to talk much about her and I didn't know what strengths and talents, if any, she had.

I knew she was strong—her upper body and arms fully rounded and muscular, strength gained, I'm sure from her years of pulling herself around on crutches—because she would sometimes help me carry boxes of shoes and put away the stock. But I had no idea those muscles could pull her straight up a ten foot wall. Could those same muscles get her down?

I positioned myself in front of Merissa, in front of Harriet and in front of Cheryl and carefully mouthed these words. "Come Down Now!"

It was at that point that my sister Shana stepped forward, one hand raised and uttered her magic word, "Ommmmmmm!" in a long sustained moan.

I had to admit it did silence the crowd.

"Everyone join hands!" she called out, and before I could put a stop to all this nonsense, I saw everyone reach for the hand next to them.

"Just what do you think you are doing?" I cried out to her.

"Creating a ring of energy," Shana said, her voice cool and melodious, "Enough energy to cushion her fall."

It was useless to explain that Fifi was deaf as a doorknob and wouldn't have a clue what any of us were saying or doing down here. As for any energy generated by this human ring, I would as soon believe that the earth was flat.

Fifi looked at me, then she looked at Shana, then she looked at Cheryl whose arms are held out in front of her and she jumped.

That was not exactly what I meant. I had hoped for some gradual, graceful descent. Nevertheless, she was down and safely cradled in the strong arms of Cheryl, who proudly and happily trotted her all around the showroom basking in their shared glory.

"Can she climb trees?" Harriet Moskowitz, Director of the Central Park Conservation Association called out. Merissa looked at her and smiled. "Mon Petite Fifi climb trees all over Haiti. Her momma and papa, they have banana tree plantation. Fifi climb before she walk."

This part of Merissa's family history was new to me, but certainly accounted in part for the French connection. At any rate, it seemed to delight Harriet, who said it was very difficult to find anyone in the city experienced in climbing trees and many of the trees in Central Park can only be pruned with the help of someone in the tree.

Voila! A productive and paying job for Fifi. Two problems solved at once. And I sold Cheryl the gold shoes, size ten, Ralph Lauren at a special one-day store discount for ninety-nine dollars.

If only all my problems could be solved so easily. As soon as all the excitement calmed down, I was left once again with a heavy heart. So vivid was my recollection of Kim assisting in the store, that I was jolted when Cheryl explained, a little embarrassed to have caused such a ruckus, "I'd never have asked Fifi to fetch that shoe, if Louise was here."

"Louise the Loser?" You still remember her? She was fired two and a half years ago!"

"I remember her," Cheryl says, "She always put away size ten for me."

"You liked her better than Kim?" My beautiful, gentle, Kim. Murphy had called last night to say I could claim the body, and I had spent the evening planning a memorial service.

"Kim? Kim didn't do much for me," Cheryl said. "I think she was prejudiced against big women." Cheryl adjusted her blonde upsweep with one large ringed finger, refastened her hair clip, an oversized daisy covered with rhinestones and waved goodbye.

Merissa came up behind me and we both watched Cheryl walk off unsteadily in her three inch yellow Prada heels.

"Mon Dieu," Merissa says "*Cette* Mademoiselle need some help from someone know something about style,"

I turned to look at her. The presence of Merissa reminded me of another mystery that needed to be solved. And so, I asked "Did you help her with a red Jimmy Choo shoe I had in the closet?"

Merissa smiled at me. "A red Jimmy Choo? *Alors* Madame Emily.

What you talking about? What anyone goin to do with one Jimmy Choo? If you had two I would keep them *por moi* "and she turned her back on me and walked out the door.

Chapter 6

The end of the 19th Century was the era of novel leathers. Shoes suddenly appeared in dozens of tanned and dyed skins—alligator, reptile, even kangaroo.

It was damp and dreary in the All Faith Chapel on Mott Street. I had conferred with Merissa, the two of us being the closest thing to family Kim had in this country—probably anywhere, given that her parents had left her on the steps of the orphanage, and we had decided that it was fitting that a memorial service be held in Chinatown where she lived, so that any friends she made in the neighborhood could attend.

Since, so far as I knew, Kim had no religion whatsoever, Merissa and I searched around until we could find something that would accommodate a certain foggy spiritual affiliation. In other words, a place where my sister Shana—lapsed Jew and proponent of several Eastern religions—myself—cultural Jew but spiritual agnostic—my neighbors, Angelina Grosso—lapsed Catholic and pagan—and Harold Shapiro—Member of the Jewish Re-constructionist Temple whatever that was—Merissa—lapsed Catholic with an affection for Voodoo—Fifi—I wouldn't even guess at that one—and an assortment of my best customers; Hispanics, ladies of the night, crossdressers and Kim's friends might relate to.

The All Faith Chapel was a somewhat drafty space behind a store front, and when the "leader" took me to see it, there was a large wooden cross set up in the front, which he assured me was only for today, tomorrow, being Saturday, the space was to be used by a Jewish group, whose leader, a woman rabbi, played the guitar.

There were homemade banners on the wall with sayings in different languages and a few tattered bibles lying around on the wooden benches. The whole thing reminded me of color-war long ago at Camp Brookwood in the Catskills but I had hopes our fond spirits would fill the small space and transform it into everyone's spiritual haven.

To this end, Merissa had brought a Haitian 'flag" with her made of sequins that honored one of her home spirits, while I brought honey and sponge cake, traditionally served after Friday night services in the temple I attended years ago. My neighbor Angelina contributed a sky-blue silk Japanese kimono that we draped over the podium along with an embroidered napkin from Bonita and Harriet's sterling silver candle stick.

Shana scattered around some white powder that at first I feared was cocaine but which she assured me was merely a special kind of incense manufactured by her ashram in the Berkshires.

You never know with Shana.

Friends and classmates of Kim from The New School brought photos of her that were taped around the room.

We had had Kim cremated—or rather Merissa did since it was clearly beyond me to retrieve her mutilated body from the morgue.

"Madame Emily," Merissa told me, "Moi. I will pick up *le petite bebe. Mort et Mort*, mon ami, Merissa has been to the morgue before. "Same as any place I ever see filled with dead folk. You think you put pretty dress on dead girl, she live again?" Merissa shook her head. "No way. I get that gal, bring her to a place to cleanse her soul. Set her free from this world."

I looked up at the cracked and peeling ceiling. Hope her soul escaped somewhere nice, is what I thought. In my purse, I held a small pouch with Kim's ashes.

We had posted a note on the door to Emily's Place, about the time and place of the memorial service, and taken out an ad in the Chinatown Daily News. I posted a note on the door of her building as well, and I put an announcement in the student newspaper at The New School. My biggest terror was that poor Kim, so neglected in life, would be once more neglected in death, with only a few stragglers showing up to honor her memory.

Boy, was I mistaken. The Chapel seated fifty people and by the time the Leader of the congregation closed the doors, there was standing room only.

People kept coming up to me and shaking my hand, dozens of Chinese people, the elderly babbling away in sing-song language I'd never heard before; little kids telling me how Kim helped them with their homework. Then there were the young people from her class.

"My best friend!" said a dark-haired young woman called Judy.

"Such an artist!" a blonde haired boy remarked.

"The most talented student I ever had," reported Professor James Keernan, a tall, pale man I had never heard of before.

And then, to my horror, who should approach me but Tweedy

Guy himself, hand extended. Maybe he thought I would not recognize him, but, of course, I recognized his professorial costume and his Italian shoes right off. And well polished they were too—especially for the occasion.

I avoided his outstretched hand and tried to look more closely into his face, but he was wearing a hat and those glasses that get darker when you're in a lighted room. Tall, regular features—no horrible scar, patch over his eye, twitch, or anything that would mark what I knew was his sinister character.

"I think we've met before," I said to him, "Kim's house."

He shifted his weight from one foot to the other "I'm afraid you are mistaken," he said. "I've never been there. Wonderful girl, Kim. How are you related?"

"We were very close friends," I told him. "How are you related?"

The question took him somewhat aback. "Related?" he answered, "Teacher and student. Quite talented. A real loss to us all" and with that, he turned on his heel and took a seat on the aisle where he could easily escape when he wanted to.

I tried to calm myself by looking over the crowd, my crowd—all the friends and "family" from Emily's Place; Merissa, and Shana, Bonita, my cleaning lady, my best customers, Harriet Moskowitz, Sasha Brodsky, Manuela Gomez, Heidi Rubinowitz and Harold Shapiro, my fabulous window-dresser. Even José who delivered the newspapers and Charles, the mailman, neither of whom knew her very well. I guess they came for the refreshments that would follow the service.

Even my eighty-year-old neighbor, Angelina, who hardly ever left her apartment, was splendid in a red satin kimono, a black turban and yellow high-heeled shoes.

And then I saw Murphy the Cop. The sight of him, like Phillip Quinn brought back the tragedy of Kim's death in a very visceral manner. I had to sit down.

None of this prevented me from noticing that Murphy was looking more spiffy today than when last we met. He had on a blue jacket and light blue shirt, open at the neck and his silver streaked hair was neatly combed.

Sure, after you hit fifty most men walk by you as if you were a lamppost but some of us can still command a little attention. I kept myself trim with yoga and tennis and my salt and pepper colored hair is short and curly. I have a silver streak inherited from my dad, may he rest in peace, that runs from the part in my hair across my forehead that Larry once said lights up my whole face. In short, I look pretty good for a woman my age. And Murphy looked to be about my age.

I caught his eye but we were too far apart to talk and the service was about to start.

We had asked anyone to speak who wanted to speak, and one after another, people rose from the audience to talk about their special feelings for Kim.

Fortunately, Phillip Quinn did not decide to speak. Fortunately for him, because I thought at that point I would have attacked him with the two inch stacked heels I was wearing. I was convinced he had something to do with Kim's murder. Why else would he lie about what he was doing there?

When I looked over in his direction, I saw he had already left.

One young man waved an orange banner and chanted something that Shana whispered to me was a Buddhist prayer. A young woman lighted a candle and mumbled something in Spanish; Merissa sprinkled chicken blood onto a plate and painted the face of the Leader. I uttered the only Hebrew prayer I knew, the one you do before you eat, but I figured no one would be able to tell the difference—a prayer is a prayer—and if there was a Jewish God, he would recognize the good intention.

Shana gathered a group of people who circled the podium seven times round, a ceremony usually performed by Orthodox Jews at weddings. At the end of the service, we all joined hands and sang a few hymns, including "We shall overcome," which I'm not sure quite fit in, but as long as it made some people feel good, it was okay with me.

The service must have touched people because even José and Charles came up to me to pay their respects before they ran for the honey cake.

Charles, always so reserved, tipped his cap and said, "She was prettier than her picture."

I looked around at the photos pasted up around the room. There was Kim wearing a New School tee shirt; Kim with a bunch of Chinese kids doing finger-painting; Kim standing against the fender of a convertible. Kim in a perfect Lotus Pose. She looked beautiful in all of them. But none of them had the glow of life. I was touched by the sensitivity of Charles the mailman.

José, usually flip and outrageous, just shuffled his feet and shook my hand.

When it was all over, I made my way over to Murphy.

"Good service,' he said, "Something for everyone."

I thought I detected a note of sarcasm but I decided to ignore it.

"Good to see you here," I lied. Actually he made me sad, even though he was attractive. "Do you always attend the services of all the murdered people in the city?"

"No. Only the ones of special interest."

He leaned closer to me and whispered in my ear, "As a woman well versed in T.V. detective work, don't you know criminals often return to the scene of their crime?"

Bit of a put-down, that, I would say. Obviously he was still annoyed that I was able to find Kim's phone—and a good suspect—before he did. However, in the spirit of the occasion, I decided not to take the bait.

"Well," I replied, "This isn't exactly the scene of the crime."

Murphy shrugged. "Sometimes they come back to be sure the victim is really dead."

"That's a creepy thing, to say." He was beginning to really annoy me.

"Murder is a creepy business. Is there anyone here you don't know?"

That question made me pause. "As a matter of fact," I told him, "I've never even heard of most of them before."

Murphy's right eye-brow twitched. "I thought you told me she was almost a daughter to you?"

"That doesn't mean I know all her friends." I retorted.

"I guess not. You didn't know anything about Phillip Quinn until you ran into him at Kim's apartment."

Now it was my turn to challenge him, "And what, if anything, did you find out about Phillip Quinn.?"

"So glad you asked," Murphy quipped. "He was her life-drawing professor—and her lover."

That shut me up pretty quick—at least for a minute. I should have kicked Quinn while I had the chance.

"So she had a boyfriend I didn't know about." I conceded, "Most young women keep those things to themselves."

"He wasn't your average boyfriend. He was her professor. And he is married. Interesting that he left pretty quickly. I wonder how many other "boyfriends" *are* or *are not* here that you didn't know about."

Now I was really getting angry. "You have no right to insinuate these things. Kim was a student, an innocent, a throw-away child just trying to survive."

Murphy cocked his head. "How well did you really know this girl? I'm beginning to wonder if you really are 'her next of kin'."

"What do you think?" I challenged him, "That I made up a whole story just to get hold of the body? Do you think I'm a suspect?"

"Everyone is a suspect until we finish the investigation. "

I shook my head. That's what I mean about cops. You can never trust them. As soon as you think maybe you can be friends, they turn on you like a snake. "What about Quinn? Now we know he probably had a motive! Maybe Kim was about to break up with him. Maybe she threatened to tell the Dean. And what about Kim's phone? Did you find out anything?"

"Yeah," he answered. "She called you, as we know. And Quinn called her, after she was murdered. That means he didn't do it."

I sat back down on the bench. "I don't think it means that at all. He could have called as an alibi."

"Don't think so. Guys like that aren't murderers. They are just taking advantage of low-hanging fruit. Young, pretty girl, worships her professor—the guy who knows everything—the father she never had. What more does he need? Doesn't have to kill her to get what he wants. We've got to keep looking. Why don't you leave the police work to me. What's a smart woman like you doing with a shoe store anyhow?"

I felt my face getting red. "It's a long story. Let's just say I'm an underachiever. What about you?"

He smiled. "Me? I'm just a dumb Irish cop."

I remembered our exchange about Dickens. "Not so dumb, I'd bet." We smiled at each other.

He extended his hand. "You know, if the dumb cop and the underachieving shoe monger joined forces they might really be able to accomplish something. Did you remember the name of the one shoe guy?"

I took his hand. It was warm and strong. I decided to ignore the 'shoe-monger' comment in the spirit of cooperation. "Ok. All I know is the person's on-line tag is Goodie One Shoes. I can't even tell if the person is a man or a woman. Whoever the person is, he or she talks in rhymes." I dug in my purse and took-out the print-out from my computer. "And he seems dangerous. Made these comments about my needing to 'make amends' as if he had some personal grudge against me or something."

Murphy moved over to a corner of the bench. Most of the

mourners had left. Even Shana had gone, I didn't know where.

Murphy read the print-out carefully. "Goodie One Shoes. Wouldn't you think it would be Goodie One Shoe?"

I shrugged. "Maybe the person isn't very good at grammar."

"Or maybe," Murphy suggested, "There are multiple shoes but only one shoe of each pair."

"Or, now that I think about it, maybe it also has to do with the other shoe, the one the woman is not wearing."

"Touché," Murphy said. "Just keep your conversation going and let me have copies. You're right though—there is clearly some threat here." He rose to leave and put his arm on my shoulder. It felt nice to be touched. "Make no mistake. Whoever this person is, he or she might be dangerous. And you are a woman living alone."

How does he know I live alone? "I appreciate the concern," I said, "but maybe I could be more helpful if I knew a little more about this murder." I had never mentioned the strange delivery of the red shoe. "Can you tell me what kind of shoe was found with the body?"

Murphy shook his head. "Remember the snake in the garden of Eden."

I shivered. Now Murphy was quoting Goodie One Shoes. "At least," I tried again, "What color the shoe was?"

He shook his head again. "Believe me, the less you know about the details, the better it is for you and the entire investigation."

He looked out over the empty space of the Chapel. Sad and dingy now, with all the warmth of our ceremony forgotten. "Was there anyone *not here* whom you would expect to come?"

Now that was an interesting question. I thought for a moment. "Juanita Rodriguez, Teresa Fitzpatric, Henrietta Morgan, Paula Friedman. They were all pretty good customers who knew Kim pretty well. Guess they had other things to do today. Lots of people feel it's more important to honor someone in life, rather than death." I skipped over Cheryl Smith the transvestite; she had told me she didn't much like Kim. "And Fifi—Merissa's niece. Merissa told me she was too upset to come."

"You'll send me these people's addresses?" he asked.

I nodded.

"Who was that pretty blonde, led the circle dance?"

I bit my lip. It was always the same. Men loved her. "My sister Shana."

"Keep an eye on her," he cautioned.

I knew my sister was prettier than me, but she's such a ditz-head that I couldn't believe a smart man like Murphy would be interested in her.

Before I could react to Murphy's comment about my sister, there was a strange ding-a-ling—like, if Tinkerbelle had a phone it would have a sound like that—and Murphy reached into his pocket and took out a very small phone and turned his back to me.

Back turned or not, my hearing was still pretty good for a woman of a certain age, especially when she was really interested, and this is what I heard:

Murphy said, "Of course, Little Belly. What Big Belly says, Big Belly will do." A pause while the other person answered. Then Murphy again, "Aww. I'll be there. I promised, didn't I? When Chief Big Belly promises, he always shows up. I'll be there. Trust me."

And then Big Belly took a few steps further away from me and I couldn't hear anything else. I heard enough to make my heart even heavier than it was. Murphy was married, had a kid. And that phrase "Trust me." Two little words with a history of the deepest deception. Murphy put the phone back in his pocket and turned to face me. "My daughter." he said, "She takes ballet. She's in a recital."

I supposed I was in a very emotional state over Kim because all of a sudden I felt this overwhelming desire to cry. I bit my lip and looked down at my shoes. Ralph Lauren pumps in real black alligator. Not much comfort. I looked up and met Murphy's gaze. "When is the recital?"

"Now." He said. He shuffled his feet. "I'm not very good at these things," he explained.

"Bring her flowers" I told him.

"Flowers?" He snorted. "She's six."

"Bring her flowers." I said again. "Trust me."

Our eyes locked for a moment and then Murphy put his hand on my shoulder. "Thanks." He said as he walked toward the door. "I'll be in touch."

Chapter 7

The ideal erotic prize in 18th and 19th century China, was the "golden lotus," feet measuring only 3 inches. Husbands would often proudly display their wife's tiny lotus shoes on a plate.

Murphy might believe that Phillip Quinn was innocent but I wasn't willing to drop that lead so easily. He was obviously a scum bag, cheating on his wife and having an affair with a student less than half his age, so he was already guilty of plenty in my book.

Yes, I would try to follow up with Goodie One Shoes, but I had a plan of my own. Unfortunately it required some help from a lawyer I used to live with, my estranged husband Larry.

Since I hadn't seen Larry, except accidently, when we would sometimes run into each other at Zabar's appetizing store, or talked to him, except to remind him that I wasn't talking to him, in three years, my suddenly asking "for a favor" was a little awkward.

I had walked out on him but we had never gotten divorced. He didn't push it because it would cost him a bundle, and I didn't push it because there didn't seem to be any point.

I didn't need a decree to tell me I was free. But Larry couldn't seem to rest happily with this arrangement. He couldn't get over the fact that I had left him. He was hell bent on getting me back. Then he could leave me and feel he had gotten the last word.

Anyway it wasn't our anniversary. Strange as it seems, Larry called every year asking if he could take me out to dinner for our anniversary—I always said "no!" Or my birthday, when he would make a similar attempt to get my attention—or even his birthday when he tried to make me feel guilty for the way I had treated him, as if I was the one who had a Cock-eyed Cossack lover on the side instead of him. Given that there was no easy excuse to call him up, I admit I was stumped.

I was sitting on the floor of my living room/dining room in my Lotus Pose which I hoped would bring me some inspiration when Larry solved the problem by calling me. It seemed Larry had read Page three of the *New York Times*, learned about Kim's murder and he felt I was a good candidate for the role of next victim.

Wish-full thinking is more like it. Knock off the old lady once and for all. Marry the Slavic slut and live happily ever after. "I don't think I'm the murderer's type," I told him. "He goes for the young girls."

"Don't be such a smart-aleck," he reprimanded me, "These creeps will go for anyone who wears shoes."

He had some idea about wiring my apartment with burglar alarms. I could just hear sirens going off every time a passing dog rubbed up against the window. But, to tell the truth, I was feeling a little nervous these days—especially after my interchange with Goodie One Shoes, and it was a good way to get him in a position to talk about Phillip Quinn. And so to his surprise and my own, I invited Larry for dinner.

Now, I very rarely cook—seemed like such a waste of time in a city where within one square block you can choose between Mexican, Indian, Turkish, French, Chinese, Thai and Italian restaurants. Since working took up most of my time, and it didn't seem worthwhile to cook for one, I had been cooking even less since my split with Larry.

So how to account for the fact that I suddenly had a desire for a home cooked meal? Go figure! I cooked a turkey with sausage stuffing, sweet potatoes, cranberry sauce and pecan pie.

It had been three years since I cooked Thanksgiving dinner and I was missing it. For the past three years I made sure I was traveling somewhere—Montreal, Jamaica, Mexico—any place that had no Thanksgiving.

Before that, we used to have a really fun time at Thanksgiving. His mom and dad; my mom and dad, Shana and her latest boyfriend, and Larry's Aunt Miriam at ninety-three dancing around the living room after a couple of bottles of wine. I would be starting off with positive memories. Besides, Thanksgiving dinner was just about the only meal I knew would always turn out right. So the fact that it was May and not November, was not a deterrent.

When a huge bouquet of flowers arrived, I decided that Larry was obviously feeling guilty about something. Either he was still seeing his Borst Baby or he had found some new piece of trash. But I had promised myself to be welcoming—hey, I invited him, right? So I bit my tongue and pretended to be genuinely pleased. I even thanked him for the flowers.

It helped a little when my neighbor, Angelina, always at the ready with some phony garbage near her door giving her an excuse to come out in the hall, popped out of her apartment to check out my guest.

"Ohhhhhh," she gushed, when I introduced her, "So this is your EX, so handsome."

Henry, her gray parrot squawked his welcome in the background

"Not an EX anything," Larry retorted, with his usual lack of charm, "But thanks for the compliment."

Angelina smiled and jingled her bracelets. She was given to wearing an arm full. Today's were silver and made little tinkle sounds when they banged into each other. She patted her red hair and walked toward us in a wobbley sort of way.

"Wow!" I said, "Great shoes!" Angelina used to be chorus girl and her legs were still muscular. At eighty plus she still wore three inch heels around the house. She hiked up her green silk kimono and did a little two step.

"These shoes have seen some things, Dolly, believe me. I still have my legs—'cept when my arthritis kicks up, slows me down a bit."

Cut steel buckles on black satin slides. Probably 1930's or 40's. Her feet were small, but wide. "What size do you wear?" I asked her, "Maybe I can find you something at the shop."

"I'm really a size six but size seven feels so good I wear a size 8," she chuckled.

Even Larry smiled now. "How do you girls walk in those things?"

"We don't walk, honey, we strut" Angelina said, "Ta, Ta!" and with that, she turned and walled unsteadily back to her apartment.

At first I thought even Larry felt a little awkward, when we shut the door. He didn't know where to throw his coat; he didn't know where to sit. There really weren't a lot of choices. I only have two rooms—one 'everything room' which included a closet-sized kitchen, a dining area and living room—the second room was a small bedroom in the back. I was partly underground and the living room had no windows—my bedroom faced the back garden—so the whole apartment was a little dark, but I thought of it as cozy.

I was usually only home at night when it was dark anyway. When I was not working, I was out wandering the city. I walked around the Museum of Natural History; visited the great Whale, explored the Rose Space Center and found out my weight on Mars. I hung out at the Barnes & Noble superstore on West 83rd Street and read books for free. If the weather was fine, I meandered through Central Park, put down a blanket on the Great Lawn, or rented a row-boat. So who needed a big apartment in New York City? The whole city was my living room.

This apartment was my turf. Here Larry was the stranger.

But after a few glasses of wine, we seemed to settle in together, forgot ourselves and actually had a good time.

So here we were, sitting across from each other and I had to admit I was feeling a little nostalgic. Until of course, Larry got up from the table, took a turn around the living room and said, "You don't have to live like this you know."

"Live like what?" I demanded.

"Like a refuge without a penny to her name, in a basement apartment with half a window and a leaky toilet."

"It's a maisonette," I explained, "and I'm not competing with any refuges for anything."

Larry shook his head. "Natasha isn't competing with you for anything. You're my wife."

"And Natasha?"

Larry rubbed his eyes. "Let it go Emily. Let it go. I explained all that. It wasn't anything. She was just a girl in a new country. I was trying to help her."

"Yeah right. More like she was a new cunt from an old country. Is she living with you?"

"Of course not. That's all over. She went back to her husband." He sat down. "She wanted me to bring her mother and her two sisters to New York to live with us. She had an uncle who was selling stolen furs in Queens. She wanted me to hire him as my accountant. She had a cousin who smuggled cigarettes. She wanted me to get him a liquor license. She thought I could help the whole family."

He reached across the table for my hand. "I love you. I've loved you since we met in high school at Erasmus Hall in Brooklyn. What do I want with a Russian girl?"

I withdrew my hand. "We both know what you wanted with that Russian girl."

"It's over Emily—I swear it's over. It was over before it began."

"Does she still work at the firm?"

Larry squirmed in the chair. "I didn't hire her. I can't fire her. She's smart. She does her work. Everyone likes her."

"I don't like her."

Larry fidgeted. "You're a hard-hearted woman," he said. "Anyone who could flush my beautiful Tiger Fish down the toilet, has to be made of steel. Natasha makes more money than her husband. They have a little kid; a mortgage. She's a survivor."

"Right. The kind of survivor who sees where the money is— and is smart enough to know how to make an old guy feel like a big shot. And your cruddy fish-tank was smelling up the entire living room."

I had forgotten about the fish. They met the same fate as Larry's chess pieces, although I choose a more suitable engine of destruction. One by one down the toilet bowl.

It was amazing to me that a man who was as smart as Larry in the court room could be so dumb in the bedroom and have any affection what-so-ever for a bunch of stupid fish.

I got up and walked across the room. I had to admit I felt a little sorry for Larry sitting there, a button missing from his shirt, a stain on his tie. Although he was several inches taller than me, he looked smaller now, his shoulders slumped, his hair greyer than before. But he was a lawyer, and good at pleading his case. Good at getting the jurors to vote in his favor. I was having none of it.

I was happy the way things were. I did not want to fall into the nostalgia trap. He deserved everything he got. He was still seeing Natasha, everyday.

"If you really care about me," I said, "you can help me in another way. I need some information on someone who might have killed my sales girl."

Larry had not known the murdered girl he read about in the newspapers was that close to me. He had never met her, never knew she existed. In fact, he had no idea of just how close to me she really was. I kept most of my feelings to myself. Kim was mine and I didn't want to share her—especially with Larry. I wasn't about to tell him that I sometimes thought of her as the daughter we never had.

If he was worried about me before, now he seemed really agitated. He jumped up from his chair. "Your salesgirl!" He muttered, "Your salesgirl!"

And then I told him what I knew about Kim and Phillip Quinn When I had finished he pushed his chair away from the table and got up.

"What are you telling me? That you want me to investigate some pervert who screws illegal aliens."

I searched for some more appealing way to say it, but settled for the bare truth. "Yes, that's about it."

"I'm an estate lawyer now. I do wills and estates. I'm not in the Vice Squad," Larry said. "You should mind your own business and stay out of it. This Kim could have been part of an opium ring for all you know."

"I know what kind of lawyer you are, "I shot back, "The kind that argues with everyone. Kim is my business. She came into my store and bought shoes from my shop. She was hardly more than a child, and a victim." I paused. "There was a time when you defended victims for a living—before you sold out."

Larry twirled around, "You had no trouble enjoying the money I made for all those years. It was a choice we made together."

"I guess I have changed my mind about what is really important." I threw back.

"Listen. I didn't come here to argue with you. I was hoping, hoping…" His voice trailed off. "What are you doing selling shoes? A woman like you? Intelligent, educated. A God damn Ph.D.! You're just doing it to punish me!"

There he went. Just like old times. It was all about him."What's wrong with selling shoes? My father did it!"

"Yes. Your father did it because he had no education. Your father would twirl in his grave if he could see you now."

Larry just didn't get it. He didn't understand all I was really getting from the store. The friends, the sense of community, the sense of real independence.

"You just don't understand," I began, "all those people are my friends."

Larry smirked. "Right, friends who are hookers and transsexuals like that tall, skinny one who works for you!"

What was he talking about? How did he know anything at all about Emily's Place? As far as I knew, he had never been there. "What were you doing at Emily's Place? Buying shoes for Natasha?"

Larry shook his head. "Of course not. I was just curious to see where you were spending all your time. "

He looked at me with big, sad eyes. "You're still my wife, you know."

Right. It was a good thing Larry did not know how to play the violin, or he would make me cry. He was very good with an audience. "And at my store you met hookers and transsexuals? The tall, skinny one. Merissa? You mean Merissa? You are calling Merissa a transsexual?"

Larry nodded. "Ever take a good look at her hands? Big hands are a give-away every time."

I was speechless. Merissa? A man? Of course not! It was just like Larry to make me doubt everything I was so sure of before. When I finally calmed down enough to speak, I said, "I think you should leave now."

Larry sat down heavily on the chair and stared at the remains of the turkey. "What do you want me to do about the Chinese girl?"

I shrugged my shoulders. "You're the lawyer. I'm not sure what we can find out but we need to know more about this Phillip Quinn. I have a feeling he was committing more than adultery."

"I'll see what I can find out." Larry wrote Quinn's name and address down on a piece of paper and reached for his coat. "I guess I should be going." He brushed the crumbs off his coat and glanced once more around my apartment. "You don't have to live like this," he said again. "You are punishing yourself."

"Maybe I really like living here," I suggested. "You know that old saying, "You can take the girl out of Brooklyn but you can't take Brooklyn out of the girl." I walked him to the door. It was kind of sad. We both seemed to be disappointed in the evening. With each other. It had started off so well with the turkey. "I'm sorry about your chess pieces."

"What about the fish?"

I smiled. "The fish are probably happily swimming around in the Hudson as we speak. Do you want a doggy bag? There's lots of turkey left over."

He shook his head. When he tried to kiss my cheek I turned away. When he was gone I double locked the door. I looked around the kitchen with the dirty dishes still on the table. Larry never did clean up anything.

"My dog chewed up one of my Armani silver sandals. I wrote to the company but they have no replacement policy. I'd have to buy a whole new pair. I would even consider doing this, even though it is outrageously expensive, but they no longer sell that style. Is there anywhere I can get just one shoe?"

I was late going to my web site to see if any interesting queries had come in. I send out an on-line newsletter once a month—a kind of shoe miscellany, that contained various assorted facts about shoes, shoe designers, celebrities and their shoes of choice, plus my now famous—at least locally—advice column, with stuff culled from my blog. Usually I checked it out at night before I went to sleep but I had a bad case of *turkey torpor* that made me too tired for anything.

The "one shoe" query caught my eye but it had come from one Roberta Della Fiore, not from Goodie One Shoes, so I figured it was nothing to get excited about. I wondered how many people actually did need one shoe for one reason or another. I remember I once dropped a bottle of olive oil on a pair of pink linen shoes I had dyed to match an evening gown. What a mess! And then there was the time I broke a strap; lost a rhinestone bow, broke a heel...yes. When I thought about it, there were plenty of reasons people could use just one shoe.

I remembered a short story by Italo Calvino, called the "Planet of Lost Socks." He had wondered what happened to all those single socks that disappear when you put them into the washing machine. You put two in but only one comes out. He envisioned a small planet circling around in space filled with all the lost socks of the Earth.

It was a sweet conceit, but not a very practical solution to the problem. I wondered if there might actually be a new business opportunity here—in a second hand single shoe exchange.But then I thought of Goodie One Shoes and Kim and decided that this was an idea whose time had not yet come.

"Dear Roberta, I'm afraid currently there is no company that will replace just one shoe. If you have a chronic dog-chewing problem, or are the kind of person who might drop soup or drip beer on one of your shoes, the best idea would be to buy a duplicate, spare pair of shoes whenever you go shopping.

Another good idea might be to find a friend with similar tastes and habits to split the cost of the extra pair of shoes. That way, you both get to have a spare and you only have to pay for a pair and a half."

I copied the question and the answer and "pasted" it on to my newsletter.

"Sometimes I think my boyfriend likes my shoes more than he likes me. He remembers all the colors of my shoes, but when I asked him one night, to tell me the color of my eyes, he guessed blue and mine are brown. What should I do to make him care more for me?"

Elsa Kropatkin

Another common problem.

"Dear Elsa, You have a couple of choices. First of all you can wear much less memorable shoes. I would suggest brown or black low heeled pumps. Certainly avoid laces. The other solution is to get a new boyfriend. Not only is he inattentive but he wasn't smart enough to guess your eyes were brown—the more common, dominant color. In a choice between a beautiful shoe and an unappreciative man, my advice would be to choose the shoe. Replacement men are easier to find."

I had just copied and pasted that Q and A as well when a new query appeared:

"Cinderella lost a shoe; the color of it was dark blue. Whatever was she to do?" It was signed, Goodie One Shoes.

This message didn't seem to have the veiled threats that the other messages had. Had he forgiven me for whatever he imagined I had done? Thinking about him still gave me the creeps. I reminded myself, there was still no evidence of a connection between Goodie One Shoes and Kim's murder. But even without that connection, he seemed dangerous.

I took a deep breath and willed myself to respond as if this was just another query from a customer: *"Don't despair; Just buy another pair to present to the lady fair."*

There was a short pause and then: *"That's easy for you to say. But I will have to pay. How about a loaner shoe? It's only for an hour or two?"*

"No deal. Get real. No longer new, I'd get little money for the shoe."

I stopped typing. My major objective was to find out whether or not Goodie One Shoes had anything to do with Kim's murder. And if that person was guilty, where he or she could be picked up. But how to get this information was another question. I decided to go for location first.

"I know someone with shoes of blue, who might be willing to lend them to you. Do you live close to Emily's Place? Tell me your size, just in case."

I waited a few minutes but there was no response. I was afraid I had scared the person off.

And then it came: *"I'm close enough in thought and deed; Here's some advice for you to heed; Be careful who becomes your friend. He may lead you to your end."*

That response was more than I had bargained for. He must have been referring to Murphy. And if he knew about my dealings with Murphy, it meant he was closer to me than I imagined.

I shut off the computer and stared at the blank screen. Tough New Yorker that I was, was I really scared of words written on a computer screen? Actually, yes. Nevertheless, in the words of a best-selling self-help book, in certain important situations, one should "feel the fear but do it anyway." I took a couple of deep breaths and turned the computer back on. I printed the name Goodie One Shoes in the Find Box, and hit enter. There before my eyes, the computer began listing contacts that went all the way back to three years ago—when I had first opened the store.

As I opened them, one by one, I could see why I had taken no notice of Goodie until recently. Almost all of the communications were rather ordinary requests for information about when a particular shoe might be available; whether or not I had stocked a particular color or not, what was the difference in fit and durability between the average Italian and French shoe, how to attach a custom buckle to a shoe, what was the most popular heel height in America, and so on. And, none of these queries were in rhyme. So when did things begin to change? Just recently, it seemed. About the time of Kim's murder.

What could have turned a rather ordinary person with a shoe fetish into a dangerous predator? Was it a suggestion of violence found in my window display? Or was it some imagined slight or hurt—he mentioned something about a sister a couple of times—that now demanded retribution?

I clicked a few more buttons on the computer and tooled around the early months of Emily's Place. It seemed suddenly as if I had burrowed into a time warp like a child wrapping herself with a warm blanket on a cold night. Here were the first entries on my Blog—notes on my first couple of sales—copies of inventory orders—emails from my first assistant Louise the Loser.

She had a bad cold and couldn't come in on Saturday. She was sure she had sent out those shoes ordered by Sophie Belkin. She swore she had opened the shop at 9:00am sharp on Tuesday. What a piece of work! Imagine her stealing from me all those months!

Of course, thinking about Louise made me think of poor Kim, her replacement, and soon my visit to the past began to fill my heart with sadness. I went into the kitchen and made myself a cup of coffee. I was still trying to recover my composure when the doorbell rang.

I looked through the peephole and saw a mailman's uniform.

"Hello Miss" Charles said when I opened the door. He held out two letters. "Special delivery."

I glanced at the envelopes. "Just a minute," I said, "This one isn't for me."

Charles held the letter up to the dim light of the hallway. "Says Shirley Levine, right here." He pointed to the lettering.

"I'm Emily Levine," I said. "Remember?"

Charles removed his cap. His head was as bare and smooth as a stone. "I thought it was for your sister."

"My sister lives in the Berkshires." I told him.

"José told me she was visiting."

God Damn! Is it like this in other neighborhoods? In the South Bronx does everyone know whose divorce checks have stopped coming? "She's only here for a few days and her name isn't Levine. Levine is my married name, not my family name."

"Oh," he said, "José told me her name was Shirley."

"Shana," I corrected him.

He nodded. "I knew it was one of them Jewish names." He put

the letter back in his pouch, while his eyes looked beyond me into my apartment.

"Whatever." I said. "She's not here now and it's not for her." I signed for the other letter, locked the door and sat down at the kitchen table where there was better light. There was no return address. Some bill I hadn't paid? A complaint about my lewd manikins? I ripped open the envelope. Inside was a piece of ivory toned paper with a charcoal drawing on it. It took a couple of minutes for me to focus on the pattern of squiggles and lines. And then I remembered what it was and where I had seen it.

It was a quick sketch Kim had done of herself. A few long lines for her shoulder length hair, a slender dash for her eyes and mouth—but the likeness was inescapable. And yet—there was something "off" about it. A distortion in the tilt of the chin and cheek—something that turned a beautiful face into a grim, unflattering, older version of itself.

Strangely, Kim had been very attached to the drawing. She kept it pinned up on a small cork board above her bed.

For a moment I just stared at the drawing, at the envelope with its non-descript, computer generated name and address. Could that have been a side of Kim I had never noticed? Her own portrait of Dorian Gray that reflected experiences her innocent beauty never revealed? Or was it merely a recording of her first, unsure steps as an artist?

And then I began to cry. The memory of Kim's delicate features that I knew in my heart truly represented her nature, our sweet hours spent together, the promise of her talent, was more than I could bear.

And then I stopped crying and stared up at the ceiling. Slowly my hands tightened into fists. The police had sealed Kim's room. This picture could only have been sent to me by the murderer himself!

I closed my eyes. The scene of my last visit to Kim's apartment and my encounter with Quinn were etched clearly in my memory. Quinn. Her drawing teacher. Her pervert lover. It was Quinn who must have killed her and was now mocking my sorrow and his escape from punishment. Was he daring me to catch him? Or was he threatening me with the same fate as Kim's?

I walked over to the door and made sure the chain was on. Why would the murderer want to send me Kim's picture? Why was he mocking my sorrow?

Shana was meeting friends for a pre-conference get-together and was sleeping over at someone's studio. It seemed strange to be alone again. Every noise in the street threatened me. The sirens and fire engines that went with the pavement in this neighborhood, suddenly seemed to signal some disaster in the making.

Yes, I was scared, but I was also mad as hell. No two-bit Romeo dressed up in Professor's tweeds was going to get the best of me. I would prove he killed Kim and make him pay.

I needed to tell Murphy about the drawing and the latest message from Goodie One Shoes. Murphy. The thought of him was immediately comforting. Maybe because I felt so vulnerable, so unprotected. A policeman would be nice. I wonder what it would be like to go out with a cop. What interests he might have besides books and murder.

Maybe he would even want to come over and question me face to face right away. I pictured him putting his arms around me and kissing away my fears. Leading me to the bedroom and beginning to undress me. Unbuckling his gun, detaching his handcuffs…For the first time in my life I wondered about the erotic possibility of handcuffs.

It took less than a minute to decide that handcuffs were not for me. It might be fun to use them on Murphy, but I am quite sure that would not be his way to play the game.

I found his contact information and dialed his phone. The phone rang five times until the message machine picked up.

"Leave a message" Murphy's voice commanded. No nice music, not even "Your call is important to me, please leave a number. "I stared at the phone for a few minutes, and then I hung up.

Chapter 8

In the 70's, Helene Verin glorified the everyday scene around her by drawing inspiration for her shoes from the pattern of the piano keyboard and the checkered cab.

"Here's the thing," Shana said after breakfast a couple of days later, "Police people can be very sensitive. You've got to try to connect with them."

I rolled my eyes. Sensitivity was not very apparent with the "police people" I had encountered. I had finally gotten Murphy on the phone and told him about the delivery of Kim's self portrait.

"Don't touch anything!" he had warned me, but of course it was too late. Was I supposed to wear gloves before opening my mail? He sent someone to retrieve the drawing and then he claimed as usual that I had "contaminated" the evidence and smeared all the fingerprints. All he could confirm was that the letter was sent by a "John Doe" from the main Post Office on 34th Street. That narrowed the field to just about anyone in New York City.

At that point, I decided it was hopeless to expect Murphy to uncover any useful information or show me respect and attention in any way what-so-ever and I was fed up with his refusing to give me information he did have—such as the color and maker of the shoe that had killed Kim. So I enlisted Shana to do a little investigating of our own.

Shana and I had slept late—it was Merissa's turn to open the store—and after she had had a bath with her cast hanging over the edge of the tub, she looked bright and happy.

I had studiously avoided looking at her tattered belly-button but the rest of her looked good. No malnutrition. No dark circles under her baby blue eyes. No tangles in her blonde hair. In other words, as regarded my sister Shana, when nothing was bad, things were good. At least I could stop worrying about her for the moment.

"So" she continued," when we get to the police station, try not to antagonize anyone."

"Since when do I antagonize people" I snapped.

Shana put her hand up. "Just let me do the talking. I have a way with people."

Right, I said to myself. All the wrong people.

I sat back down on my chair and bit my lip. There was no sense arguing with each other. This was one time we would have to work together.

"Emily's Place is like the St. Patrick's Cathedral for shoes in New York City," Shana insisted. "Sooner or later the killer is going to be drawn there—if he's not already there, and to you as high priestess." Shana smiled at me. "Larry is worried about you."

"Larry worries about himself." I answered her. "He was just afraid of looking bad if I got murdered. It would be embarrassing for his corporate clients to find out his estranged wife was killed with a shoe."

"He is not that bad a guy" Shana insisted. "It's just that your auras clash. As for Murphy the Cop, unless he is really as sexy as you say—and especially if he is as sexy as you say—he should be kept out of your business unless you really are in danger. First off, we've got to gather information."

The plan was to visit the precinct where Murphy had his office and see what we could find out. I had looked up the address on his card and was surprised to find out that it was precinct 87 on the Upper East Side. I put the dishes in the sink and we set out toward 96th Street and the cross town bus.

It was crowded on the bus and we held on to each other. About half way across the park someone stomped on my foot and I let out a yelp. When I turned to see who it was, all I saw was a large, dark sweater and hood—heading towards the back door of the bus.

When the bus finally stopped at Fifth Avenue, a number of people got off, and I even found a seat. But my big toe ached like crazy. That would put me out of tennis for a month if it was broken. I was beginning to think this whole exercise was a big mistake when we finally got to the 3rd Avenue stop.

It had been decided that Shana would report that her pocketbook had been stolen on the cross-town bus. I didn't want to run the risk that Murphy would recognize my name on the Police Complaint form, and together we would try to get whoever was on duty to talk about the murder. Since Murphy was stationed there, we figured the people around him would know something.

I reached over and took Shana's purse, a small woven thing with tribal designs that looked like it had come from Afghanistan in 1960. "Remember," I said to her, "you felt someone tug on your arm and when you looked down, your pocketbook was gone."

"Can you hold on to my book too," Shana asked, handing me a copy of "Murder on the Orient Express."

I opened my purse.

The first thing I noticed was that I had more room than usual in my handbag. The second thing I noticed was that my wallet was missing.

"Oh! Noooo!" I moaned. "I can't believe this. My wallet is gone!"

Shana's eyes opened wide. She looked up into the sky. "Karma." She pronounced. "We're already attracting bad Karma. Anything to do with crimes and criminals will change the atmosphere. We should have worn orange. That's a lucky color."

I turned my bag upside down. There was my Mocha Berry lipstick, my keys, and my CVS discount card. There were a few dirty tissues, an empty eye glass case and a few cards with vendors names on them. But my wallet was gone.

"Did you have much money in it? Think," Shana implored, "what about your credit cards and keys?"

"I think I only had about twenty dollars. I have my keys." I was really happy about that. But all my credit cards, department store cards and my driver's license were gone.

My legs felt weak. I looked around for a place to sit, but there were no benches on Third Avenue. I felt violated—dirty. Someone has felt around in my purse and pulled out my wallet. And my big toe still hurt. And then it hit me. That guy who stomped on my toe, stole my wallet. He had just created a diversion so that I was busy thinking about my toe instead of my pocketbook. Now in addition to feeling violated, I felt angry, and stupid. "Damn it all to hell! How dumb am I? A kid from Kentucky, ok, but me? New York born and bred?" I leaned on Shana and rubbed my toe.

"Don't waste your chi blaming yourself. The situation is much larger than either of us. Just try to hold on to your sense of outrage," she counseled. "The Police Station is just down the street. Now at least we won't have to lie about a stolen wallet. And you can be the victim instead of me." Shana took back her purse, and patted me on the shoulder. "Here we are," she said, pushing me in front." Break a leg!"

This particular police station did not inspire confidence. The outside door was heavy and it took both of us to shove it open. Inside there was a kind of anti-room that smelled from mildew. The walls were snot-green and the dark gray carpet stained. Seated on a bench against the wall were a couple of African-American kids in their early twenties wearing baggy jeans and black sweatshirts with the hoods pulled down low around their faces. Actually, they were dead ringers for whoever it was who robbed me on the way over.

We walked past them, clutching our pocketbooks close to our bodies and through the entrance to the next room, where a policewoman sat behind a large metal desk. In back of her was a wall of steel filing cabinets. Another policewoman, seemed to be trying to make sense of various pieces of paper and deciding how to file them away.

Shana approached the desk.

The Police woman behind the desk did not raise her head. She seemed to be reading something, hidden from view by the desk.

"Hello?" Shana called out politely.

The lady raised her head. Kind of pretty but a little overweight, light brown gal, who looked to me to be about thirty years old.

"Yes?" she said, looking kind of annoyed.

"My sister just got robbed on the cross-town bus." Shana reported, and pushed me forward.

"Can your sister speak for herself?" the police woman asked in a nasty tone of voice.

Now I must admit that I was so shaken up by my robbery that I seemed to have lost my bearings for a few minutes, but the tone of this lady's voice immediately called me back to myself. I was not going to be victimized twice!

I bent over the front of the desk and said, in my loudest voice: "I sure can—even though I am a woman of a certain age, I can still walk and talk!" So much for the "sensitivity" of "police people."

That took the policewoman a bit by surprise. At least it shut her up for a minute. Shana too. The police woman who was fumbling with the files stopped and stared at me.

Now that I had their full attention, I said, "I want to report a robbery on the cross-town bus."

The Police ladies exchanged glances. "Where did you get on the bus?" The one behind the desk asked.

"On Broadway and 96th Street." I replied.

"Oh well," the lady behind the desk said, "You've got to go to the precinct on the West Side." She picked up whatever it was she had been reading and lowered her eyes.

"Excuse me?" Shana questioned in a perky voice. She leaned her cast on the desk, nudged me gently aside and stared at the police woman with her baby blues.

The police woman at the files—a white woman about twenty-five, also a little overweight, held up her hand. "It's like this," she said, as if talking to a kindergarten class, "You were robbed on the crosstown bus, so you need to go back to where you got on the bus, to the precinct in charge of that area. I think it's somewhere on West 67th Street."

"But I discovered I was robbed on this side of the park," I explained.

The lady behind the desk shook her head. "Where did the robbery take place?"

"If I knew that, I would have grabbed the guy," I answered.

At that point, Shana let out a moan, dropped her purse and slowly keeled over, grabbing on to my legs with her one good arm as she let herself gently down on the floor.

"It's her heart!" I cried out. For a moment, I really thought it was. All those hours of meditating and stuffing herself with exotic substances had finally done her in.

Now both police ladies sprang into action. "I'll call 911" said the one behind the desk.

"Can I get you some water?" said the one at the files.

Shana raised her head—and pinched me on the leg. "If you could just help me over to that bench," she gasped, "I think I'll make it. A little water would be fine. I don't think I need 911. I have some medicine in my bag."

She picked up her bag and fumbled around inside for her pills. I saw her extract a Tums from a roll before she threw the rest back in her bag. By the time the glass of water arrived, Shana had pretty nearly revived.

"Thanks so much," she mumbled. "So sorry for the trouble." She shifted her position on the bench. Occasional deep sighs escaped her. "Does anyone have a rosary," she asked plaintively.

Both policewomen looked nervous.

In the meantime, I had recovered my composure. "I was robbed on this side of the Park," I said decisively. "Actually, just before I got off the bus."

The dark skinned policewoman rummaged around on the desk and handed me a form. On the top she wrote her name: Rosa Valdes.

The light skinned woman applied a cold compress to Shana's forehead. Rosa called her Denise.

While I filled out the form, Shana observed the decorations in the office. "Lost Dog." She read a poster near the desk, "Show dog. Pomeranian. Stolen from car, Thursday March 12."

I turned to look at the picture. A white puff of fur with eyes.

"I thought a Pomeranian was a flower." Shana said.

Both policewomen smiled.

"No posters about the shoe murderer. I thought for sure there would be posters of The Most Wanted Shoe Murder—something like that." Shana commented.

Rosa shrugged. "Can't put up a poster 'cause we don't have a sketch of who did it."

"Well, how else can you spread the word that women are in danger," Shana questioned, "I imagine everyone in the city is upset about that murderer. How about a description? It wouldn't hurt if people were on the look-out for the guy who did it, even without a picture."

Rosa flopped down heavily on the chair behind the desk. "We don't have a description of who did it. We don't even know if it was a man or a woman."

"What?" I said, looking up from my complaint sheet, "What woman would use an expensive shoe to kill someone, when she could wear it instead?"

Both policewomen chuckled.

"Yes, and I heard it was one of those famous brands—the one those women from Sex in the City are always talking about..."Shana chirped.

"Oh," I said, "Jimmy Choo?"

Denise laughed. "That's it! Don't know much about Jimmy Choo. I spend most of my days and nights in these." She stuck out her foot displaying a black sponge-soled shoe shaped like the webbed foot of a duck. Standard Police footwear, I surmised.

"That," I said, "could count as sexual abuse in my book,"

Denise smiled. "I guess so, but when you need to stand on your feet all day, you need something comfortable."

"You could wear something prettier. It could be red or blue—with some kind of heel. If it were the right shape, it could be a weapon," Shana suggested.

Rosa scowled and put her hand on her gun. "Any weapon I need I got right here. My off-duty shoes are made for dancing. Got me a pair of silver Prada would knock your eye out—figuratively speaking of course." She raised herself from her chair with some effort and then did a little tango around the desk.

It's what I always say. Doesn't matter what age, race, political beliefs or educational level a woman has. Shoes can be a bridge between all differences. Made you wonder about the fall of the Berlin wall. Motivation is a very empowering thing. The designer shoes were all on the Western side.

Shana made little clucking sounds with her mouth. "Tsk, Tsk. Bet the poor woman didn't get much chance to wear those red shoes."

Rosa nodded her head. "There was only one shoe. All the women in the Chinatown precinct were searching for the mate. Dead girl didn't need expensive red shoes. Murphy—he's the special detective assigned to the case—thinks the murderer made off with it."

Shana and I exchanged looks. Bingo!

I was so pleased I wanted to hug everyone in the room but I forced myself to remain calm.

"Is the shoe here? Shana asked looking round. "What do they do with all those things they find at the crime scene?"

"Oh, no," Rosa said, "Don't keep valuable stuff like that here. That is EVIDENCE."

"Yeah," Denise continued. "They don't trust us with EVIDENCE. EVIDENCE is kept locked up downtown somewhere in an EVIDENCE ROOM."

"Right," continued Rosa. "Girls like us, we might be tempted to take some confiscated Crack or something if it were left lying around in the local precinct—like the apple from the serpent."

"Only the MEN have keys to the EVIDENCE ROOM." Denise volunteered.

"Murphy. He has the key to the red shoe. Probably hops around with it in the Evidence Room." Rosa continued.

I stared at Denise. I was sure I had seen her flinch a little when the name Murphy came up.

"Oh," I said, "Is this Murphy the kind of guy who likes to dress in women's clothes?"

Now Denise really did flinch.

"Of course not!" she responded in an annoyed voice. "Don't go starting any stupid rumors," she threw back at Rosa.

Rosa clapped her hands together and laughed. "Only kidding," she reassured us, "Murphy is a hunky guy. Denise has a thing for him. Can't resist teasing her a little when I get the chance."

I was about to ask if Murphy was married—I knew he had a daughter—when Shana cut in.

"Poor dead girl," said Shana. "Ohhhh...do you think someone could make me a cup of tea? Herbal would be great."

I was beginning to think it was time to finish up this game before there was a change in the Karma. I glanced at my watch. "It's so kind of you," I said to Denise who was now opening a drawer of the filing cabinet that held a tea bag and some sugar, "but I don't think we need to bother you much longer."

Shana was beginning to push her luck—and ours. I would love to stay to try to find out more—some interesting facts about Murphy's personal life—but I felt I should be content with what we found out so far—even though the news was not good. And what if Murphy himself should suddenly appear? That would be embarrassing.

I handed my complaint sheet to Rosa. "I'd like to thank you both for being so nice to my poor, sick sister here," I nodded my head at Shana. "She seems to be feeling much better. It seems you ladies could use a new pair of shoes for when you are off-duty. I have a shop across town and we have discounts for our special friends."

I searched around in my violated but now fairly empty purse and dug out a couple of cards.

"Emily's Place," Denise read. "I've heard of Emily's Place. It's famous!"

"Hey," Rosa stared at me, "I even know someone who works there."

"Don't tell me," I said, "Does her name begin with Merissa?"

Rosa laughed, "Guess Merissa gets around."

I helped Shana get to her feet. She smiled and extended her hand. When Rosa took it, Shana held it, gently opening the fingers. She stared at the palm. "I see a long life-line here," she said. "What sign were you born under?"

Before Rosa could answer, I pulled Shana after me, out of the door.

Chapter 9

Restriction is the key to eroticism for a shoe fetishist. Slowly unlacing a boot; gently unwinding a bound foot, the ultimate release.

After we left the police station we hailed a cab. I was exhausted. We kept congratulating each other on how well we had played our roles, who said what when, who did what then.

The truth was, as good as everything had gone, I was worried and depressed. I had gone searching for knowledge I wasn't meant to have and now I was stuck with it. The image of the serpent and the apple kept popping up.

I had calmed myself with the idea that the shoe, so mysteriously deposited in my mail chute was a perfectly innocent "gift" from some customer. What had I been thinking? I had hidden important information from a police investigator. What was the matter with me? I had watched enough television to know that that made me an accessory to the crime. The result of all my snooping around—successful as it was—was to turn me into a scared shop-keeper who could easily either be murdered herself, or be arrested as a criminal.

Shana, on the other hand, was thoroughly delighted. "Maybe I should stay awhile and help you solve some of your other problems," she suggested.

I shivered. Shana as my roommate for an extended period of time was not something I felt I could bear. Even though I loved her. Especially because I loved her. At least in the Berkshires she wasn't likely to be murdered. New York City was a different story altogether. Especially now. At any rate, it seemed I had nothing to fear from that direction. About twenty minutes after we returned home, Shana packed up her back-pack, kissed me good bye and told me she was off to her conference and would be staying with a friend. She promised to keep in touch.

First thing I did after saying good bye to Shana and double locking my door was make a list of the credit cards that were stolen and start calling the companies to put a stop on everything.

Then I searched in my bag for Murphy's card and number. It was time to tell him about the strange delivery of the red shoe. And then I remembered that the card had been in my wallet.

That was embarrassing. I would have to call the 89th precinct, talk to Rosa or Denise and then have to admit that I knew something about the shoe murders and needed to contact Murphy.

Or, I could go to work at Emily's Place and try to forget about murders, Murphy and motives and wait until Murphy called me. That is what I did.

I was more tired than usual when I came home that night. It had been a long day, what with my searching after forbidden knowledge and then being stuck with it. But I was alert enough to sense something wasn't right as soon as I opened the door to my apartment.

Bonita Gonzalez had worked as a cleaning lady in my apartment for three years and in all that time she had never failed to lock the door behind her.

First thing that caught my eye was a broken flower-pot with earth spilled out on the carpet, my scrawny ivy plant's limp leaves and thin stems splayed across the floor in a failed attempt to wrap themselves around the nearest chair. And then I saw that the door to my bedroom was firmly closed.

"Bonita?" I called out. "Shana?" Although Shana had told me she was staying at a friend's during the conference, you never knew when the "Karma" would change and her "chi" would propel her in a totally different direction.

It was that time of the early evening when dark shadows fell across the streets of the city and only a few rays of light found their way inside my apartment.

I was beginning to get that tight feeling in my belly that meant something was seriously wrong. Someone was in my bedroom. I felt as sure of that as the fact I was standing in my middle of my living room. For a moment I felt like turning tail and running out like a scared rabbit, but the truth was, I had no place to go and no one to call on for immediate help, so I took a couple of deep breaths, quietly opened the closet door and picked up one of my dress boots—a gorgeous Prada number in plumb with a three inch heel—I figured if someone could kill with a shoe I ought to be able to protect myself with one—opened the outside door again in case I had to make a quick exit—and knocked on the door of the bedroom. Absolute silence greeted me. I turned the knob of the door and saw a figure lying face-down on my bed.

I think I must have stopped breathing completely while my eyes adjusted to the gloom of the bedroom—and then I saw a naked leg, with bright red toe nail polish—and blonde, tangled hair matted in some dark substance, that even as I stood there seemed alive and slowly running down her back. Something long and dark protruded from the back of her head

And then I shrieked "Shana!" and rushed to the bed.

I dropped the boot I was holding, fell on my knees to the floor and grabbed her bare shoulder with both hands, desperately trying to turn her over. It was the first time I had ever understood the meaning of the term "dead weight." With a final push, I managed to turn the body, which slowly slid to the floor, the head wobbling in a strange manner, as if it were about to fall off.

There was blood everywhere and I kneeled beside the body and lifted Shana's blood splattered face to my lips. Only it was not Shana. It was my housekeeper, Bonita Gonzalez. I suppose I started to scream at that point and as I backed out of the room, I crashed into another person, who now sat on the floor next to me, screaming even louder than I was. It was my next-door neighbor, Angelina Grosso and Henry the Gray Parrot was flying circles around us both.

I guess between the two of us—or shall I say the three of us because Henry was squarking loudly as well—we made enough noise to rouse the entire neighborhood and when I turned around my bedroom was filled with most of the people on the block, from the Federal Express delivery man, Sam Holloweran to the numbers runner, 'Neddy No-Show" who hung out on the corner, to the ladies who played bridge in front of one of the brownstones down the block when the weather was fair, to Francis Nigel in 3C who I hadn't seen since last Christmas when she came home drunk and had lost her key.

And last, but certainly not least, was George Washington Green our heroic superintendent who had come to supervise whatever crisis was occurring on the ground floor. Whatever gave me the idea there was no one to help me?

"Don't touch anything!" George Washington bellowed.

Too late. For a moment I pictured Murphy and his attachment to pristine evidence , but I was so relieved to find myself surrounded by friends and neighbors, and the discovery that the murdered woman was not my adored sister Shana, that I just didn't care.

"I called the police," Francis Nigel called out, and with that, Neddy No-Show and at least three other people I didn't recognize, made a bee-line for the door.

George Washington bent over me and offered me his arm to lean on, and I pulled myself up to a standing position and then helped Angelina Grosso to stand up as well. For a moment we hugged each other while Henry fluttered overhead.

I took one more look at poor Bonita, dressed only in a bra and panties, with what I could now see clearly was a blue high-heeled shoe sticking out of her head. Even covered with blood from the bedroom doorway I could see it was a Dolce & Gabbana, probably size eight. And when I turned around, there was Murphy the cop.

Seemed he was the NYPD specialist in murdered women—the on-call guy for homicide. I had to hand it to him. When Murphy cared enough, he knew how to travel at the speed of light.

He shooed everyone out of the apartment, except for Angelina and Henry. He picked up the blanket from my bed, covered the body, shut the door to the bedroom and then he started in on the "Evidence." "Holy Mary Mother of God" I heard him mumble under his breath.

"Tampering with evidence again, I see," he said, when I explained how I had turned her over to see who it was, but his eyes had a gentle look and I could sense a softening somewhere under that starched blue shirt. Imagining what was under Murphy's clothes seemed to come easily to me—even under the most bizarre circumstances.

"Oh my," said Angelina smiling, "So nice to see you Officer." She smoothed her wild red hair down with the palm of her hand while Henry settled watchfully on her shoulder.

"My pleasure," said Murphy. He took her arm and led her to a seat at my kitchen table.

He motioned for me to sit opposite them and took a silver pen and little black notepad out of his pocket.

"Tell me what happened," he instructed me.

When I was finished, he turned to Angelina.

"And what did you see?" he said to her. "I know how perceptive you are."

Translation—she was a busy body with her eye glued to her peephole and hardly anything got by her.

"I feel so bad," Angelina said, waving her hands. "I didn't hear a thing. You see my soaps go on about 3:00pm. There's One Day at a Time, and Dallas, and even Henry likes to watch them, and it's really

Goodie One Shoes

terrible, the troubles those people have. I don't suppose you watch it—there's this really wealthy family but everyone hates everyone else so I wasn't up and about in my usual way until after 5:00pm. I didn't have a clue anything was wrong until I saw the outside door to Emily's apartment was open." She adjusted the folds of her sky-blue kimono and smiled up at Murphy.

"So," Murphy said, "You didn't see or hear anything unusual until 5:00pm."

Angelina nodded. "One of the girls had just shot her lover, who she found out was the illegitimate father to her friend's daughter and…"

Murphy held up his hand. "I understand perfectly," He said to her. "It helps to know that the murder was probably committed between three and five o'clock." Murphy rose from the table, took Angelina's arm and walked her back to her apartment.

He must have made a call to his back-up because not more than ten minutes later about four guys in plain clothes arrived and started dusting the place for fingerprints, crawling on the floor, opening and closing my windows, checking the lock on the door, opening drawers and peering into all my closets. If I had not felt violated before, I certainly did now. Now too, the full horror of the scene I had witnessed descended upon me.

"The lock was not forced or broken so the victim either knew her assailant or she was careless about who she let in." Murphy told me.

"I used to tell her all the time not to answer the door at all, because anyone I know would know that I am working during the day. Anyone else who would ring the bell would be…I don't know…the wrong address, or someone trying to sell something." I put my face in my hands. Poor Bonita. She had come from Guatemala four years ago and was just trying to earn enough money to pay her rent.

"Why didn't she phone me?" I moaned. Ever since I had missed Kim's call the day of her death, I had kept my cell phone close by. Bonita was constantly talking on her phone—laughing, gossiping—it was almost a part of her body. Why didn't she use it to try to save herself?

A detective came out of the bedroom with some red thing encased in a plastic bag. He conferred with Murphy for a minute and gave him the bag. Murphy held it up. "Ever see this before?" he asked me.

I looked closer. It was crumpled up but it looked like a red tee shirt. A red tee shirt with a large Evil Eye imprinted on it. I gasped.

79

"Shana's tee shirt!"

"My men found it on the floor near the bed. The victim was probably wearing it when she was attacked. If it were your sister's, how did the dead woman get it?"

I explained how Shana and Bonita had exchanged tee shirts a few days ago. "My sister's boyfriend sells them. They are made of bamboo."

"Bamboo." Murphy repeated. He gave the bag a shake and then put in on the table.

"Dead girl's name and address?" he asked.

"Bonita Gonzalez. I only know she lived somewhere uptown, in Spanish Harlem."

"Do you know who she lived with? Parents? Kids? Relatives?"

I shook my head.

Murphy slammed his notebook shut.

"Is this another one of your employees who jumped ship?"

"I wouldn't know. There's more of a chance she climbed through a hole in the fence."

"I suppose you never asked." Murphy was not in a mood to be friendly.

"And, of course, you were paying her off the books—no withholding tax for social security or any other tax."

What was it with this cop? Instead of trying to comfort me, he was attacking me. Where did he come off lecturing me about paying people off the books? His grandmother probably came here and cleaned peoples' toilets for whatever they would pay her and his grandfather probably did jump ship.

I folded my arms across my body and said, "So arrest me."

"Yeah, maybe I will. It's a good thing you have an alibi and were working until 5:30pm at Emily's Place." For a moment we glared at each other and then Murphy opened his little black book again, and took out his silver pen. " Do you know anyone who might have wanted to kill her?"

I shook my head and then I remembered something. "There was a boyfriend. Ten years younger. She said he was crazy about her. Wanted to marry her." I hesitated, "I told her it wasn't a good idea."

Murphy cocked his head and looked at me. "You don't approve of marriage?"

"She told him she had a green card. She didn't."

Murphy's blue eyes did not even blink. Perhaps this was not a new story in the Big Apple.

"His name?"

I may forget where I put my keys, but strange bits of knowledge lodge themselves in the crevices of my mind.

"Juan Diaz."

Now Murphy did blink and scowl. "The John Doe of the Hispanic World. He'll be married the day after he reads about the murder in the papers to someone who really has a green card, and head out for the territory."

"Huckleberry Finn," I murmured.

"Yeah," Murphy said, "But now-a-days he'd be named Juan or José and the territory he'd head for is New Jersey."

"So you don't think he's a suspect?"

Murphy bit the end of his pen. "Not likely, but if we find him we'll question him."

"Her phone! Bonita was always talking on her cell. Juan's number must be in there!"

Murphy looked over his shoulder at the men creeping all over my bedroom. "So far we haven't found a phone."

I felt my eyes begin to fill with tears. Bonita was someone who I really only knew casually. She had come into the store, like so many other stragglers, looking for work, and since she couldn't speak much English and I couldn't speak much Spanish, I thought maybe I could let her clean up my apartment once a week.

There was something about her that made me trust her--maybe it was her blonde hair—dyed of course—but she seemed to have made some effort at being glamorous in her tattered clothes—that reminded me of Shana. She was slender and fragile looking, and so I let her into my life. But how to explain all that to Murphy the cop?

"So," Murphy said, "You hired her because she looked like your sister Shana."

This took me a little aback because I knew I have not said a word aloud.

"Her name." Murphy continued, "Bonita means pretty in Spanish."

I had to hand it to Murphy. I really hadn't thought of that before. "She was a good woman," I said. "She worked hard, was always laughing and singing. I even recommended her to Harriet Moskowitz, Director of the Central Park Conservation Association; a rich widow with a huge apartment on Park Avenue."

Murphy scribbled a few notes and walked around the apartment conferring with his men. "Anybody else have the key to your apartment?"

"Shana and George-Washington Green, the superintendent," I reported. Someone came in and carried out the body. "The missing shoe you want to look for is a Dolce & Gabbana, size eight, last year's style, cost about nine hundred and fifty dollars; twenty percent less at Emily's Place"

Murphy's right eye-brow twitched. "Where would a cleaning lady get the money for a shoe like that?"

We looked at each other silently. "No," I said. "I don't think she was turning tricks on the side. And besides I would bet she wears a size seven."

For a moment, Murphy stared off into space, and then he shrugged. "Might have gotten them from that rich widow you mentioned. Don't you women give your cast-offs to your maids?"

I winced. I didn't think of Bonita as a maid. More like a poor relative. She would clean, sing, bring me little specialties—a flan, a piece of spicy Mexican chocolate—ask my advice—compare notes about men with Shana. But I had to admit Murphy might be right in the case of Harriet Moskowitz. She would have no use for her shoes the next season and she might well have given them to Bonita.

Besides, I knew that Harriet did wear a size eight.

"I'll check it out," Murphy says, "I hear you paid a visit to my precinct. Something about a red shoe."

I threw up my hands. "I wanted to tell you but I lost your number. Someone put a red designer shoe through my mail chute a couple of weeks ago. I didn't think too much about it before, but now I think it will match the one you found with Kim's body." I gulped, seeing his quick intake of breath.

"And you didn't think it worthwhile to mention this before?"

"You didn't tell me…I didn't know that the shoe had anything to do with Kim's death."

"Where is that shoe now?" he asked me.

"It's gone."

Murphy opened his mouth as if to say something really nasty and then seemed to think better of it. "Find the red shoe," he directed, "and I'd change the lock on your apartment, There's a good chance the murderer took Bonita's key when he left."

I nodded.

"Any connection that you know of between Kim and Bonita?"

I shook my head.

"I can think of one," Murphy said, "You."

Both these women had worked for me. They had even met once or twice in my apartment—but what did that mean?

"Anyone you know want to murder you?"

It did not take me more than a minute to come up with a list of suspects. "My estranged husband Larry, of course, but he wouldn't have the guts. Besides, he hates blood. If he were going to kill me it would be poison all the way. And then the President of the Upper West Side Decency Association who claimed I was corrupting the youth in the area by the provocative poses of my manikins. And then the Director of the West-Side Chapter of Pro-Life, who threatened to put me in jail for supporting a Planned Parenthood office next door. And then..."

Murphy stopped writing and looked me in the eye. "Think about it," he says. "Someone might be murdering important people in your life, hoping to hurt you. There is a reason the murderer sent you that drawing of Kim."

I looked at the ceiling and fought back the tears that threatened. Kim—my beautiful Kim—and now poor Bonita. "I feel bad about Bonita but she wasn't my best friend."

"Okay, but maybe the killer wasn't looking for Bonita; he was looking for Shana."

I staggered to a chair.

"Weren't they about the same size?" he went on, "Blonde. And the tee shirt. If your sister wore tee shirts with the evil eye around town, how easy for someone to make a mistake."

God, it all made sense. Too much sense. I felt like screaming.

"What about Quinn? I asked Murphy, "Maybe he wants to hurt me because he knew I saw him at Kim's apartment. Maybe he was looking for me when he killed Bonita."

Murphy fiddled with his pen. "I don't think so. You don't look anything like your sister."

There was no need to rub that in. I took a deep breath and then I told him about the latest emails from Goodie One Shoes—and how the tone of his earlier communications had been so different. He certainly did seem to blame me for something.

Murphy tapped his little notebook. "There's something here we are overlooking. You are overlooking—something very obvious, hiding in plain view."

Right. Suddenly it was all my fault.

"Think about it. Goodie One Shoes may well be the key to the whole mystery. We know he has it in for you—we just don't know why. And whoever sent you that drawing is surely playing with your head."

And then I heard that strange, little Ding-a-ling that I remembered from Kim's Memorial Service. Murphy reached into his pocket for the little phone and took a walk to my bathroom.

It was painfully clear that I knew very little about Murphy the Cop. I admit I occasionally pictured him with his clothes off. I wondered if he thought of me at all. I sat down in the living room and stared at the ceiling. Was I of any interest to him outside of a nuisance involved in a couple of his murder cases?

When Murphy returned he sat down beside me. "My daughter." He said simply. "Thanks. She loved the flowers."

I nodded. I was pleased that a personal note had been added to our relationship. "She knows how to dial the phone?"

Murphy smiled."She knows how to press a couple of buttons on her cell phone."

Of course. Damn! My age was showing.

"She has her own phone?" I tried to cover up my embarrassment.

Murphy nodded.

I scowled.

"What?" he said to me.

"She's only six. I never had my own phone until I moved into my own apartment three years ago."

Murphy raised one eye-brow. "I bought her a phone so she could call me whenever she wants—not when her mother gives her permission."

"Her mother doesn't know she has a phone?"

"It's none of her business. It's a secret between me and my daughter. You think that's bad?" Murphy asked.

"What do I know about kids?" I responded. "I never had any. The closest thing I ever had to a kid was a gerbil when I was thirteen."

Murphy laughed. "What happened to your gerbil?"

"It choked to death on a chicken bone I fed it—on my birthday."

That's not funny," Murphy said, "things around you dropping dead."

For a moment we looked at each other.

One of the detectives approached and whispered something in Murphy's ear.

He put his hand on my shoulder. "Got to go downtown," he said. "It looks like the murderer found Bonita harder to kill than Kim. The shoe alone couldn't do the job. He finished her off by slitting her throat."

This last bit of news made me break down completely. Murphy made some comforting noises but I was too distraught to decipher them. Nevertheless, it felt good to know he tried. Maybe we could be friends after all.

Two more plainclothes men emerged from the bedroom with plastic bags. Another one stretched a tape in front of my bedroom door.

For the first time I realized I was not going to be able to sleep in my bed for a while. As a matter of fact, I couldn't imagine ever sleeping in that bed again.

As if he could read my thoughts, Murphy said, "I think you'll have to sleep somewhere else for a couple of days."

For a moment I felt desperate. Where could I go? I thought immediately of my old apartment on Central Park West—with doormen—elevator men—Larry—to protect me. No. I would not give in to that. "I think Angelina has a pull-out couch."

I would much rather camp out at Murphy's place but that did not seem to be an option, at least in his mind. I watched him as he packed up his notes and moved around the apartment talking to his men. It seemed he had already forgotten me.

"We'll be in touch," he said as he squeezed my shoulder before walking himself out.

Chapter 10

In Victorian times modesty dictated that women wear high boots to cover their ankles. However, the intricate lacings resulted in the opposite effect—men found that more titillating than a flash of flesh.

"*Woman drowns her three kids*, page two of the Metro Section. There is a good story on page three about a drunk cop who ran over a woman and her baby—husband was really distraught," José happily reported the next morning, as he handed me the paper. "And, I almost forgot, there's another one of those shoe murders on page four."

I turned away and pretended to busy myself straightening a couple of shoes on display. I should have known it would be in the papers when I saw the happy grin on José's face. As usual he had enjoyed the gory details while not paying much attention to names and places.

I grabbed the paper without glancing at the article, put it down on one of the seats and headed to the back room to measure out the coffee. I was certainly not going to mention the victim was another person I knew. Or that the murder actually took place in my apartment. I didn't want to speak about the murder at all.

"Where is your friend Charles?" I asked him, in an attempt to change the subject.

José yawned. "Don't know. He comes and he goes. A real loner, that one."

I waited for the warm smell of coffee to revive my spirits while José chatted happily on about "drunk cops" and "drowned children." He roamed around the show-room, oblivious to my own silence.

When the coffee was ready, I carried out a couple of cups and set them down on the table between two of the seats.

José put down his stack of papers and walked to one of the display tables, fingering the shoes. He picked up a patent leather boot with a steel heel.

"Pow!" he said, swinging it around his head. "I bet this could do the trick!" His mother must have dropped him on his head when he was a baby.

Unable to restrain myself any longer, I picked up the newspaper José had conveniently folded to page four. A grainy black and white picture of a body covered by a blanket—the blanket that once was on my own bed. When was this photo taken? I could not remember any reporters around. The headline read "Cleaning Woman Murdered in Upper West Side Apartment." No address. The last line stated "The murder weapon was a shoe."

Again, they were deliberately omitting the style, color and maker of the shoe. Even the location of the wound. I pictured Bonita's tangled blonde hair with a blue shoe stuck in her scalp. I would never again hear her little songs, the lilt of her laughter.

When I picked up my head again, José was gone, and the boot with the metal heel had been carefully replaced. I glanced at my watch. Merissa was late. Not like her. Sure, she had the occasional hang-over, but most of the time she was so eager to fondle the shoes that she would beat me to the shop. I was just about to call Merissa on the phone when she rushed in, trailing her coat and scarf and babbling away as if to make up for lost time.

"*Mon Dieu*! Don't know what happened to the time, rolled off the bed in the middle of the night, bump *mon tete* on the drawer, no comb, blouse all crumpled up, got to clean up my place…" She walked past me into the bathroom. "So *comment allez-vous* Madame Emily, Hmmmm?"

She was moving so fast I couldn't keep up with her.

And then the bell tinkled; first customer.

I glanced into the show-room. It was Yetta Melnick, one of the elderly widows in the neighborhood, who probably had not bought a pair of shoes since 1953. She came in for the company.

"Be right there," I called and grabbed Merissa's arm before she could escape into the show-room. When she finally lifted her face, I could see why she was in such a hurry to avoid me. Her lip was swollen and she was wearing sun-glasses. I gently removed her glasses. One of her eyes was half shut.

"Wait just a minute," I said. "We have some things we need to discuss."

Merissa scowled. "*Plus tarde.* We got ourselves a customer."

"No we don't" I said, "We got ourselves a situation."

Merissa gave in. "If you say so, Cheri."

She allowed me to lead her to the back room.

"Who hit you?"

"Nobody hit nobody. I fell off the bed. Told you that. I got careless, is all. Nothing to worry about. Nothing to talk about. Merissa take care of herself."

Here was the thing. I did not meddle in the lives of my employees—or my friends, for that matter. Everyone had things they kept to themselves. I respected that. Someone wanted to cry on my shoulder—I would listen. But truth was, I did not want to know too much. If I did, I would have to worry that Gladis Firth could not possibly pay her rent, and that Mary Williams husband would never come back to her, and that Beverly Plotkin's son really was a dope addict.

And what could I do about it? Hey, I'm not Mother Teresa. I had a store to run; I had bills to pay. And my worry time was taken up with Shana.

So I lent a friendly shoulder. Sometimes I slipped a few bucks under a door. But mainly, I tried to mind my own business. But then the question always came up, as it did with Kim—how much is enough?

I never asked Merissa where she went after work. I know she liked to party. Take care of Fifi. I had seen some of her friends—men, women, cross-dressers. It was her business, right? But I worried about her. I had always worried about her. Not, because like Fifi and Shana, she was naive—but because she was too courageous, too fearless to worry about herself and too proud to ever ask for help.

It occurred to me that Merissa had not read page four in *The New York Times*. I thrust it in front of her. "There's been another shoe murder. Someone murdered Bonita, the woman who cleaned my apartment. I found her." For a moment my voice caught in my throat. "It was horrible. There was blood all over."

I could say that Merissa turned white but of course, she couldn't. Nevertheless, I saw that something was happening. The muscles in her face seemed to go limp. She put her dark glasses back on and grabbed hold of my arm so tightly it hurt. "Your cleaning lady murdered? What you talkin' bout girl? What you sayin?"

"Here! It was in the papers. They didn't mention the name or address."

Merissa lowered her head and seemed to crumble, right there in front of me, like a castle made of sand, until she collapsed in a heap of blue silk and tears on the floor.

Merissa and I had worked together for three years—shared the bathroom, the coffee and the cleaning up—shared the vision of how to make Emily's Place one of the most famous shops in Manhattan.

But there was a side of Merissa's personality she always kept under wraps—a vulnerability she never allowed me to see. Now, painful as it was to see, it made me feel closer to her.

It felt comforting to share my grief with Merissa but she had never met Bonita. "I think she died quickly," I murmured. "In the end, he slit her throat."

She began to sway back and forth and moan. "I got to talk to you Madame Emily," her fingers dug deeper into my arm. "Me and Fifi, when I find her, we got to move on."

"What are you talking about? "What do you mean when you find Fifi? Where is she?"

"Fifi! *Mon petite* Fifi! She gone! She disappeared. Everything gone! Those shoes you give her? Gone! That coat I buy her? Gone! Even her pillow. It gone!"

"She must have known where she was going if she took her things," I said. "Didn't you tell me she does this from time to time? Runs off with a man? Then comes back?" I pictured Fifi as a big balloon with a happy face, slowly floating over the West Side—out over the Hudson River, until she disappeared from sight.

"I got to find her now. We got to go!"

"Go where? "

She stared at me, her eyes wide. "We go to Canada. We go to Haiti. We got family in Haiti."

"Haiti? Are you crazy? No one has anything to eat in Haiti. People are dying like flies in Haiti!"

Now I dug my fingers into her arm. "You can't leave Emily's Place! I need you!"

Merissa's eyes roamed over the showroom. "We got to go. Something bad happening here. Something bad going to happen to you. To Shana."

I was getting really frightened now. If something was so bad it scared Merissa, it must really be terrible. I bent over closer to her. "Shana? What is going to happen to Shana?" I did not really worry about anything happening to me. I'm tough. Whatever happened I would get though. But Shana? Shana was a babe in the woods. It was bad enough that she could hardly manage the Berkshires. But in New York City? With a murderer loose?

Merissa moaned again. "I hear things. Bad things. Someone get you. Want to make you suffer. Kill your sister."

I grabbed Merissa's shoulder and shook her."Who? What did you hear?" But Merissa only shook her head. And slowly, in front of my eyes, I saw the shell begin to close once again around Merissa. Her face began to relax. The lids of her eyes began to lower. She licked her lips, and she rose. But I would not give up."What about Shana?" I asked her. "Murphy thinks the murderer might have been trying to kill Shana. Bonita is—was—blonde too."

"You got to be careful. That cop, he on to something, he say someone want to hurt you. You got to get Shana back to the country. Then she be safe. Merissa will take care of you."

I was happy to learn that Merissa cared as much for me as I cared for her—but what did she know that she wasn't telling me? I grabbed her glasses and looked into her one good eye.

"What happened to the red shoe?"

Merissa turned her head. "Nothing happened to it. It's in the closet where we hang our coats. "

"It wasn't there the other day."

"You just didn't see it, dark back there on the floor and your eyes not so good."

I bristled. "I may not be able to read the clock from across the room but I sure can see a red shoe when it's in front of my nose."

Merissa pulled her glasses out of my hand and settled them back on her nose. Then she took me by the hand and led me to the closet in the back room. She reached down and pulled out my umbrella. There, right behind the umbrella, was the red shoe.

I stared at it for a moment as if it were a hot coal—or perhaps an evil omen—and then I replaced my umbrella in front of it, without a word.

"Forget about the red shoe, and stop worrying about Merissa. *Mon Dieu*! Merissa has lived in tougher places than New York City. She just got a little careless. Won't ever happen again. Surely not."

I clutched her shoulder. "What if the murderer is stalking all the people I care about? What if he is stalking you?"

Merissa snorted. "*Mon dieu*! What if? What if? If the queen had balls she'd be king." And with that, she turned around and walked back into the show room.

I finally put up the "Closed" sign about 6:00pm. My head was reeling. I sat down in the back room. For the first time all day I finally had a chance to think. And what I thought was not good.

What had really happened to Merissa? What might she know about Bonita's murder? And where had Fifi gone? What could have so frightened Merissa that she would think of Haiti as a safe haven?

And how did the red shoe magically appear again? A heap of mysteries sat on top of my brain like a pile of dirty laundry.

I suddenly realized I was hungry. I had been so busy all day that I had not eaten. I was rummaging around in my mini refrigerator—my backroom is small but since I spend so much time here I've outfitted it with some of the comforts of home—looking for some cheese to put between two slices of bread when I heard it.

A sound that made me drop the cheese and stand stock-still. The creak of the mail chute in the front door. A soft, thud, as something landed on the carpet. I peeked into the front room. On the carpet lay a crumpled paper bag. I finally got up enough courage to pick it up and look inside. I found one blue satin mule, adorned with a white marabou pompom and a three inch metal heel. Dolce & Gabbana—size eight.

I closed my eyes and tried a few "Om's" that my sister had told me would bring instant relaxation. She was wrong as usual. I had last seen its blood-soaked mate sticking out of Bonita's scalp. I dropped it like a hot potato. Poor Bonita. Her laughter echoed in my mind. When I opened my eyes the crumpled brown paper bag was still lying at my feet and the shoe was right there next to it.

I picked up the bag. No name, no Bendels, no Saks, no Bloomingdales, nothing. Just a plain brown paper bag. I tried to remember what the other bag looked like, the one with the red shoe but nothing came to mind. I had thrown that bag away. Before I knew it had probably contained the mate to a murder weapon.

I shoved the blue shoe back into the bag. With a start, I remembered my last Goodie One Shoes message. I rummaged around in my drawer until I found a copy of the print-out I had made for Murphy. "Cinderella lost a shoe—the color of it was dark blue."

Oh my God, I was beginning to think that Murphy was more right about things than I had originally given him credit for. Goodie One Shoes was a prime suspect.

I took a couple of deep breaths, walked back to the store room and hid the bag in the back of the closet right next to the red shoe, behind my umbrella.

Then I called Murphy and left a message on his machine to call me as soon as possible.

When I finished work the next evening, Murphy was standing outside in front of a police car.

"I think you need to put a quarter in the meter," I said.

Murphy looked at the meter and smiled."One of the perks of the job."

"Someone dropped off the mate to the blue shoe," I told him. "Put it through the mail chute."

"Hope you still have it. Or has it disappeared like the red one?"

I was about to tell him the red shoe had returned when he said, "I thought we'd take a little ride."

Now this was interesting. Maybe, I told myself, Murphy is interested in me. Maybe he will ask me out for dinner. I had felt a thaw the last time we met.

Murphy opened the door and I slid in beside him. This was kind of fun. I had never been in a police car before. And it was nice to be this close. My leg brushed against his and our shoulders touched as he put the key in the ignition.

The light on the top revolved in a circle, bathing us with alternate rays of red and yellow. His police phone picked up muffled conversations of other cops. The car smelled from cigarettes and coffee. There was a roll of lifesavers on the dashboard. "Thought I'd give you a lift downtown to the lab," Murphy said. "We need your fingerprints."

Damn! Romance did not seem to be a high priority with Murphy. I was beginning to feel offended. "Are you going to tell me I'm a suspect?"

Murphy concentrated on the traffic ahead of him. "It's procedure. We need your prints so we can tell them apart from someone else's—someone's who don't belong there." A truck stopped short in front of us and Murphy stepped hard on the brake. "New Jersey," Murphy groused, "That guy's from Jersey. They never learned how to drive." He drove through the next red light. "Also your DNA. I need a sample of your DNA."

Now I was offended. "My DNA? What are you talking about?"

Murphy pulled the car over to the side and parked in front of a hydrant. "Bonita had skin under her finger nails. She scratched her killer. It's our first real clue. We ran it through all the local criminal files. No match."

I felt like punching him. "Why would I murder Bonita—in my own bedroom? It makes no sense."

"Also Shana. We need her fingerprints and her DNA. You two are the only ones we know of so far who were close to both the victims." He started the car and pulled out again.

I stared straight ahead and said nothing—mad as Hell.

"And Shana. Your sister. Maybe her boyfriend is importing something else besides tee shirts. Maybe Bonita was their drug connection."

I was rendered speechless. I had a strong urge to grab the wheel from Murphy and crash his car into the garbage truck I saw in front of us.

It took me a few minutes to regain my composure and then I said, "Are there any other 'procedures' you have planned for Shana and me? Perhaps a mammogram? Maybe we are really men in disguise?"

Murphy pulled the car over again to the side and turned to look at me. "I'm sorry, okay? I'm getting pressure from the Commissioner. People are talking about a "serial killer," preying on women. I've got to follow procedure. "

He offered me a lifesaver.

I refused.

He unwrapped one for himself and threw the wrapper on the floor. Then he reached under his seat and took out a small battered cigar box. "Kim's room is still off limits. Since nobody lives there the lab boys are in no hurry to finish up. But I brought you a few "personal effects" I thought you might like to have."

He handed me the box. "You'll have to sign for it," he said, extracting a sheet of paper from his jacket pocket.

I glanced quickly at the paper to make sure it was not a confession and then I scribbled my name on the bottom. I did not trust the guy but I was touched by this gesture. My eyes began to fill with tears.

Murphy put his arm around me and lifted my chin so I was looking directly into his eyes. "Listen. All this is just routine. We are ruling you and Shana out—not in. Didn't find the boyfriend or the phone. But we found a couple of interesting clues that may pay off down the road—a few red threads—synthetic. Could be from the killer's clothes."

The police had sealed my bedroom for two days. At least they accomplished something. In my mind's eye I saw poor Bonita's mangled body on my bed. "Who claimed the body?" I asked him.

"Turns out she had a sister who did have a green card."

I was relieved I was not her next of kin.

"And we found a strange, crescent-like imprint in the blood on the floor of your bedroom. Not sure what that might be. We found traces of copper, steel. I thought it might have been made by a bracelet."

"A crescent?" I said. "How big a crescent?" Clever bastard. He had managed to turn my anger into curiosity.

And with that Murphy opened the glove compartment and whipped out a photo of a partial semi circle, that looked to me about three inches long, with an indentation beneath it.

I put Kim's cigar box down carefully on the floor in front of me. I turned the photo around a couple of times and then I saw it. "I'd say it was the tip of a shoe print—size eight."

Murphy seemed to choke on his lifesaver and I patted him on the back—hard.

"I suppose you know the style number and maker,' he said when he recovered.

"No. I don't see any other marks. You said there were traces of metal?"

He nodded.

"Could be some kind of tap or decoration." I handed him back the photo.

Murphy turned on the ignition. His police radio mumbled. The top light gyrated.

"Hey," I said, "Does this car have a siren?"

"Sure," Murphy answered.

"Let's turn it on," I suggested.

And he did.

Suddenly I felt so much better.

Chapter 11

Western fetishists tend to enjoy domination and hence favor high heels, metal studs and other hard-edged ornaments, while those in the East, particularly in China, prefer passivity, and believe the tiny bound feet of their women promise erotic bliss.

Two days had passed and I hadn't heard anything more from Murphy the Cop, other than permission to reclaim my apartment. Kim's box remained closed. I did not yet have the courage to open it. I needed to wait for the right time and place. I had ordered a new mattress on-line, picked up a blanket and pillow on sale from the linen store on Broadway, gritted my teeth and moved back in.

My bedroom looked like a motel room. The furniture was all there but all the life was missing. The top of my dresser that usually held a pile of papers and some scattered cosmetics, now displayed a row of lipsticks, lined up like soldiers, in front of three mascaras lying log-like in size order behind them. Papers were held together with a rubber band, stashed on the side table. Photographs around the room had been rearranged and stared out at me, all at the same angle, like pictures at a gallery. The books usually scattered around the floor near my bed were stacked in a neat pile on top of the radiator.

The whole room smelled from disinfectant. The death that had taken place there suddenly appeared like my own.

I threw my dirty clothes on top of the bare mattress, pushed over the lipsticks, threw my books back on the floor, picked up the window shade and looked out into the garden.

It was Saturday and the sun was shining. It was Merissa's weekend to work at the shop, and I was free to do whatever I wanted.

I picked up Kim's box and propped it on top of the kitchen table. MONTE CRISTO, Cubano. Where would Kim have gotten an old Cuban cigar box? There was so much about Kim I had never had a chance to find out.

I took a deep breath and opened the box. Inside were a few yellowing photos. Kim as a child, four or five years-old, holding hands with an older woman—her mother? A heavy-set Caucasian woman. The Missionary who had saved her? I would never know. A group photo of children about five or six—a missionary school? There was a small gold ring with a single pearl I had bought her for her birthday; a few old Chinese coins and a small, plastic comb in the shape of a butterfly.

So little left of a life. I fought back the urge to cry. I looked once again at all the photos. I held each coin in my hand. And then I lifted up the comb.

There was something wrong with that comb. The other objects felt right—infused with Kim's spirit or something else I couldn't quite name—the comb was different. I carried it over to the window in the bedroom. A cheap, Chinatown souvenir. Something my Kim would never have worn.

Sure, she was Chinese, but she hated the cheap merchandise sold in Chinatown. And she never wore anything in her hair. I went to the phone and called Murphy. He answered on the second ring.

"Thanks for giving me that cigar box with Kim's things," I said. "I appreciate it."

"My pleasure," he answered.

I hated to ruin what I hoped might be a beautiful friendship by challenging his judgment but I'm not very good at beating around the bush. "There's a problem" I said simply, "That comb you gave me in the cigar box? It's not Kim's."

I did not hear anything but I bet Murphy was cursing under his breath. "And how would you know that?" he asked me at last.

"She hated cheap Chinatown souvenirs and she never wore anything in her hair."

Murphy was quiet. Then he said, "I found it on the floor, next to the photos and the coins that had spilled out of the box. The place was a mess—things thrown all around. The lab didn't find any fingerprints on it, or any DNA. I figured it came out of the box."

"You figured wrong," I told him. "It could be the murderer dropped it."

Now I did hear Murphy cursing under his breath. "Someone might have given it to her as a gift. That old lady down the hall could have lost it there. There's no reason to believe the murderer dropped it."

"Sure there is. No fingerprints. No DNA." I reminded him, "If it was Kim's comb, there'd be prints at least. The murderer didn't leave prints anywhere—must have been wearing gloves."

"You're telling me the murderer was a Chinese woman who liked cheap hair combs?" Murphy was really pissed off now.

"Far be it from me to try to tell you anything," I said, "except that Kim never owned or wore that comb."

"I'll take another look at the lab report," Murphy said, "Maybe there was something about that comb I missed."

"Thanks," I said, and hung up. I stared for a few minutes at the comb in my hand. Was Kim murdered by some jealous Chinese girl? And what was Quinn's role in all of this? And Goodie One Shoes? I knew nothing of her friends or life in Chinatown. All I knew at this point was that I was getting a headache. I needed some air.

I decided to go for a jog in Central Park. Not exactly a jog—because of some arthritis in my knees, but rather a race-walk around the reservoir—something I had not had the time—or the spirit—to do since Kim was murdered.

I put on my jogging, now walking shoes, sweat shirt and sweat pants. A good walk around the reservoir would clear my head just fine. I took my key, shut out the lights, locked up.

For more than the twenty years I lived on Central Park West, I jogged every morning. Then I had to give it up for race-walking about a year before I moved to Broadway. Since then I had given up those walks. Part of starting a new life. Part of realizing that Broadway was three long blocks from Central Park.

Now I walked as briskly as possible through the roadblocks of weekend visitors; shoppers, sight-seers, people walking their dogs, homeless men rummaging through garbage cans, delivery people of all shapes and sizes carting cartons of food and merchandise, elderly women with their walkers and nurse's aides, Italian tourists chattering away, vendors selling African statues and second-hand books until I finally made it through to Central Park West.

It felt good to finally enter the park. I race-walked down one of the pathways till I reached the reservoir. Then I started around the Jacqueline Kennedy jogging track, named for her because she actually did sometimes walk around it. I even saw her do it.

It was glorious now to circumnavigate the reservoir. The vista across the water to the buildings on Fifth Avenue and Central Park West was picture-post-card perfect. The late afternoon sun came through the clouds like slivers of silver and gold and lighted up the reflection of the trees in the water.

As I got into my stride I noticed how quiet it really was, here in the middle of the park, in the middle of one of the busiest cities in the world. I passed another woman walking with hand weights, and then a man, jogging backward. And then I was entirely alone.

Alone in New York, almost anything can happen. Especially in Central Park. On the West side of the reservoir the shade fell more densely. The leaves of the cherry blossoms, not yet in bloom, rustled in the wind.

I turned my head. Behind me I saw a man walking at a good pace. He was wearing a sweat shirt with a hood and sweat pants, much like my own.

I quickened my pace and glanced back again.

He had quickened his and was gaining on me.

I began to jog.

So did he.

I noticed that he seemed to drag one leg and was no longer gaining on me.

I slowed my pace.

So did he.

As a long-time jogger and race-walker, I often engaged in these strange undeclared races with people. You'd be just jogging along, minding your own business and then, all of a sudden, someone would pass you. You'd feel challenged and pretty soon, you were increasing your pace to pass the other. Then the other would pass you and you him or her until one of you got tired and left. And so, I wasn't particularly concerned but I couldn't forget about him either.

I increased and then decreased my pace.

He did the same.

Obviously, he did not want to catch up to me or pass me.

So what, I wondered, is his game?

A few yards ahead of me a group of young men in gym shorts entered the path talking to each other in German. I breathed a sigh of relief.

Now, I had enough courage to see if this man was deliberately shadowing me—or if he was just out for a little exercise.

I stopped dead on the track and slowly turned around.

He stopped.

For a moment we stared at each other, and then I took off in his direction.

He hesitated for a moment, and then, threw something far out into the reservoir.

We both watched as it made a large arch upwards, caught the glint of the sun, and then splashed down with a plop into the water. Then he walked quickly off the path and into the surrounding woods.

When I got to where he had been, I stared into the woods and then out into the water.

For a moment, a silver shoe with a bright red sole floated out there. And then it sank like a stone.

"You're home early," Larry greeted me at the door to my apartment.

"Awk! Awk! Home Early! Home Early!" Henry called out from my kitchen where he was happily perched on the top of my wrought iron chair.

There was Larry, my estranged husband, and a couple of short, dark skinned men who looked like the ancient Mayan statues in my ex-living room back on Central Park West, walking back and forth in the living/dining area carrying wires and tool boxes.

Seated at the kitchen table, sipping tea was my neighbor Angelina and of course, there was Henry.

"I see you've made friends," I nodded to Angelina who rose somewhat unsteadily from her seat.

"Yes, indeed, Dolly. Your husband is quite the gentleman. Reminds me of Henry Fonda, he does. Knows how to please a lady."

At the mention of "Henry," the Parrot flew up in the air, made a few swoops at the Incas attempting to attach some wires to my window-sills and then returned to his perch on the back of one of the kitchen chairs.

"Yes, I'm sure he does, though Russian ladies are his specialty."

I kissed Angelina on both cheeks, avoided Larry's offered cheek and steered myself into the living room area. I sat down on the couch and unlaced my running shoes. The last thing I felt like dealing with today was Larry. And yet, as I sank into the cushions and heard Larry giving orders to the workman, Henry squawking happily in the kitchen and Angelina alternating throwing kisses in the air and reprimanding him gently, I felt content. More. I felt safe. I had to admit to myself that it was the first time all day when things felt somehow "right."

Habit. Twenty-plus years of having Larry take care of me. But enough was enough. I rose from the couch. "How the hell did you get in here?"

Larry shrugged

"I guess it's time I was going," Angelina said. She made some kind of circular motion with her hand, a signal for Henry who immediately perched on her shoulder. "Ta, Ta!" she called out, waving a handkerchief she had stashed in her bosom, and spreading a sweet, musky odor into the room.

I locked the door behind her. "So how did you get in?" I asked again. "This building is supposed to have good security."

"Ah." Larry said. "Where there is a will there is a way. I merely buzzed the super—one George Washington—I do believe—told him I was your husband, come to install a burglar alarm in your apartment—and he came down in a jiffy."

"George doesn't do anything in a jiffy."

"A twenty-dollar bill helped speed things up."

I sputtered. So even George Washington couldn't be trusted. "And Angelina?"

Larry laughed. "Do you think anyone could come in or out of here without her and her mangy bird noticing? As soon as I opened the front door she came out into the hall. Said her bird recognized me. So it was only neighborly of me to invite them in. Poured a little Vodka in her tea so now we're friends for life."

Larry put his hand on my shoulder. "That's why it's so important that we install this security. A camera in the hallway so you can see who is standing in front of the door before you open it. They still haven't caught that guy who's been killing women with their shoes."

"Shoe." I corrected.

Larry looked at me quizzically.

I had figuratively speaking, put my foot in my mouth on that one. All I had to do now was tell Larry about the Phantom of the Jogging Path, the Shoe Mailman and the fact that my cleaning lady was murdered in my bedroom and he'd probably stick me with a couple of body guards. I cleared my throat. "I read in the papers the killer leaves only one shoe."

"Whatever." Larry continued. "One shoe or two, a murderer is loose out there and you're alone in here."

I looked away. I could not argue with that.

Larry took my arm and led me to the kitchen table."Brought you an éclair from Payard." He pointed to a plate of assorted desserts in the middle of the table. It looked as if Henry had helped himself to a couple of them. One of the problems with being married for so many years is your ex-mate knows all your weaknesses.

"Thanks." I said and went into the bathroom to wash my hands. When I came out, I saw Larry had cleared away the crumbs and poured a cup of coffee for me. The only time he had cleared the table and made coffee for me in all our years together was when I had cut myself with a carving knife one Thanksgiving.

I recognized a message here. It seemed that since I had left Larry the balance of power between us had shifted. Increasingly, it seemed, he tried to please me.

He sat at the table opposite me and helped himself to the pear crisp. It seemed to me he had lost weight. For a couple of minutes we quietly enjoyed what were probably the best desserts of their kind in the city.

"I got some information on that Quinn guy." Larry said wiping his lips. He reached into his briefcase and took out a file. "First off, He's been a tenured professor for fifteen years. Unless we can prove that kid was under sixteen or he raped her, no one is going to touch him."

"But she was his student!" I protested. "When I went to school any sexual relationship would have been unethical! Besides, she may have been over sixteen but she was from another culture. She was like a child!"

Larry grunted. "Times have changed in case you haven't noticed. When you and I went to school you weren't allowed to have boys in your room. Now they live together in the dorms and take communal showers. But I did find out something else."

I looked up. I saw how he was a really effective lawyer. First he beat you down; then he picked you up. A jury would be putty in his hands.

"Quinn had been fired fifteen years ago for sexual harassment in a small college in Colorado. The girl involved disappeared. It was rumored that she went back to Mexico, where she had family—but no one has been able to check that out—small towns in Mexico, like China, don't keep good records—especially about citizens who disappeared from their country years ago."

"I knew it! "I cried out. "I knew there was something wrong! You've got to find out more."

Larry held up his hand. "That will require some more research."

I held on to Larry's jacket. "You've got to follow up on this, Larry," I begged him. "He could be Kim's killer—and the killer of other women all over the city!"

"I'm not a private investigator." He shook the folder in front of my face. "This took me a lot of time. Calling in favors. Asking for new favors. This could cost me plenty."

I sat back on my chair and stared at Larry. For a few minutes I had forgotten who he really was. "It might cost you a few lunches with your Cozzack Cutie" I said, "Too busy talking on the phone to pay her proper attention."

"Oh come on!" Larry retorted. "Give me a break! The former Governor of New York State came out on T.V. telling everyone about his multiple affairs and his wife stood with him, staring up at him with love in her eyes. I make one mistake and you run away from me."

"One mistake that I caught you with. Who knows how many others there were."

Larry winced. "I swore to you...I..."

"Yeah, yeah yeah..." We had been through this before. I was surprised I still cared. I thought now that I could forgive him the sex. It was the relationship I could not forgive. "Anyway, that was—is—one very long mistake, you are still making."

Larry glanced over to the workmen who were talking quietly to each other in Spanish.

He lowered his voice.

"How badly do you want this information on Professor Low-Life?"

I played with my fork. This was the real Larry. Who did not really care about anyone or anything except winning. The consummate deal-maker. Back them into a corner and then give them a way out they are not likely to refuse. I was not going to fall for that. "Not enough" I said, shaking my head. "Guess I'll just leave it to the police."

For a moment Larry and I looked at each other, each reluctant to turn away first. I was aware of feelings for Larry I thought were long gone, but I did not know exactly what to call them.

Finally, Larry reached for his coat. "I think these guys are almost through," he said, indicating the workmen. "Don't be such a smart aleck. People are being murdered in this city. You've left a perfectly beautiful home for what?"

I figured that was a rhetorical question so I did not answer it. At the door, I offered Larry my cheek. He gave me a small peck. For a moment I remembered Larry's lips pressed hard against my own. I remembered our arms, our legs, entwined. I remembered our lives and bodies joined together. I turned away.

He motioned towards Angelina's door across the way. "Damn bird ate up two apple tarts," he said, and headed down the hallway.

Chapter 12

The history of humankind is a testament to the importance of the shoe. Records of the Eqyptians, Chinese and Hebrews repeatedly reference shoes, and the holy Bible mentions them frequently.

"Not much to report, today," José said, handling me the paper. "Couple of old ladies mugged on page three. Rich guy strangled to death in East Hampton, page two." José smirked. "Must be one of them HOMOSEXUAL murders."

He pronounced the word "homosexual" carefully, as if afraid some part of it would stick to his tongue and alter his gender.

"Can't understand it," he said, "Whole idea of man with man makes me sick."

He smiled at me, and winked. "Specially when there are all those nice women around to play with."

I ignored José and opened the paper. It seemed an important part of José's masculine identity to flirt with me.

I picked it up with a combination of terror and curiosity. "No women murdered last night?"

"Not unless I missed something," José answered brightly. "First thing I look for."

I breathed a sigh of relief and took a quick glance through the metro section. I had been up half the night, sure that I would find another woman murdered by a shoe in this morning's paper.

José yawned. "Worried about something?" he asked. "I would be, if I were a woman living alone."

He stared at me, sympathetically. "Lots of women live alone these days. Can't understand it."

I gave him my most severe look back. "I'm not alone," I lied.

"Sure you are, 'less you've hooked up with someone new in the last day or two. "

What did he say? I was beginning to get that creepy, crawly feeling you get when you see a water bug coming at you across the kitchen floor. "I'm not alone," I repeated. "I have a bird."

José laughed. "Sure don't have no bird. Only bird in the whole neighborhood is Henry who lives next door."

I slammed the newspaper down. I had had enough of people knowing my business. Wasn't this New York City? The great metropolis where everyone was anonymous? Where people didn't meet each other's eye in the street? Where no one ever said hello to a stranger? Where people could live on the same street and even in the same building and never learn each other's name? So how come this creep knows all about me? "Where there is a will, there is a way" Larry had told me. He certainly had no trouble gaining access to my apartment. And I didn't have much trouble finding out where Philip Quinn lived. In the end, New York City was just a big village where anyone could find out anything.

"Hey! It's not my fault people tell me things," José said, looking accusingly at me. "Lots of lonely people in this city. Lots of lonely women in this city. Lots of people happy to see José and tell him their troubles." He stood up and gathered the rest of his papers to his chest. "Guess you don't need José around to tell you things you don't want to know."

I bit my lip. Now I had hurt his feelings. I looked at his ragged jacket; his tattered cap. He had come to me for a little human interaction before he started his dreary day and what had I done? I extended my hand.

"I'm sorry," I said, "Guess I'm just a little edgy this morning. Didn't sleep too well last night."

José took my hand and smiled. "Sure, don't think nothing of it. Happens to everyone."

He winked at me again.

I smiled. "Have a nice day," I said as he walked out the door. I watched him slowly make his way down the street. For the first time I realized he had a slight limp. Like the man on the jogging path. Then it occurred to me that the shoe murderer might only be interested in one shoe because he only had one good foot.

I slept late the next morning. I did not want to arrive early and open the store. Just the thought of José's gleeful announcement of the latest murder as he handed me the paper gave me the shivers.

I picked up the phone and canceled my delivery of The New York Times. And then I went back to bed. It wasn't fair to blame the messenger for the message but José's messages were getting me down.

I hoped it was one of Merissa's good mornings and she would

open. If not, the customers would just have to come back another time.

And then the phone rang. It was Murphy.

"Hi! I said in my brightest voice, "Thanks for calling back." It was hard for me to keep the sarcasm out of my voice.

"Yeah. "he said "I was up all night taking care of a murdered woman. Figured if you could make the phone calls you weren't an emergency."

"There wasn't much help you could give the dead lady," I retorted, "whereas I could have been in big trouble."

Although it was hard to hear a sigh over the telephone, I was pretty sure I heard one. "Could've." He repeated. "Are you okay now?"

"We need to talk, I have some information about these shoe murders you need to know."

Another sigh. "Hit me," he said. "I've got an emergency on the other line."

Come on! He was the one who'd asked me to tell him about Goody One Shoes. Now he was acting as if he was doing me a favor. "If the last murder had anything to do with a silver shoe, you might want to find the time to talk to me."

I detected a slight intake of breathe. "Where are you?"

"I'm home. Decided I need a morning off."

"I've got to go home and clean up a little," he said, "check into the office. I'll be over in a couple of hours."

Cleaning up sounded like a good idea to me. I jumped into the shower. The cool water cleared my head. I got dressed in jeans and a long sleeved black tee shirt just tight enough to show I still had a good figure and glanced at my watch. I called the store. No answer. Merissa must be busy.

I called Merissa's cell. No answer. I left a message for her to call me as soon as she could.

There was just enough time to run to the bodega and get some chocolate chip muffins. I had a feeling Murphy would appreciate a sweet.

When I opened the door, Angelina's door latch across the hall clicked and she peeked out—hair still disheveled. "You're late this morning," she announced. "Everything all right?" From inside her apartment Henry echoed, "All Right? All Right?"

"Yes, everything's all right. Just a little tired, is all. Need anything from the bodega?"

"Just the newspaper," Angelina said.

I stared at her. "Don't you get the paper delivered?"

"No," she said. "I usually pick it up at the corner when I go out for my walk."

That really stopped me. If José did not deliver her newspaper, how did he know so much about her?

I locked my apartment door and walked to the door of the building. Peering into the street I saw a group of teenage girls walking hand and hand on their way to Brandeis High School a couple of blocks away. I saw a man with a poodle, and the mail man wheeling his load of letters ahead of him. No sign of anyone with a limp.

I walked quickly down the street until I caught up with Charles the mailman. It was comforting to be close to someone in a uniform, even if it was just a mailman's.

"Hello," I said.

He tipped his hat.

For a couple of minutes we walked in lock step next to each other.

"Haven't seen you around Emily's Place for a while," I ventured.

"Been busy," he replied his eyes straight ahead.

We walked in silence for a couple of steps.

"How are the shoes?" he asked.

"The same." I remembered this guy was not much of a conversationalist. And then it occurred to me that he would know pretty much everyone in the neighborhood if this limping guy was in the neighborhood which was anyone's guess. It was worth a try.

"Would you happen to know anyone round here who has a limp" I asked him.

He shrugged and continued walking in a straight line. "Few people, Yes" He walked more slowly.

"There's Mrs. Rabinowitz, lives at 390. She had a hip operation two weeks ago."

He walked a little slower.

"Barney Klinger. He was hit by a car a month ago. Still can't walk right."

He took a few more steps.

"Marion Friedman. She had bunion surgery."

"Mr. Esposito…" He stopped.

"He died last month. Still haven't rented the apartment."

We paused together at the corner and waited for the light to change.

"It was a mistake." Charles said.

"What was a mistake?"

"The maid who was killed in your apartment."

The light changed but we stood at the corner, motionless. "What do you mean?" I asked, holding my breath.

Had he read about it in the newspaper? The article about the murder didn't list the address. But Charles delivers my mail. Someone in the building must have told him.

"A maid. Nobody wants to kill a maid. They have no money. They don't do bad things. They only clean. The killer must have made a mistake."

The cars started up again. The roar of the traffic made it hard to hear. I leaned closer to him.

"Even me" he said. "Sometimes I make a mistake. Your buzzer system. Sometimes I ring Angelina Grosso in 1A and George Washington Green in 5C buzzes me in. The killer went to the wrong apartment."

"What was he looking for?" I yelled over the traffic din.

"Drugs. Drink. Anyone want anything else, they got to go out of the neighborhood."

And then the light changed and we each headed off in a different direction.

There it was again. The intimacy of one of the world's largest cities. How was it possible that so many people knew your business? Not only knew it but commented on it? As for anyone in the neighborhood with a limp—it was as I suspected. Asking if someone had a limp in the neighborhood was like asking if anyone looked suspicious. It would be everybody.

At the twenty-four hour hour Korean place I picked up two morning papers and an extra chocolate chip muffin for Angelina and went back to my apartment building.

Once inside the hallway. I saw Angelina's door was open and there was Murphy sitting in her living room balancing a cup of coffee on his lap, with Henry perched right next to him on the arm of the sofa.

"Yoo, hoo" Angelina called, "Emily, we're in here."

Henry flapped his wings and winked at me, but he was clearly more interested in Murphy.

Murphy put his cup down and greeted me at the door. "This lady was kind enough to invite me in, while I waited for you." he said, glancing in an obvious way at his watch.

"I'm sorry," I said, annoyed. "I was just out for a few minutes." I handed Angelina the newspaper and a muffin, and led Murphy across the hall.

Larry could have saved a bundle on the security system. Angelina was just as good.

I fiddled with the key a little before I succeeded in fitting the key into the lock. I could feel Murphy's breath on the back of my neck and smelled his after shave lotion.

He made me nervous. I could so easily imagine him putting his arms around me, kissing my ear. I motioned for him to sit down at the kitchen table and took out the chocolate chip muffins. It seemed a little late to offer him coffee.

He reached for a muffin.

"Damn!" He took out a handkerchief and wrapped it around his finger.

"Damn cut opened up again."

"What happened to your hand?"

He scowled. "Helped myself to a slice of apple pie next door and the knife slipped. Old lady has a collection of sharp knives in her kitchen that would make a butcher jealous."

"She likes to cook,"

"Right. Pasta. Lasagna. We're talking about noodles. She has a knife in there, could gut a pig."

"Italian food is more than pasta." I told him. "Thanks for coming over,"

He nodded. "So, what was that about a silver shoe?" I could see that Murphy was not one for small talk. He took a bite of the muffin and waited for me to go on.

"Took a few hours off and went for a walk along the jogging path in Central Park yesterday. Not many people out that time of the afternoon, about 4:00pm. And then I noticed somebody behind me in a hooded sweatshirt who seemed to be following me."

"Man or woman?"

I hesitated. "A man."

"Are you sure?" Murphy questioned. "How could you tell? You told me the person was wearing a hooded sweatshirt."

"He looked like a man." I thought for a minute. "He walked like a man. He had a limp."

Murphy chewed slowly and looked at me across the table.

"A woman could have a limp. Did you see his face? Did he have a mustache or a beard?"

I put my uneaten muffin down and rose. Why was he challenging me? Didn't he think I could tell the difference between a man and a woman?

"He was dark skinned, could have been African American, Hispanic, maybe Italian."

"Sounds as if he or she could have been Indian, maybe even Jewish." He shook his head. "Not a lot to go on here. Tell me about the shoe."

I circled the living room. "I got a little scared. There weren't many people out that time of day and the sun was beginning to go down, so there were lots of shadows. When I speeded up, he speeded up. He could walk pretty fast, even with his limp. When I slowed down, he slowed down. When I saw a group of runners come on the track, and I wasn't alone any more, I decided to see what was really going on."

Murphy took another bite of his muffin and motioned for me to go on.

"So I turned around and headed towards him. That's when he stopped in his tracks and threw the shoe into the reservoir."

"You saw him throw a silver shoe into the reservoir?"

I nodded

"Describe the shoe."

"The sun sort of glinted off it so I couldn't see it that clearly," I explained. "All I could see was that it was silver, and it had a strap and a red sole."

"You're sure it had a red sole?"

"Yes. Yes! And I'm sure it had a strap. It was silver with a red sole and a strap."

I stopped for a minute. "I'd say it was about a size seven or eight—three inch tapered heel, peek-a-boo toe—French. Gotta be Christian Louboutin, Spring, 2007"

Murphy almost fell off the chair with that one.

I must say I was beginning to enjoy myself.

"Did it float?" he had the nerve to ask me.

"Shoes don't float." I said, "unless they're made of plastic. Leather is heavier than water. It sank like a stone."

"I think I'll have a cup of coffee now, if you don't mind. So how can you tell it's Christian Louboutin, 2007, size eight, from fifty yards away?"

I chuckled. "How can you tell a Mercedes from a Honda? Bordeaux from a Burgundy?"

I quickly set up the coffee pot and watched as the coffee slowly filtered down into the glass container below. I put in two sugars and brought it to the table.

"Thanks for remembering," he said, taking a sip. "I don't know about Bordeaux and Burgundy but I can tell a Guinness from a Pilsner, and Starbucks from Maxwell House." Murphy took another sip and got up from the table. He circled the room like a lion in a cage. He ran his fingers around the edge of the moldings as if checking for dirt. Then he moved to my book shelves. He took down a copy of Emily Dickenson's Poems, and leafed through it.

"Your name sake?" he asked.

"I'd like to think my parents named me after a great American poet, but in fact, I was named for my great Aunt Emily Jacobovitz. She was very sickly as a child and the Rabbi said to give her a middle name of *Alta*—Yiddish for the Old One, and it worked. She lived to be ninety-seven."

Murphy chuckled. "Even better than being named for an unhappy spinster who died young."

He replaced the book and took down James' PORTRAIT OF A LADY.

He opened the book and flipped through it. "Isabel Archer," he says. "Quite a gal. What drove you from Isabel Archer to Merissa LaBelle?"

"Downward mobility," I quipped. "And the fact that I prefer my friendships to be with living people, not dead ones."

He replaced the book and ran his hand along the edge of the front door.

"Who wired the apartment?" he asked.

"My ex."

He turned to look at me. "How Ex is your Ex? He still seems to worry about you."

I shrugged. "Ex as in Excess baggage. I like to travel light."

Murphy sat back down at the table."You're a strange one. Not Isabel Archer and surely not Emily Dickenson. Not Emma Bovary and Not Moll Flanders."

I laughed. "As long as you don't identify me with one of the hags in Macbeth."

He ignored that remark and went on. "You're more like one of those caped-crusaders—but without the cape—like Wonder Woman. At least you seem to think you're Wonder Woman." He stroked his beardless face. "Neighborhood social worker, defender of the underdog. You must think you have super-powers to confront that hooded person on the jogging path. Anyone with any sense would have run away as fast as possible."

"There you have, it. I'm just a stupid shoe saleswoman. Just like you're a stupid cop." I got up from the table. "You seem to have an advantage over me. You know a great deal about me and I don't know much at all about you."

"It's my business to know about you," he shot back. "What do you want to know about me?"

"What's a smart man like you doing as a cop?"

He laughed. "It's not downward mobility for me. Believe it or not, it's upward mobility."

He played with his coffee cup. "I grew up in the Bronx. My father had a liquor store. There were four kids. Not much money. Did you ever read Angela's Ashes?"

"Course," I told him. "I taught the book in Freshman English."

"Well, it wasn't quite that bad—but there was a lot of drinking and very little money.

When I was a kid, the cops from the PAL kind of adopted me. Taught me to box. Taught me how to take care of myself and others. In my neighborhood, being a cop with a steady pay-check is definitely up-wards mobility."

"What about your marital status? You seem to know all about mine."

He laughed. "You like to play,' I'll show you mine if you show me yours?'"

He displayed the fingers of his left hand. No ring. "Not married. Divorced. One kid. Now we're even."

"Not quite," I told him. "What kind of shoe was used to murder that girl last night?"

"No shoe," he said. "She was shot in the chest during a robbery in Greenwich Village."

We looked at each other without speaking.

"The next shoe murder hasn't occurred yet, but the killer is getting bolder. He is delivering the shoe to you before he actually kills the woman."

I poured Murphy another cup of coffee and one for myself. My hand shook and some of the coffee sloshed around in the saucer. Why was the murderer stalking me? Would I be his next victim?

"I guess we need to dredge the reservoir in Central Park," he said. "That's going to mean trouble."

He wrapped his hands around his coffee cup. "For one thing, I will have to deal with the Park Conservancy. A bunch of nuts if I ever saw any."

I wondered whether or not I should admit I was a member. I decided to keep quiet. "But why show the shoe to me?"

"Why send you the drawing of Kim?" Murphy retorted.

I stared across the table at Murphy."He's playing with me. The murderer is playing with me—mocking me—trying to frighten me."

Murphy made a gesture with his hand that meant, "More, give me more."

"What?" I asked him.

"Suppose," he said to me, "You start with a description of the shoe."

"I already gave you a description." Men are so dense. "I'll show you, It just so happens I own an identical pair."

I walked into my bedroom and opened my closet door. Now, I will admit that organization and housekeeping in general are not my strongest suits. Nevertheless, when it comes to my shoes, they are arranged carefully, by color and date in my closet.

It took me no more than a couple of seconds to find the silver shoe—and one more to realize the mate was gone.

I grabbed the single shoe and rushed back to the kitchen table.

"My men noticed it was missing when they checked the room after Bonita's murder."

I sank down in the kitchen chair.

My shoe closet had been raped! For a minute I felt like crying. Get a grip, I told myself. They are only shoes. "But why?" I cried out, "Why me?"

"Someone wants to hurt you for some reason—and it's not the guy who owns the shoe-store down the block. This is personal. Someone really hates you. He is going to try to kill you eventually but first he wants to play with you a little. Make you squirm. Kill your beloved assistant Kim and your sister Shana. The question is why. When we can answer that, we'll be able to find him. So think!"

I shook my head. Yes, it all made sense in the abstract, but not in the real world. I couldn't imagine anyone hating me that much.

"Did you owe any vendors money? Did you have an argument with any of your customers? Did you fire anyone?"

Bingo! Lights began to go off in my head. "Louise the Loser! She's the only person I had ever fired. But that was two and a half years ago."

Murphy took out his little pad and pen. "Time for her hatred to fester. If she had trouble getting another job. If she needed money. If

Goodie One Shoes

she had other problems in her life."

He looked at me. "Don't tell me she's one of your charity cases who just happened to get to America by digging a tunnel from someplace in Mexico—that you have no idea who she is or where she came from, or where she lives?"

"Not exactly what you say. But yes, I did feel sorry for her. She was born here. Lived a few blocks away with her brother. Dropped out of school and needed a job. Caught her stealing and fired her after only a few months. Had the nerve to ask me for references a couple of months ago." In my mind's eye I could see her clearly. Neatly dressed, dark hair tied back in a pony tail, pleated skirt, cheap shoes, usually some kind of sandal with socks. Only one who ever worked at Emily's Place who really didn't seem to like the shoes.

In some ways I could see she might fit the picture Murphy was trying to paint. But I couldn't imagine her being able to overpower these dead women. Louise was a small woman. Kim maybe, but Bonita? Bonita was tougher. She wouldn't succumb easily.

But now Murphy seemed real excited. All of a sudden his face glowed with renewed energy. Murder turned him on. I promised to send him Louise's address later in the day.

"You told me someone put the blue shoe through your mail chute?"

I nodded. 'There's more. The red shoe has reappeared."

Murphy jumped up and took a turn around the room. "Those shoes are evidence. They can give us clues to the identity of the murderer."

But I was still confused. "None of this makes sense. Why bring them to me? Why not just throw them into the Hudson River?"

Murphy smiled. "It's the criminal mind. Why did the Zodiac murderer keep sending notes to the police? Part of the excitement is to try to outsmart the police. It's like an elaborate game. But you can't play it alone. You need someone to play against. You need someone who can appreciate what you have accomplished—and who knows the price of losing. That's where you come in. Who but another worshiper of shoes can understand the lure of the shoe? The irresistible need to handle, smell, maybe wear the shoe—or at least see someone else wear the shoe. And to feel the fear of the stalker?"

I was beginning to see his point. It was all pretty depressing. Not to mention, scary. Some killer-pervert had picked me as his soul-mate.

And then I heard that strange ding-a-ling sound.

Murphy reached into his pocket and took out the little phone.

"Yeah... Right... That's what you say... Now's not a good time... We'll see about that!" and he closed the phone hard.

"Sorry," Murphy said.

"Your wife found the phone?" I suggested.

"She's my ex-wife and I don't want to talk about it." He sighed, then asked, "Have you heard from Goodie One Shoes?"

I opened the drawer of my desk in the living room and withdrew a print-out of my emails with Goodie One Shoes.

Murphy folded them up and put them in his pocket."You need to take these threats very seriously. The fact that you were shown that shoe—before a murder has taken place—is a message from the killer that you may be next on his list." He paused. "Then again, he may be just playing with your head. He might even have planned all this as a distraction while he stalks and kills someone else you care about."

I shivered "Do you think Goodie One Shoes is the murderer?"

He shrugged, "Right now we don't know enough. Could even be Angelina Grosso. She has the knives—and she'd have the limp if she suffers from arthritis which would be a good bet at her age. And that red thread we found—could be from her wig. I know that hair isn't real."

I winced. "Not Angelina, She's my friend. And besides, she couldn't rape her victims."

Murphy's eyebrow twitched. "Could be she had an accomplice."

"Right. There's always Henry, her bird. And besides, she has no motive." I added.

"I don't know about that," Murphy said. "Haven't you ever heard a woman say, 'I'd kill for a pair of shoes like those?'" All of a sudden his eyes looked tired again and his step appeared heavy. I was not sure if he was happy to have the information I had provided or depressed over the thought of having to follow it all up. At the door he paused and took my hand for a minute. It was warm and firm and he drew me closer. "I need you to take special precautions. You can exchange emails with Goodie, but keep your distance. Don't give away any personal information. Don't even think of meeting with him. You need to be more careful. "

His face was just inches from mine. For a moment I thought—hoped—he would kiss me. He put his hand on my shoulder. "You are not Wonder Woman. You do not have super-powers. You shouldn't go anywhere alone for a while."

"Right," I said to him. "Any ideas about who will want to

accompany me all over the city?"

For a moment our eyes locked. Then he looked away. "Stay put, for a while," he counseled. "Stay off the jogging path on the odd hours. Come home in the daylight. Look behind you before you put the key in your door. Lock it as soon as you enter." He put his hand on the door knob. "As for the rest, remember Sister Carrie and how she was able to seduce the man on the train with a steak. I'll be in touch," he tossed over his shoulder as he walked down the hallway.

I locked the door and took *Sister Carrie* down from the shelf. I wondered if he had made a mistake, or his message was quite intentional. It was the salesman who had seduced Sister Carrie with a steak. Not the other way around.

Chapter 13

In 18th Century Europe, a noisy metal device on the bottom of shoes kept delicate slippers above the mud, muck, and cobblestones.

Murphy came into the store the next day to get Louise's address and to retrieve his evidence, or EVIDENCE as Rosa and Denise would say it.

When he saw me crawl into the closet on all fours and fish out the red shoe to which a bit of rug fuzz now clung, and the blue one, in its paper bag, he bit his lip and rolled his eyes. He was not happy.

"What?"

"Thanks so much for taking such good care of the evidence."

"I didn't know this was evidence at the time I received it."

Murphy grimaced, then put on some plastic gloves and reached for the shoe and brown bag. Talk about locking the barn after the horse had run away.

He held up the red shoe. "Bet every hooker on the West Side has handled that one." If facial expressions could talk, Murphy's would be cursing loud enough to break my china coffee cups.

Suddenly there was noise coming from elsewhere. Inside the showroom, I can hear Harold Shapiro's sharp tones in some kind of verbal conflict. "Be right back," I said to Murphy and went toward the ruckus.

There, standing beside the Designer "Previously Owned" table were Harold Shapiro and Cheryl, the transvestite, having a tug of war with a shoe.

"I saw it first!" Harold called out.

"Not on your life!" Cheryl responded, giving a fushia-colored Platform Chanel shoe a final yank that almost sent Harold sprawling.

"You son-of-a-Bitch" yelled Harold.

Out of the corner of my eye, I saw Murphy slowly emerge from the back room and advance toward the area of conflict.

Merissa was advancing from the opposite direction.

"Hold on. Hold on." I said, calmly but firmly.

I placed myself between the two warring parties. I had been through things like this before. Almost weekly, as a matter of fact.

The "Previously Owned Table" was Merissa's idea and I had joked with her about it, suggesting that she had really thought it up just for herself because she seemed to buy, or shall we say "exchange", so many of the shoes. But then I found out that it was much more complex and original than that.

We were talking one day a couple of years ago about how expensive some of these designer shoes were, even though we gave every customer a discount. After all, Jimmy Choo could still run you a thousand dollars; Prada two thousand and Armani about the same. Who on Upper Broadway had that kind of money to spend on shoes? Maybe on a month's rent, but on shoes? Let's face it, even with the investment bankers moving in, most of the people in the neighborhood were single moms, divorcees, widows, or aspiring actors. The gang on Central Park West shopped on Fifth Avenue, not on Upper Broadway. The women on the Upper East Side rarely crossed the park for anything other than a therapist's appointment. So why stock precious objects like a Christian Louboutin pump with a carnal red sole, or a Herman Delman black satin slide with a peek-a-boo-toe? My argument was just because I liked to look at them. I liked the feel and the smell of them. Some people had diamonds; I had shoes.

But Merissa was more practical. She shared my love for the shoes but she also believed that if enough people felt like we did, we could figure out a way to make these beautiful shoes into a profit center. After all, I was in business to make money, right? If all I wanted to do was to fondle shoes, I could go to Bendels.

So Merissa and I decided that if we had the shoes, the crowd would come. All we needed was a little faith and an imaginative sales pitch. We decided right away that we had to discount the shoes even further. Even if they had the money, people liked a bargain. That had always been one of the lures of the Upper West Side. The apartments were just as big as those on the Upper East Side, just as close to Central Park, but the prices were lower. The other difference was attitude. The West Side had it all. A kooky, creative, mixed racial, religious and sexual identity that reflected independence of spirit, independence from Corporate America, and often times, independence from any regular pay check.

That led us to the concept of selling second-hand shoes. So, first off, we adopted a well-known luxury car slogan and called our shoes,

"Pre-owned," instead of "Used."

"Used Shoes," sounded even worse than "used Cars." It conjured up pictures of misshapen shoes distorted by bunions, crushed counters, worn-down heels and scuffed sides, smelling of unwashed feet. But "Pre-owned," is sexy. "Pre-owned" thumbed its nose at virgin shoes and promoted the idea of experience. New shoes are tight and uncomfortable whereas "gently worn pre-owned shoes" had been broken-in. They conformed softly to the shape of your foot; they exuded a warm shine, like old-world elegance. They were scarce and rare in the marketplace, available only to the chosen few who knew where—a few seasons late—they could be found.

Even Merissa was surprised by the success of "The Previously-Owned Table." We knew women would love the shoes, but we hadn't figured that some of them would love cash even more.

Here was a typical scenario: Bored house-wife comes into the store dragging her reluctant husband. "It's my birthday," she claims loudly, "I want a pair of Prada shoes." But she knows that her husband is never going to dish-out a thousand dollars for a pair of shoes, so she brings him to the Previously-Owned Table. There, lo and behold, are a pair of sensational Prada shoes for just three hundred seventy-five dollars. Wife swoons, "I've never had a pair of Prada shoes,' she whines. Hubby pays up and the two leave hand in hand.

The next week the wife returns with the shoes, worn once. We buy them back for twenty percent less in cash and put them out again for ten percent more than we paid. The wife has a fist-full of cash, and we get to sell the shoes all over again. We end up selling the same pair of shoes over and over again, making much more than the original thousand dollars and everywhere along the line, we made people happy. Some women really loved the shoes and kept them as long as they wanted and still got decent money for them when they got tired of the style—and then could buy another pair. Others, were really more interested in getting the cash than the shoes.

And so, when I saw Harold Shapiro at the Previously Owned Table, it made me wonder. I knew Harold was gay, but I never knew he was a cross-dresser.

Today Cheryl was wearing a red-haired wig in a bee-hive arrangement on top of her head that matched the scarlet of her full skirt. Her blouse was white with big black dots and her earrings were chandeliers of cascading pearls. She wore a pair of white gloves. It must take her hours to coordinate her outfits.

Goodie One Shoes

"May I have the shoe please?" I requested politely.

Cheryl protested, "But I had it first."

"I don't allow any fighting at Emily's Place," I said, motioning her to hand me the shoe.

Harold sneered. "It is definitely my shoe. Merissa was holding it for me."

Cheryl gave Merissa a dirty look and handed me the shoe. It was a size ten.

"There is one fair way to settle disputes of this sort," I said. I reached into my back pocket and took out a quarter.

"Heads or tails?"

"Heads," yelled Harold.

Cheryl mumbled "Tails."

Murphy leaned over and whispered in my ear. "I'm out of here, Good luck!" And he headed out the door, with his EVIDENCE stuffed into his briefcase.

I flung the coin.

It came out heads.

Cheryl, swung her skirt viciously around so it almost hit Harold in the face, and scowled at me. Harold smirked triumphantly. I wondered what he was going to do with them.

Merissa threw her hands up. "Sorry Cheryl."

"Rules are rules," I said to Cheryl, and folded my hands across my chest. "Come back next week. We always have something new."

Cheryl took out a handkerchief from her handbag and nosily blew her nose. When she lowered her head, I noticed a comb in her hair in the shape of a Chinese fan. My God! Cheryl. Cheryl loved to wear cheap hair ornaments—Cheryl had a red wig!

I remembered the red threads Murphy found with the murdered Bonita. I pictured the cheap plastic comb in Kim's cigar box. The comb Cheryl was wearing was not exactly the same but could have been a sister. Same cheap plastic. Same red and white rhinestones. Could Cheryl be a murderer?

She was certainly big enough to overpower both Kim and Bonita. And she didn't like Kim—said Kim had it in for "big women." Even admitted she liked Louise the Loser better. But if she were the killer, there must be some connection between her and Bonita. And what of Quinn and Goodie One Shoes?

I would have to deal with all that later.

I grabbed Cheryl's arm. "That Chinese fan in your hair, it's so pretty."

"Glad you appreciate it," Cheryl beamed. "Just between us girls, it's nine ninety-five in Chinatown."

I took a chance. "You have another Chinese comb—looks like a butterfly. I've been looking all over Chinatown for that comb but I can't find it. I'll trade you a pair of shoes for yours."

"So nice to have someone notice." Cheryl adjusted her blouse and pulled herself up to her full height." I guess this just isn't my lucky day. It broke in half when I tried to stick it in my hair yesterday and I threw it away." And with that, she walked out the door with as much dignity as possible.

Chapter 14

**Pointed shoes originated in France.
They were said to be the invention of a Count of Anjou who wanted to hide his deformed feet.**

"OMMMM. Hope everything is good. My conference is done but I thought I'd hang out in the Big Apple for another couple of days. I should land at your place around midnight. I forgot my key. Blessings."

My telephone message machine glowed with her ' chi." My sister Shana landed places after midnight like a witch on a broom. And she had promised me not to go places alone after dark. Good God, it occurred to me that Shana probably knew nothing about Bonita's murder. I knew I wouldn't be able to rest until Shana was back in the Berkshires.

Despite the clues found in Bonita's murder it seemed the police were no closer to finding the murderer. I had been so excited when I realized Cheryl wore cheap combs from Chinatown in her hair—that she actually admitted she owned the very same style comb that now lay in Kim's Cuban Cigar box—found at the scene of Kim's murder. Pretty incriminating, no?

Murphy however, was not buying it. "Those combs are a dime a dozen in Chinatown. There's no way to prove this Cheryl person ever owned that exact comb. It's not like the lockets in Victorian novels that prove everything. Besides, what would be her motive?"

I had not figured that out yet. I knew she didn't like Kim much, but that hardly served as a motive for murder—or did it? "Find out if Cheryl has a sister," I asked Murphy.

"Sure he said, "What's her address?"

It was then that I realized I had no address for Cheryl. She always paid in cash. The only address I had was her email—to notify her for sales. I was thwarted for the time being, but I couldn't get over the feeling that Cheryl was somehow involved in Kim's murder. Of course, that still left Bonita's murder. Poor Bonita. Maybe I should have advised her to marry her boyfriend, Juan Diaz. Could have changed her luck.

I glanced at my watch. It was only 9:00pm. I expected it would be a long evening. I turned on my computer and decided to check out my records for the two shoes, the red Jimmy Choo and the blue satin mule, Dolce & Gabbana.

The police seemed to assume that the dead women were wearing their own shoes. And that the shoe murderer took home one of the shoes as a souvenir. If so, the women probably bought the shoes themselves.

But there was something about both those size eights that bothered me.

Yes, size eight was the most popular size shoe worn by American women, but I knew for a fact that Kim wore a six. And I had never fit Bonita for a pair but I would bet she wore a seven.

Moreover, it was darn unlikely that my cleaning woman would be wearing a designer shoe—in the wrong size—to clean my apartment even if it had been a hand-me-down gift. And I was pretty sure Kim had never owned a pair of designer shoes. So the only conclusion was that the murderer must have brought along his own size eights to put on his victims. But why size eight?

Well, I knew that men with fetishes were particular about their props. There had to be a certain order to the game, certain words that needed to be said. Size eight might just be one of those random details.

First I checked my list of buyers for any man's name. I looked closer at the first screen. Jimmy Choos purchased this year. Yes, there were several men's names but all are husbands or boyfriends of customers. One name was a surprise—Harold Shapiro.

Why a size eight? The shoe Harold had won in the coin toss was a size ten. And what was going on with Harold and these women's shoes anyway? Had he or his partner Peter become cross-dressers?

Next, I flicked to Dolce & Gabbana. I scrolled quickly down. A few more husbands and boyfriends. No Harold Shapiro. I breathed a sigh of relief.

To check my hypothesis that the purchaser was a man, not a woman, I phoned Murphy's private number. I was lucky. He picked up right away.

"Listen," I said to him. "I have to ask you an important question. The shoes that were found with the bodies of Kim and Bonita, did anyone try to see if they actually fit on each woman's foot?"

There was a pause. I imagined Murphy thinking up some way to save face. "The shoes were squashed and full of blood. There wasn't a conducive situation for trying them. Kind of like the O.J. Simpson glove."

Right. Murphy must be the only cop in America who really thought the glove didn't fit. "Do me a favor," I said, "measure Bonita's feet and take the blue shoe from the Evidence Room and see if it fits."

"Where are you going with this? The morgue is not a shoe store."

"I don't think the shoes will fit. I think the murderer brought them and tried to fit them on the victims. So you should search these scenes again to find the shoes that did belong to the victims. "

Another pause and then Murphy said, "And suppose you are right. Where will that get us? We are still looking for a guy with a shoe fetish who murders women."

Now it was my turn to pause. He was right. We might be closer to the mechanics of the murder, but not to the murderer.

"By the way," Murphy told me, "Louise the Loser left the city about six months ago. Her brother told me he lost touch with her. I've got a couple of people working on it. And that comb you said wasn't Kims? There were no fingerprints—no DNA—but we did find a few red synthetic threads."

I clutched the phone. Was I a great detective or what? Now we knew the same hand committed both crimes. No more of the bullshit about "extra-curricular activities" or "drug connections." And I came up with the best suspect yet! I felt like howling with glee but I was afraid I had already shown Murphy up so much he probably hated me.

"Woman's intuition" I said modestly.

"There were so many threads all over Kim's apartment I didn't pay attention to these. All the dust and lint from Chinatown was stuck in her rug. You should have sent Bonita over to give it a good cleaning."

The mention of Bonita brought me back to myself. Murder was nothing to gloat about.

"It was only after we found the red threads under Bonita's fingernails that the ones in that comb became important," Murphy explained. "Links the two together for sure."

"Anyone would have overlooked them" I tried to comfort him.

"I told you we'd be a good team at Kim's memorial." He reminded me.

I smiled. This seemed to me a bit of revisionist history but I let it go. "So what about Cheryl? Is that enough to arrest her?"

"Not by a long shot. Unless we can prove those red threads came from her wig. That would put her at the scene of both crimes. Without that, I don't even have enough to get a search warrant. All I have is your "woman's intuition" that a comb you never actually saw in Cheryl's hair not only belonged to her but that she dropped it while murdering a girl without a motive."

Sneaky bastard, that Murphy. At the end of the conversation he had succeeded in making me feel like a dunce, instead of him.

Eventually I must have fallen asleep because I was awakened by a loud clap of thunder. I looked at the clock at my bedside. It was 4:00am and Shana had not yet landed. I looked out my window where the rain was coming down in sheets. Where was she? Sailing on her chi between the raindrops? I found Shana's cell number in my wallet and gave her a call.

"OMmmmmmm" said her voice on the recording. "Krishna isn't here right now. Please leave a message."

"Where are you?" I spoke into the phone. "I'm worried. Please call me."

I finally fell asleep again as the sun came up.

The next morning I overslept. When I finally opened the shop, about 11:00am, there were a few nasty notes from disappointed customers. And one that sent a chill up my spine:

Dear Emily, Not here I see, too bad for me. I came to worship at the shrine. The disappointment is all mine. I thought I'd give your wallet back but now I'll plot my next attack. Till then, I wait to share some fun, even if it's all for one."

The letters were printed in ink with no signature.

Chapter 15

Weatherproof boots were a great step forward for female emancipation, allowing women greater mobility and freedom outdoors.

Three days had gone by and thank God there were no more single shoe deliveries through my mail chute and no more messages from Goodie One Shoes.

That was the good news.

The bad news was that Shana had not returned. I kept calling her cell phone but the tape was filled up and it was no longer taking any messages. Each evening I rushed home to play my message machine. Nothing. I would have been hysterical but things like this had happened before. Shana was forty-two years old—or forty-two years young. She lived a life of loose connections. Floated here and there like a row-boat that had come loose. She had tried to be an actress, a caterer, a physical therapist. Something always happened: an accident; a missed assignment, a failed love affair, and she had drifted further and further until she came to rest, at least for a while in an ashram in The Berkshires. She had fallen for Buddhism, or more probably a Buddhist who introduced her to tantric love-making and vegetarian food.

I had felt so relieved of duty, for a while. But of course, Shana's change of address didn't much change her pattern of behavior. Remarkably, through it all, Shana maintained a carefree, optimistic attitude that was extremely irritating to me, but awesome to behold.
If she was the beautiful butterfly, gathering sweetness from the most foul-smelling flowers, I was a sparrow who built nests in hurricane-prone areas. In other words, she seemed to have learned to live with the good, while I was forever fearing the bad. I had been worried stiff the first night she didn't show. I had been angry the second night. And now I was just plain worried.

Merissa seemed to have forgotten all about her fears for me and Shana. No more talk about running off to Canada or Haiti. She just squeezed my hand when I asked her what she had heard about someone wanting to hurt us. Mumbled something vague about "talk on the street" but that was all I could get out of her.

Then I told her about what happened on the jogging path. That at least got some reaction.

"*Mon Dieu*! "she uttered and grabbed my arm. Her sleeve, a wide, bright orange silk that draped and flowed gently with the movement of her arm, fell back to expose what seemed like a series of scratches on her arm.

"Your arm! Where did you get those scratches?"

She quickly pulled the silk sleeve down over her exposed flesh."*Mon chatte.*" She said. "I pick her up when she want to go down."

She turned away and glanced into the showroom where a couple of customers were waiting. Bonita had someone's skin under her fingernails. Could it possibly be Merissa's? No. She had no motive. She loved Kim. She didn't know Bonita. Even Murphy didn't ask for a sample of her DNA.

What kind of a person had I become to suspect my friends? Merissa was more likely a potential victim. "Let the customers wait," I said to her. "You may be in danger. Remember what I told you? Murphy thinks the murderer is targeting important people in my life."

Merissa grinned."*Mon ami!* Merissa glad to be important in your life. I tell you once. I tell you again. Merissa can take care of herself."

I phoned Murphy and told him about Merissa's reaction to the news of Bonita's death—her warning that both Shana and I were in danger—but I didn't mention the scratches. I was ashamed to betray our friendship.

At any rate, he was unimpressed. "I know people like Merissa. Like to make believe they are important. Know everything. Maybe she heard something 'on the street' and maybe she didn't."

If I couldn't get anything else out of Merissa, he wasn't even going to try. If she had connections "on the street" that would help protect her and her friends, hey—go for it—was his advice.

But he did agree I should file a missing person's report about Shana.

When I got home I kicked off my shoes and lay down on the bed. A breeze rattled the shade in my bedroom. Next door I could hear Henry making a racket and Angelina's less than dulcet tones trying to quiet him down.

I could never live with a bird like that. I began to feel a little guilty about flushing Larry's goldfish down the toilet. Maybe goldfish weren't such bad pets after all. I closed my eyes. I could still smell the fetid water from the fish tank. Yes, the toilet bowl was the right decision.

And then the phone rang. "Murphy here!" he said. "We've been dredging the reservoir in Central Park for two days. No silver shoe."

I could feel my defenses go up. "I saw the guy throw it into the lake. Maybe he fished it out later."

There was a pause. "You told me it sunk like a stone."

Now I was getting annoyed. Why was he attacking me? Did he think I was making it up? "Look," I said, "I know what I saw. If you don't believe me..." I let the rest of the sentence go.

"I believe you," he said "And you were right about the shoe not fitting Bonita. It was too big."

"But, as you said, that doesn't help much," except my ego, of course.

"I guess not," Murphy replied. "One more thing. Louise the Loser? It turns out she went to Boston. Got run over by a bus about a month ago."

"Oh, my God."

"Well, she was worth a try. Sister come home yet?"

I had to take a deep breath. "No. Haven't heard a word."

There was a pause. "We found another woman murdered last night. Blonde, slight, blue eyes. Had both her shoes still on."

I looked up at the ceiling. My breath caught in my throat. Shana? These were the words I had feared for days. "Her arm," I finally blurted out, "She had a cast on her arm. And a torn belly button."

I heard some papers rustling. "I'm sorry," Murphy said. "It wasn't my case. I sent the photo and description you gave me out to other units. I need to get some more details. Try not to worry."

I hung up and stared at the photo of Shana perched on the night stand by my bed. It was when she had graduated from Erasmus Hall High school several lifetimes ago. A cap and gown posed against a bright red background. Her blue eyes looked out happily, her blonde, sun-streaked hair curled gently around her face. A Shirley Temple doll grown up.

Then I sat down on the side of my bed and cried.

The tears were still wet on my face when I heard the buzzer go off.

I jumped off the bed and pressed the intercom, my heart racing.

"It's me," Shana said in her bubbly voice, "Long time no see."

I wished I could say that I fell to my knees to give thanks to whatever God or Gods had returned her to me but all I could think of was how much I wanted to strangle her. When I opened the door and saw my beautiful baby sister, broken arm and all, I pulled her into my arms and burst into tears all over again.

I buried my nose in her hair and inhaled her sweet Shana smell I had known for so much of my life. Dirty, grungy, and hungry she might be from time to time, but her hair was always freshly shampooed.

Where the hell had she been for five days and five nights?

"Where? How? I was so worried!"

Shana kissed me on the cheek and unbuckled her knapsack. She flopped down on my couch.

"The conference was so amazing," she began, "There are all these foods that have been proven over the centuries to increase the "chi," the vital life energy," she turned to me, her face aglow. "Did you know that each part of the body has its own energy force—channels like arteries that transport chi from one organ to another?"

"What" I said to her, "does that have to do with the fact that you never returned my phone calls?"

Shana smiled and shrugged. "Oh that. I lost my phone in a taxi. Never got any messages." She giggled. "Deepak couldn't contact me either. Good thing too. I met the most interesting man…a real healer. He can just pass his hand around your body without touching it and he can tell what parts of your body need mending."

"Let me guess. He discovered your arm was broken."

"Very funny. No. He actually discovered my heart was broken."

I covered my face with my hands. How had she lived on this planet for so long without developing an ounce of responsibility towards anyone else? "Didn't you realize how worried I'd be?"

"You're always worried about something." She said. "I don't have to participate in your craziness."

I sat back and closed my eyes. I did not want to argue, criticize. To worry. And yet I always did. If I can't help my "craziness" why expect Shana to overcome hers? "So." I said to her, "you went off with the healer?"

"Yes and no. I set out to meet him but I had a slight adventure on my way." Shana's adventures were enough to terrify most sane people. I knew it would take all my chi just to listen to it.

"I was walking down this street—must have been a little after midnight, and I heard someone walking behind me." She hesitated. "I didn't actually hear him—it was more that I felt him."

I nodded. I was very well acquainted with Shana's "feelings."

"But I could feel that there was something extraordinary about this person." All the people Shana met were extraordinary. "The vibes were so strong but there was something wrong with their rhythm. I just felt this person needed help so badly so I turned around and smiled and said 'Can I help you?' and there was this person with a hooded sweat shirt shading his face and he took my hand and..." Her voice trailed off. "Then someone else jumped me from behind, and the hooded person limped off into the night."

I jumped up from the couch. "The hooded person had a limp?"

"Yes. That's what was disturbing the vibes."

I pictured once again the scary figure on the jogging path. "Who jumped you?" I asked excitedly "How did you get away?"

"That's what was so extraordinary. Someone threw me down but then he must have run away because a group of people from the conference were coming down the street and started yelling. They picked me up, brushed me off, and put me in a cab to meet Kyle."

"Kyle? The Healer?"

"Yes, He's Celtic. From Wales."

Well, she might even meet someone eventually whose ideas came from the twenty first century instead of ancient mythology—but I wouldn't hold my breath.

"Did you get a look at this person who jumped you?"

Shana shook her head."I was so surprised to find myself on the sidewalk. All I could think of was the poor guy who ran away who really needed my help."

Help with what? Mugging her—or possibly killing her? This time her Karma or something had protected her. Maybe the tee shirt with the evil eye. She was wearing one now in bright yellow.

"Were you wearing that tee shirt?"

She smiled. "They were a great hit at the conference. Sold out all I had—fifty of them."

I pictured all these women wandering around the city wearing brightly colored tee shirts with a giant evil eye on the front. I wondered if they would attract the killer or keep him away. And then I told her about Bonita.

She covered her mouth with her hand and lowered her head to her knees. Shana is a real expert in Yoga. For a few minutes sobs shook her body.

I put my arms around her and we sat entwined for a couple of minutes.

"Bonita put up a fight," I told her. "She scratched the killer. They found skin under her fingernails. "

Shana sniffled softly.

"Murphy wants a sample of your DNA."

Shana jumped up from the couch. "I'm leaving tomorrow for the Berkshires. I'll send him my spit in the mail."

I was surprised at the vehemence of her reaction."Murphy will want to question you. Your mugging may be related to the shoe murders."

Shana sat down again. "My mugging had nothing to do with shoes. I'm leaving tomorrow."

I put my hand on her shoulder. I did want her out of the city. I knew she was in danger. And yet… "You'll get in trouble if you run away. The police will think you are guilty of something."

"I'm not running away," she said to me. "I'm going home. And as for getting into trouble—I've been in trouble my whole life."

We smiled at each other then. We knew it was true.

Then I realized my sister was even tougher than Merissa and I was the most vulnerable of them all.

Chapter 16

In the 18th Century, women's shoes reflected the elaborate ornamentations of their dress and included metallic braids of gold and silver and complicated embroidery

Parked in front of my building, right in front of the No Parking sign was a dark blue Toyota. I noticed it right away because it was Alternate Side Parking day and the Toyota was the only car on that side of the street.

The idea was that you needed to move your car a couple of times a week, from one side of the street to the other, so that the street cleaning truck could clean where the street met the curb. So on alternate side parking days, a leaky, noisy vehicle pushing a big brush came by; hosed off the street and swept up crumbled candy wrappers, old newspapers and dog shit.

Sometimes, if you have failed to move your car, the police have it towed it away so when you came out to get it you think you have lost your mind and forgotten where you parked it. Is it any wonder why I don't like Cops?

So naturally, as soon as I saw a Toyota on the wrong side of the Street, it was no surprise at all to me that the person sitting inside the car was Murphy. Nevertheless, I had to admit that Murphy had made some inroads in my affection despite being a member of that distrusted fraternity. I might almost admit I was pleased to see him except for the fact that I associated him with bad things like the murders of Kim and Bonita.

I was already getting a nervous feeling about the purpose of his visit. When I got close to the car, he opened the door. "Hey!" he said.

I smiled at him and pointed at the No Parking Sign, right over his head.

He shrugged his shoulders and smiled. "Another one of my perks." Then he opened the door a little wider and I saw he was not alone. A woman was sitting next to him who looked vaguely familiar.

"Denise Rand" he nodded in her direction. "I think you two have already met."

I smiled. My wallet. The woman at the Precinct. The one who has a thing for Murphy. I looked at them together. Denise was pretty in an over-weight kind of way. Her blonde hair, bleached I was sure, worn pulled back in a pony tail tucked under her cap. Maybe Murphy had a thing for Denise.

Murphy got out of the car and we stood together on the sidewalk. "Remember I told you not to meet Goodie One Shoes no matter what?" Murphy peered down the street and then back into my face.

"I've changed my mind." He kicked his shoes against the sidewalk as if trying to get rid of a piece of gum he might have picked up. "I don't have anything. Nothing is panning out. I have fingerprints and DNA that don't match any known criminals. I have the bloody imprint of something that is either a bracelet, the toe of a shoe or something else entirely. We have a red thread that could have come from anywhere. No real clues at all. Nada. Except for expensive shoes sold to hundreds of women in the tri-state area—and some men." He looked up and down the street again. "I think maybe it's time we focused on trying to trap this Goodie One Shoes person. He may have nothing at all to do with this. He might be his own kind of pervert. But I understand stores like yours attract them like flies."

"Right," I said, "Like cops mix with the best kind of people."

He ignored me and continued. "My people are getting restless. They want some action. I have got to do something. He is worth a shot."

Okay. I would do whatever Murphy wanted to Goodie One Shoes. Stolen my wallet, hadn't he? Caused me grief and hours on the telephone canceling credit cards. He had written a poem alluding to a blue shoe right about the time of Bonita's murder with a blue shoe. Not enough to hang a murder on him, but maybe for a start. And he had threatened me. "What do you want me to do?"

"Next time he contacts you, I want you to set up a meeting. In the store. Somewhere public. I don't want you alone with him." I glanced at Denise who was watching us intently. If Murphy noted it, he ignored it completely. "Get him to come to the store. Denise can hang out. Pretend to be a customer. Figure out some reason to confront him and get some ID on the guy. He's probably guilty of something."

Murphy stared at his hands. He flexed his fingers. Large and long. His hands were big. Veins stood out on the back of his thumb and wrist. He reminded me of a character from a Dickens novel. One who had been spared hanging at the last moment but whose head and neck were always on a slant—twisted by the close encounter with death. Murphy's hands seemed as if they had a life of their own. Like they itched to squeeze the life out of someone. In Dickens he would be the executioner.

"Sure. I'll do what I can."

Murphy took a deep breath, but his fingers kept squeezing the thin air. "I don't want you to contact him. Wait till he contacts you. You don't want to scare him away—let on that you have some special reason for wanting to see him. It has to be completely natural."

"Right." I said. "I understand."

Murphy looked from me to Denise and then back again. "I would have sent Rosa but she likes shoes too much." He got back into the car and rolled down the window. "I'll be in touch." And they drove off.

Naturally, because I was now eager to hear from the mysterious Goodie One Shoes, there was absolute silence from him. Also from Shana who perhaps had lost her phone again. One day. Two days. Three days. A week went by.

I could not stand it any longer. I turned on my computer and typed in "Goodie One Shoes" in the "find" box. I made a note of his email address and then I scanned my customer base.

In the three years I had been in business, I had built up an address book of several hundred customers. As I scanned through, I could not help but feel proud of all I had accomplished.

In many ways, establishing Emily's Place was much harder for me than getting a Ph.D. in English. After all, I had gone to school for years. I had been reading novels since the third grade. I had all those professors and student advisors and deans to guide me.

I just did what came naturally. But at Emily's Place I discovered a different part of myself. A part that liked a new challenge. Learning to run a store, figuring out what kind of merchandise to order, getting credit from vendors, marketing a product—all these were things I had never thought much about before. And then, of course, there was the product itself. Shoes. An item I had always loved. And community. Let's not forget the community. Sooner or later all kinds of people came to Emily's Place. I was selling fantasy now, where once I sold knowledge. Both are valuable, but the dreamer was different from the scholar and my problem was how to entice Goodie One Shoes into the store without raising any suspicions.

Well, I had the perfect plan. A Special Sale. Only to my Special Customers. Of whom, Goodie One Shoes had to be one.

I went slowly through my list. The easiest thing would be to announce it to the entire list. This I did a couple of times a year, before Christmas and before July 4th, but that created mayhem—dozens of customers pushing each other, trying to cut the line, and not a few altercations to put it mildly.

I would have to go through my list and find, maybe twenty other customers who lived nearby and add their names to Goodie's so he would not be suspicious.

I breathed deeply, intoned "OM" for a few minutes to attract good Karma—if it worked for Shana it might work for me too—and got going: And everyone I chose would be someone I knew well, so when Goodie arrived, he should stand out.

Harriet Moskowitz
Marilyn Goldsmith
Susan Klein
Yulia Romenovsky
Sydney Morris—Yes, this Sydney is a woman.
Angel Diaz
Mary Greenleaf
Mollie Henderson
Sasha Borisky
Maria Hernandez
Kim Lee
Rona Kaminsky
Beverly Blaukoph
Esmeraldo Brown

I wondered if I should include a few transvestites who were good customers but I figured that would only confuse Denise.

So I wrote:

A Special Invitation to my Special Customers: Emily's Place is proud to offer you a pre-season viewing and 10% discount on our new Spring line. Be the first in your neighborhood to see and proudly own the new red Jimmy Choo Sandals; the plaid Kate Spade ballet slipper, the Prada black satin mule and many, many more. Sizes from five to ten available.

Join Merissa and me on Thursday, May 12 from 5:00pm to 8:00pm for wine, cheese, cookies, coffee and the best shoes in the entire city!

See you next week!
Fond regards,
Emily Levine

Was I worried about confronting a murderer? Not at all. I was actually excited over the possibility of nailing the monster who had killed Kim and Bonita. I could almost feel the adrenalin coursing through my system. Besides, I would have Denise for back-up.

I read my message over and then pressed SEND. Within minutes the responses started coming in:

Dear Emily: Now you're talking! See you Thursday, Maria.

Dear Emily: Do you have anything in Pink? I wear a size 7, Sasha.

Dear Emily: Save me a pair of the ballet slippers in red. I can't get there till 7:30pm, Beverly.

Dear Emily: How sweet you are. I don't live far. We have a date. I can hardly wait. Goodie One Shoes.

Bingo! I stared at Goodie's message for a couple of minutes and then I wrote back:

So nice of you to want to see
Our new season jubilee
What size and style are your delight?
I will hide them out of sight
Regards, Emily

An answer appeared instantly:

"I wear a size ten as you should know.
Find me something with a bow."
Goodie One Shoes

I hugged myself and turned off the computer. Even Murphy would be impressed with this one.

I was about to call and give him the news when I changed my mind. There would be plenty of time to tell him later when I could choose a time and place more conducive to the intimate exchanges I hoped to have in our future.

I dialed Denise's number instead and gave her the details. We agreed that she would wander around the store like any customer until I gave her the signal—dropping a box of shoes at her feet. When I bent down to retrieve them, I would finger the suspect.

That night I dreamed I was dancing over the rainbow in red glass slippers and that Murphy the Cop was my enchanted partner.

How had I lived for so many years without learning that nothing was as easy as it seemed when you first thought it up?

I might have remembered the fiftieth birthday party I put together for Larry—the one that was supposed to be a surprise.

It was. For me and Larry both. That was when I arrived at the door of our apartment with twenty of our best friends. When we turned on the lights there was Larry in bed with the Borscht Bombshell.

I might have remembered the vacation house I booked through the internet in Spain, that had no air-conditioning, a pool full of algae, and giant rats. Whenever we opened a shutter to get some air, bats flew into the house.

So I ought to have realized that catching Goodie One Shoes would be fraught with unforeseen difficulties. It started with Merissa.

"What you doing Madame Emily?" She confronted me. "You goin' sell out all our new shoes at a big discount? Before even the season starts? How I'm goin' to have a job ? How you goin' to have money to pay Merissa, you do something like that?"

"Give it a rest," I said to her. "I've been running Emily's Place for three years. And I haven't run out of money yet."

True, as far as it went. I would find the money to pay Merissa even if I had to sell my wedding ring—worthless to me and kept now in the vault for a special emergency—but secretly I knew she was right. Between the discounts on the shoes and the cost of the wine and cheese, this was sure to cost me several hundred dollars. And The New York City Police Department was not putting up any of the cash.

And then there was the whole rush and bother of having to order extra stock. I knew for sure the red ballet slippers would be gone in a heart-beat. They were to be sent Special Delivery and still had not arrived.

There were tables to set up; plates and napkins and glasses for the wine and cheese to be bought; all those emails to be answered and all those notes on putting shoes aside recorded and acted upon.

I could just hear Beverly Blaukoph if I told her I was all out of Prada silver sandals, size seven. I'd rather face Goodie One Shoes alone in an alley. Whatever. It was done. Now there was nothing to do but struggle through.

At half past 4:00pm I started emptying the store of the remaining customers which was no easy task. Janine Miller insisted on trying on every size six I had, even though I told her we were closing early.

When they were gone at last, I put up the closed sign and moved the displays out of the way to clear a space for the large sale table and the smaller table for wine and cheese.

Denise sat on one of the seats in the middle reading a movie magazine. She was wearing a sleeveless pink shirt dress and a pair of wide brown sandals that looked as if she had ordered them from LL Bean.

She looked thicker than normal around the waist so I figured she was hiding some hardware—maybe a gun and some handcuffs. A large tote bag sat on the floor at her feet.

I glanced at my watch. Both the shoe delivery and the wine were late. The cheese and crackers, plus some cut veggies and dip had arrived from Zabars and were shoved inside my refrigerator in the back room.

I peeked out in front and saw a bunch of people already lining up.

A few minutes later there was a gentle knock. Thank goodness. There was Charles the mailman carrying a dozen boxes of shoes on his cart. While I was signing for the shoes, the delivery boy arrived with a carton of wine.

My hands full, I looked around for Merissa. Someone needed to set out the sale shoes.

But Merissa had gone out to run an "errand" or so she told me an hour ago and still hadn't returned.

"Denise!" I yelled inside, balancing the clipboard with papers to sign on my knee. "Can you please give me a hand? This stuff needs to go on one of those tables."

Denise closed her magazine and came to the door. She looked at the mailman and the wine delivery boy and then she turned to me and shook her head.

"Not my job. I'm just a customer, remember?" and she walked back to her seat inside.

I looked so pathetic that Charles and the delivery boy carried all the stuff inside and dragged out the tables.

At this point, it must have been 5:00pm because people started banging on the doors and I had to let them in. And then I realized that half the people on the line were free-loaders from the neighborhood looking for a little wine and cheese.

I could see Denise standing now and looking over the people while I went back to set out the cheese and crackers. I figured I would toss out the winos as soon as I had gotten things organized.

It was about this time that I saw Merissa come in followed by Harold. She must have invited him, because I didn't. Harold waved to me and then disappeared in the crowd before I could grab him to help.

But Merissa dove right in. In minutes she had opened the shoe boxes and started arranging things on the sale table while I put out a couple of bottles of wine.

But then I noticed the wine was not the wine I had ordered. It was all red. No white. That pissed me off! Most of my customers drank white wine. I looked at the label of the bottle of red. "Paul Hobbs, Cabernet Sauvignon, Napa Valley. It seemed vaguely familiar, and I know enough about wine to know that California had some good ones, so I figured I would use it until the white arrived, if it ever did.

I went into the back room to get the wine opener and called Pierre's Wine Shop. "You sent me the wrong bottles," I told him. "There's no white wine."

There was a brief pause and then Pierre said, "Ms. Emily, I didn't send you anything. My boy didn't show up today. I was just packing your order up to take it over myself."

I hung up the phone and ran back into the showroom, but the delivery boy was long gone.

Could that have been Goodie One Shoes himself, come to check out the scene and see if it was safe to stay? One look at the "undercover" Denise could have sent him on his way.

I was mortified. I had hardly even looked at him. All I could remember was that he was some short Spanish guy, like so many others who worked around here. What would Murphy say? Had I flubbed it? Was this whole exercise now just a waste of time?

I felt so embarrassed I decided not to mention any of this to either Murphy or Denise. I would pretend nothing had happened and proceed according to plan. Besides, the wine could have been sent by anyone. And then I had no time to think because I had to open the bottles, set out the cheese and crackers and sell some shoes.

By about 7:00pm or so things had settled into some reasonable rhythm and I had a chance to look around. I had ejected two or three scruffy-looking characters who wandered in. Pierre had delivered the white wine and we were selling lots of shoes.

Suddenly I heard Harold's voice raised high.

"How dare you!" he shouted. "I'll sue! I swear I will sue!"

Followed immediately by Denise's voice, loud and clear: "You have a right to remain silent," she said.

I pushed my way through just in time to see Denise snap the handcuffs on him.

"Wait! Wait!" I cried out. "What are you doing?"

Denise looked at me and scowled. "This guy has been walking around touching all the shoes. I have been watching him for an hour.

Goodie One Shoes

When I saw him put one of the shoes into his sack, I knew it was him!"

Harold glared at me, but he looked embarrassed.

"Harold works for me," I told her. "He takes shoes to put on the manikins in the window."

Denise glanced over her shoulder into the window. "He slipped the shoe into his bag. Not on any manikin." She reached down and picked up a pink satin pump with a three inch silver metal heel from the floor and dangled it in front of my face. Chanel, six hundred and fifty dollars—size ten.

I bit my lip. This was outrageous, even for Harold. I would have to deduct the price of the pair from his fee. But that was between Harold and me. Goodie One Shoes he was not. He was my friend and I trusted him. "Sometimes Harold takes the shoe to his shop because he wants to change it. Cut out a toe...paste on some sequins..."

"*Mon dieu*! *Mon Amie* Harold is *tres* original! He works very hard to give us the best display on Broadway." Merissa cried out.

Angel Diaz yelled, "Take your dirty hands off our Harold!"

Rona Kaminisky shouted," Free Harold and buy yourself a new pair of shoes!"

Sasha Borisky shook her fist, "This is no place for Secret Police! Copper, Get out!"

Beverly Blaukoph stepped out in front of the crowd, "I was on J. Edgar Hoover's Red List and I'm proud of it!"

At this a cheer went up. Never mind that most of the people cheering had not been born when J. Edgar Hoover was around. It is The Upper West Side and Cops were still on the wrong side of everything.

For a moment there I thought the crowd might lynch Denise—string her up right in the window next to Mary and Sadie but that did not happen. Denise produced a key from somewhere on her thick waist and unlocked the handcuffs.

I poured her a glass of white wine and held it out to her. I poured a glass of red wine and held it out to Harold. Then I looked over the crowd. My customers. My friends.

I poured a glass of wine for myself and held up the glass. "Let's everybody drink to the new season at Emily's Place."

And everybody did.

Chapter 17

Repression and Prohibition in the roaring 20's gave rise to the most frivolous shoes of the century

It was only three days later when Merissa slinked into the shop two hours late and I knew something was very wrong. Her hair, usually pulled back in an elaborate series of braids, hung stiffly in bunches around her face. One of her eyebrows was rubbed off and her lips, usually painted bright red, were pale.

Perhaps the most alarming sign was that she was wearing flat shoes. True, they were gorgeous, jeweled sandals made by Prada, but definitely not Merissa's usual style. She gave me her 'keep your distance' look and quickly walked into the back room.

Angry. Sullen. But thank God she seemed safe enough. I hadn't forgotten that she might be a target. Of course, employer, or just friend—I couldn't ignore what I had seen. And so I followed her to the back room.

Merissa was talking on her cell phone when I came in and abruptly shut it off. She scowled.

"So?" I sat down on one of the chairs and waited.

"I don't want to talk about it." She said, "It's too demeaning."

"No one wants to demean you."

Merissa nodded. "Not you. Him."

"Who Him?"

Merissa lifted up her right foot. There was a bandage on her big toe. I touched it gingerly.

"Ouch!"

"Is it broken? Can you move it back and forth? You should have it x-rayed."

Merissa wrinkled her nose. "I'm not foolin' with this toe no way. If it's broke, then it's broke. What anyone going to do anyway? Put Merissa's beautiful foot in a cast? What I'm going to do then? How I'm going to get to work? Ever think of that?"

"Work is not the most important thing."

"Sure is to me. Only thing keeps this black girl going."

I was not going anywhere near that one. Merissa and I got along as well as we did mostly cause I knew what topics to pursue and which to let alone. Besides, Merissa's race was more in her head than on her skin. Some days she identified with the rich white folk from across the Park, and wore a Ralph Lauren dress to work, her hair combed back in a pony tail. Other times, it was her French ancestors she honored, wearing a Hermes scarf, her hair straight, hugging her face. But sometimes she felt a kinship with the poor black gals in the projects, and she'd wear her hair in corn rows, or sometimes bleached. Even her speech patterns changed according to her mood.

"Hey, your work is my work," I told her. "It's here for you as long as I'm here. If you need to heal your foot, you will heal your foot. The work will wait."

Merissa flashed me a smile. She rubbed her toe gently.

"God damn ass-hole," she mumbled. "He should rot in hell. Ruin Merissa's gorgeous foot. God damn!"

I waited until she was ready to talk.

At last she raised her head and looked me in the eye. "Freakin' guy followed me home last night. I knew someone behind me. I feel these things." She gripped the edge of the table. "Don't live long as me in this city you don't feel things. I know this dude behind me so I walk faster. Dude walk faster. It's maybe 2:00am. Dark. Where I live everyone fast asleep. Dude keeps comin'." She paused. "When he gets close enough, I whirl round and kick. Catches him right under the chin. Makes Merissa laugh out loud!" She looked at me. "three and a half inch heels I wearin'. Steel studs down the back. There's a reason Merissa loves her shoes."

I stared back at her. "You're telling me you kicked this guy? Are you crazy? He could have been the shoe murderer!"

She laughed. "Yeah! Crazy like a fox. I been going to the gym for two years—just waitin' for this. All this time. All this time training. You ever hear of kick boxing?"

"Sure. I've heard of it. That's about all I know."

"I took karate when I was *une petite fille*. Tall, skinny, *jeune fille*. Nobody messed with me then. Nobody messes with me now. Karate is ok when you are *une petite*. In *cette cite* , you need something else. Started takin' up Kick Boxing. "

Her eyes narrowed and her nostrils expanded. She looked fierce enough to scare off lots of people. "Big guy," she mumbled. "Big guy—big as me—follows me. Bet he's sorry now. Goin' think twice 'fore he follows another woman big as me."

I could not believe she could be so foolish. "The gym is one thing," I said. "But real life is another. What if he had a gun? A knife?"

Merissa made a sound in her throat half way between a snort and a grunt. "A knife or a gun? I would have kicked it clear across the avenue!"

"Okay. So you caught him under the chin. You beat him up. What are you complaining about? What's 'demeaning' about any of this?"

She extended her foot. "That son-of-a-bitch grabbed my shoe right off my foot! Grabbed my eight hundred and fifty dollar Jimmy Choo shoe and head back down the street, *tres vite*. Time I gets my balance back—this son-of-a-bitch, he gone!"

I could not help but feel awe at Merissa's courage. I sure would have run like hell. But on the other hand, when the guy followed me on the track I confronted him too. Except that was in full day light on a crowded city track. Merissa was all alone. Also, the guy following me was short and slight.

"Now what I goin' do with one Chimmy Choo ? You tell me, Madame Emily, What I goin' do?"

But what was it? Did the "big" guy want Merissa or did he simply want her shoes—or rather shoe? When he ran off was he trying to disarm her, or trying to collect something for himself? Or did he really aim to kill her and she proved too much for him?

I pointed towards the closet in the back. "Put it in there. We might as well start a collection. Did you get a look at him? "

Merissa sniffed."Who was lookin'? I was lookin' at his shadow come close—closer. I was counting seconds, breathing hard. I never thought to look at him. Too dark. Wore one of them sweat shirts with a hood. Think maybe he had a handkerchief somethin' on his face." She looked down at the floor. "Can't even tell what color skin that dude did have. Never did think about it till this minute."

I thought back to Shana's description of her mugging. Maybe Merissa's "big guy" was the same one who grabbed Shana from behind.

For the first time I thought that maybe there were two guys involved in the Shoe Murders—One big and one small.

I grabbed Merissa's hand and squeezed it.

"Let's give thanks that you're safe. If you are on the shoe killer's hit list..." My voice trailed off.

Merissa smiled proudly. "Don't I tell you Madame Emily?

Merissa, she take care of herself."

"I have got to congratulate you," I said, getting up. "You are one mean lady." But a detective you are not. What are we going to tell Murphy?"

Merissa scowled "We? Me—I am not talking to that cop at all. How he going to get me back my eight hundred and fifty dollar shoe? They don't make that shoe no more. All that cop goin' to do is make trouble." She looked me in the eye. "You think I'm goin' to any line-up and pointing a finger at *l'homme* big as me knows where I live? You got to be kidding."

I could see her point. "But what if that guy is the Shoe Murderer? If we don't do anything, he can kill someone else. Me. Shana. What about that?"

Merissa looked at me accusingly. "You told me that shoe murderer dude was a little guy. Guy with a limp. This another guy altogether."

"But what if there really are two guys, working together.?"

"Yeah. Right. There you go again, Madame Emily. Think every crime in this city is connected. Everyone in this city pure and sweet, 'cept that shoe murderer out to get us."

I got up and went to the bathroom. Why was it so hard to make Merissa understand she was in danger? We were all in danger as long as the shoe murderer was loose. I was convinced now the murderer was Cheryl and it was clear to me I had to get a snip of red hair from her wig even if I had to pull it off her head. But the more I wanted to see her, the longer she stayed away from the shop. There was nothing I could do at the moment except report this latest attack to Murphy.

It was probably about 4:00pm when Harold Shapiro arrived to freshen up our window display. After three or four weeks both Mary and Sadie would always began to look seedy. Dust from the sidewalk, dark specks from incinerators, soot from bus exhausts. All the detritus and debris of the Upper West Side of New York City eventually seeped between the folds of their dresses and settled in the cracks of their plastic skin.

It was at those times that Harold became a precious addition to Emily's Place. He would fill a pail with warm water and lovingly wash the cracked plastic of their flesh, grab a feathered duster and laboriously hunt down the grunge gathered in their skirts, plug in a hair blower, and courageously try to restyle their wretched locks—and, of course, reposition their shoes.

"Please," I begged, "No rhine-stone G-strings. I don't want to be run out of this neighborhood on a rail."

Harold wiggled his butt at me as he unzipped the garment bag. "You're so last-generation." He unloaded a couple of large feathers and a sequined gold mini-skirt. "The best is yet to come," he said, and took out his wallet. For a minute I was afraid he was going to put some condoms on their fingers, but instead he took out some little printed papers. "Tattoos, my friend. Tattoos are very now! We can put them over their private parts."

"I don't think so," I said. "I think maybe under the belly-button."

Harold gave me a very disappointed look. "We'll see. You've got to allow me some artistic license." The last time I gave Harold artistic license, he inspired a killer to murder with a shoe.

He went back to the garment bag and took out a big straw sombrero and a poncho. "I thought a little South-American theme might do, for our Hispanic friends."

I waved my hand. I was too tired to argue. And there were more important things on my mind. Like why he would steal from me? And why he would want those shoes at all?

"Don't just stand there,' he said, "Make yourself useful. Go grab me three or four more shoes from your new Spring line."

I shook my head, "You already grabbed one of my shoes from the new Spring line—and not for Sadie or Mary."

"Sorry about that. I was going to tell you later. You were busy. It was a bit of a mad house if you remember."

"What were you going to do with one shoe, anyway?"

He shrugged. "I figured I'd hide one shoe so no one else could buy the pair, and then I'd get the other one from you later."

"It was a size ten. Were you going to wear it?"

"No. Of course not. It was for my new friend." This was a surprise. Harold had been in a steady relationship with Peter, a very handsome lawyer, for ten years. "And anyway, didn't you just win a pair of size ten shoes in a coin toss?"

Harold smiled. "Sure. But you know how it is. So many shoes...so little time. A guy can't have too many shoes." He straightened up and climbed down from the window. "Peter is great. I love Peter. But he is a little square. Actually, a lot square." He peeled off one of the tattoos. "Sometimes a guy's got to do what a guy's got to do." He climbed back into the window and put the tattoo on Sadie's thigh, just under the hem of her skirt.

"So what is this guy like? What does he do for a living?"

"We don't talk about mundane things like that. It's not that kind of a relationship."

I guess not. I wondered just how much he did know about this guy though. He must realize that some of these "relationships" can get dicey.

"So what's this guy's name?" I asked him.

"Miguy."

"Miguy? Miguy what? Is that a first name or a last name."

"It's a last name, silly. His first name is Norman. It's Norman Miguy."

I pronounced the names slowly. Norman Miguy. And then quickly. "No man My Guy!" I repeated. "Don't you get it?"

Harold looked at me quizzically. "Get what?"

"Didn't you ever read the Odyssey? The Cyclops! When Odysseus puts out the eye of the Cyclops, he tells him his name is No Man. So when the Cyclops runs around yelling that he was attacked by No Man, no one pays any attention to him."

Harold scratched his head, "So? So he is No Man, My Guy. What difference does that make? I don't see the connection."

Maybe Harold did not see the connection but I did. I could not believe he would be so careless. "Listen. He is protecting himself in advance for anything he might do to you. If you are injured, and you go to the police, they will ask you who did this? You will say, No man did this to me. My guy did this to me. That's all nonsense. The police will laugh at you and walk away!"

Harold slipped a sleeveless tank over Sadie's head. "You know what? You've read too many books. No one is doing anything bad to me. People make up names when they have "relationships." That way nobody gets hurt." He turned to look at me. "I told him my name was Peter Pretzel."

It was things like this that made me feel like a Woman of a Certain Age. It was true that there had always been gay men, Still, sometimes I found myself shocked by the casual nature—and in these times—dangerous nature, of their couplings.

"I bet My Guy likes to dress in women's shoes. That's why you wanted a size ten. But you've also come in looking for a size eight, right?"

Harold looked away. "I thought my transactions with Merissa were confidential."

"Merissa doesn't have to tell me anything. I see the sales. I keep the records."

Harold snorted. "My Guy likes to play games. Sometimes he

dresses up himself. Sometimes he likes to dress up others. Anyway, it's all over between us."

He stepped down from the window and started to gather up the tools of his trade—the hair blower, the duster, the pail. "No Man is No Where, as far as I'm concerned. Just sort of disappeared one night. Never showed up. Never called." Harold scratched his ear. "It's all for the best. I like to kid you but the truth is I'm really pretty middle-class myself. All that dressing-up and shoe stroking wasn't for me. Peter and I are a better match. We're going to Italy next month for a little vacation."

"The perfect place."

He looked back over his shoulder at Mary and Sadie. "I'll bring the girls back a souvenir. Some fab necklace. Chandelier earings. Bring something for Merissa too. And Fifi."

"Fifi's gone," I told him. "I thought you knew."

Harold looked surprised. "Gone where? Saw them last night sitting on a bench in Riverside Park, thick as thieves. Fifi eating an ice-cream cone, chocolate dripping down her chin and Merissa right there holding a napkin. I'd say they were deep in conversation except Fifi can't talk."

How strange. Merissa seemed so upset when Fifi moved out, but not a word when she returned? I kissed Harold on both cheeks and walked him to the door. That was when I noticed he was limping.

For a minute my breath caught in my mouth. I pointed to his leg. "Where'd you get the limp?" I asked him, as calmly as possible.

"God damn ladder slipped out from under me. Teach me not to change light bulbs after a bottle of wine. "

"Oh," I said, "When did that happen?"

"A couple of days ago I guess. Can't remember exactly." He gave me a hug. "Don't worry about me, so much," he said. "It's just a bad sprain."

I waved goodbye to Harold and looked back at Mary and Sadie. A couple of passer-bys had stopped to admire the window. All this murder business was getting to me. It was as if a pebble of evil had been tossed into my world and even if the stone itself had not hit me, the ripples it had created were impacting my life. More—dragging me down in currents of toxic waste. I felt guilty and scared at the same time. Disappointed in myself and unsure of all the things I once took for granted. How could I turn so quickly against my friends? I shuddered and tried to dispel all the suspicious thoughts that surrounded me. You had to trust somebody.

Chapter 18

Most of women's most comfortable shoes were derived from men's styles: the Oxford, the Brogue, the Ghellie, and even the Sneaker.

"I think I have some more information about Professor Low-Life," Larry's voice was so hoarse I could hardly make out what he was saying over the phone.

"So, yes? What have you got to say?" I was feeling particularly unfriendly today and dispensed with the usual phony small talk. Murphy had called earlier to say they had never found the silver shoe in the Reservoir and they were abandoning the search, and yesterday Merissa had called in sick and left me alone all day with a store full of customers.

"I found..." the rest of his sentence was lost in a fit of coughing.

I held the phone away because I was sure any bug he had was contagious. "Why don't you take a glass of water and call me back later." He grunted something and coughed again.

The sound of his voice finally got to me. "You don't sound very good. Are you ill?"

"I thought you'd never ask. I have the flu and I've been in bed with fever for the last two days. I..." There was another coughing spell that obliterated the rest.

"You'd better not talk any more. I'm sure anything you have to say about Quinn can wait."

Then there was a sneeze.

"And Larry," I said, "Thanks for thinking of me. Get better soon." I put down the phone and stared at the floor. From somewhere deep inside feelings welled up that I had hoped were gone forever. I always hated it when Larry got sick. He was such a strong, over-powering figure in my life that when he was weakened in any way, it frightened me. I remembered him lying limply in our king-size bed, sprawled cross-wise desperately trying to find a comfortable position when he had come down with a strep throat. For two days he refused to take anything but some water. He held my hand and told me how much he loved me, and to whom to give his Rolex watch. At the time, it was to be his nephew Evan. He wanted to donate his salt water fish and tank to the Police Athletic League. Too bad. Evan had moved to California and never called. As for his fish...They were no longer an asset he needed to worry about.

I glanced at the clock. 6:00pm on a rainy Sunday and I had nothing to do. It occurred to me that it would be a good deed to visit Larry and try to comfort him. I pictured him twisting and turning on our big bed, staring at the ceiling and making lists of the things he loved to be dispersed amongst his friends.

Like the gold-cuff-links I had given him for our tenth anniversary. The picture of his mother that he kept in his underwear drawer. When you don't have children and you no longer have a wife, to whom do you give the things you love? Asking these questions made my throat hurt.

I went over to my bedroom closet and picked out a red silk blouse. It wouldn't do to visit him in black. He would take that as a bad sign. I moved my dresses aside and stared down at the rack of shoes on the floor. Right in front was the single Christian Louboutin silver shoe—a reminder of someone who wanted to murder me. I pushed it aside with my foot. Then I kneeled and picked up a fuchsia silk slide with a two inch heel, its front embroidered with gold thread surrounding three glittering rhinestones. The label stamped in gold letters was faded but still readable—Bergdorf Goodman. I had worn those to my thirtieth birthday celebration. Larry had taken me to *The Four Seasons* for dinner and had surprised me with a table full of our friends.

I reached further back to a black satin shoe with an open toe and ankle strap. On its front was a tassel with two black sequined balls. The heel a slender rod of black patent leather, three inches tall. I had worn it to the dinner when Larry became a senior partner at Klein, Franks.

I did not have to read its label. I had seen an ad in a magazine at the hair-dressers and torn it out. "Tango shoes," authentic Tango shoes from Argentina. I sat down on the bed and dangled the shoe. The Tango. A dance of passion. Yes. There had been real passion between Larry and me.

I put it back on the rack next to its mate and reached down for another pair of shoes. The dove-gray leather pumps I had worn to the party Larry threw for me when I finally got my Ph.D. Since I had left Larry there had been few celebrations of the sort that called for fancy shoes. Strange. When I left him I did not take many things. But I took all my shoes. My whole past life was somehow in these shoes.

I stared at the closet. Paint peeling on the sides. A musty smell mixed with the acid scent of moth balls. This closet was my archeological dig. Way at the back of my closet—its deepest layer—were the shoes I wore to my wedding. I kneeled down and stretched my hand way back until it came into contact with soft leather. I pulled out the shoe and put it against my cheek. The leather was still soft, though cracking in a few places.

More boot than shoe, I had ordered it specially made from Altman's, a now-defunct Fifth Avenue department store that had been one of the first stores in the city to actively promote European design.

I put it down and slipped my foot into it. It still fit perfectly. The leather had yellowed. The silk laces hung limply on the sides. I had just graduated from college when we got married, at the Park Manor on Flatbush Avenue in Brooklyn. A swanky affair. But the truth was, money was tight. I told my father I would borrow a dress from my best friend who had gotten married the year before, if he would let me spend the money on a custom-made shoe from Italy.

I took off the shoe and ran my finger down the two inch heel. It had taken eight weeks for me to get the shoes. I was scared stiff the manufacturer had taken the money and gone out of business. I thought I would have to wear sneakers to my wedding. But then they arrived. And I had them still.

Why? Surely I would never wear them again. No daughter or granddaughter to whom the shoes might have some meaning. And yet, I kept them still. I kneeled once again and replaced the shoe carefully in the closet. From the front of the closet I pulled out a pair of red patent-leather pumps with a mid-sized heel. Comfortable. Practical. Pretty enough. They would do for a sick-call.

Alberto tipped his cap and opened the heavy brass door to 980 Central Park West. "Nice to see you Mrs. Levine," Alberto said, reaching for the Zabar's shopping bag I was carrying.

Larry might be sick but he would have to be dead not to enjoy the smoked salmon from Zabars. It had been a Sunday morning ritual when we lived together. Lox and bagels, cream cheese with chives, chocolate pound cake and fresh orange juice. I still bought my coffee at Zabars but usually avoided the other foods. Too many memories. Of course it was dinner time now, not breakfast, but what the hell.

Alberto walked over to the intercom to buzz Larry that I was on my way up. I waved at him. "Don't bother," I said, "He knows I'm coming, and he's got the flu. Might be asleep."

Alberto hesitated. He wasn't sure what to do. He had been trained to announce any visitors. But I was not really a visitor. Or was I?

I walked into the lobby and took a deep breath. Alberto followed carrying my shopping bag. It had been three years since I was here. My home for twenty years. I was not sure if my desire to learn more about Quinn or my concern for Larry brought me here but I was glad I had come.

My heels sank softly into a crimson and gold oriental carpet, covering much of the cream-colored marble floor. A soft defused light came in from the double polished chrome doors leading out to a private garden in the back of the building.

There had been endless arguments about that garden—as about most things having to do with the coop. The young, Wall Street types who had arrived in recent years wanted luxury accessories to match the multi-million dollar prices of their apartments. Like doormen and elevator men to wear white gloves; air-conditioning in the lobby; authentic art-deco furnishings.

The older share-holders, like Larry and me who had been there since it was a rental filled with musicians, writers, and professors, wanted automatic elevators and bare marble floors. We had clearly lost.

I looked at the ceiling—hand-painted clouds and twenty-four carat gold stars. An echo of Grand Central Station. I had forgotten—or had no longer noticed when I lived here.

"Hello Mrs. Levine," Eddie the elevator man said, taking the Zabars bag from Alberto. "Beautiful day."

"Yes," I said. "It is." The fact that it was raining out had passed him by, but I did not feel like correcting him.

The inside of the elevator had been done over. Lined in deep chocolate walnut, trimmed with polished chrome, and sporting mirrors on every side, I was confronted with my image everywhere I looked.

Another change was how quickly and silently we arrived at the fifteenth floor. No longer creaking and sighing, the elevator moved stealth-like a Mercedes ascending to the heavens.

Eddie waited while I fumbled in my purse for my key. He had been trained to wait, to be sure the visitor was admitted. For a moment we both hesitated. Should I ring the bell? Was I a visitor or a wife?

"It's ok," I told Eddie, "You can go." Eddie nodded. Never contradict a share-holder.

I fit my key in the lock and the door opened easily. Larry had not changed the locks. Something I would have done immediately.

The entry foyer was full of mail and newspapers. He must have made some effort to put it all on the old roll-top desk that sat there for that purpose, but much of it had tumbled onto the floor. What if Larry was so sick he could not attend to the simplest things? I bent down to pick up what I could. And then I remembered that Larry was always a slob. It was me who used to pick up the mail and newspapers. I dropped the papers I had picked up and walked through the apartment toward our bedroom.

I tried not to look left into the living room, or right into the dining room for fear of what I would see—but curiosity got the best of me.
In the living room, books, a couple of jackets, spread over the couch. On the far wall, a new fish-tank. The water was murky and it smelled. Inside I could see a few bulgy-eyed fish negotiating their way through the turgid water and some holes in the coral reef Larry had provided.

I glanced into the kitchen and saw a sink full of dirty dishes. I decided to skip the dining room. I would have thought that these signs of his falling apart would make me feel good, but they did not.

When I got to the bedroom, I found Larry sitting up in bed reading. "Hi!" I said.

He was so surprised his book fell to the floor and his glasses slid down after them.

"I don't look that bad, I hope," I said, bending down to pick up his book and glasses. "GUNS, GERMS AND STEEL" I read the title out loud. Exactly the kind of violence-filled, historical survey Larry liked.

Larry fumbled with the covers and pulled his old ratty robe around him.

I smiled. I didn't often succeed in making Larry feel uncomfortable, but uncomfortable he surely was. I held up the Zabar's bag. "I brought you some lox and bagels. thought you might need some nourishment. And since you were nice enough to find out some information for me. I thought I would repay the favor."

Larry coughed. "Thanks," he said, and reached for the bag.

I had automatically started puffing up the pillows and clearing away some of the mail stuck in the covers when the bathroom door opened and a woman came out. I dropped the Zabar's bag.

The woman, Larry and I all stared at each other for what seemed like a long time. And then Larry coughed. When he recovered he said, "Emily, this is Natasha, my secretary. Natasha, Emily."

"This is Natasha your secretary," I repeated. I had once read that politicians repeat things just said to them in order to buy the time to figure out a response. I folded my arms and stared at her. "I think we've met before."

I had spent so much time hating this woman, my rival, my competitor, my enemy—and trying to remember what she looked like, that when I finally saw her again, I felt disappointed. I had thought of her as tall, and blonde, with high cheekbones and full lips. Kind of like one of those sinister foreign women who are always showing up in James Bond movies.

In fact, she was short and stocky with dyed red hair. She wore a baggy floral print dress that looked like it had once been used to cover a chair. Put a babuska on her head and she would look just like a peasant digging potatoes in the field. I was beginning to feel better.

Natasha said, "I came to bring him papers to sign, and some special borscht I made to help his health."

"Borscht" I repeat. "How nice. Can I taste?"

Larry, sensing trouble, gathered the covers around him and said, "Natasha was just leaving." But no, Natasha was now happily leading the way to the kitchen. I followed. Larry, coughing and grunting paddled barefoot behind us.

Natasha proudly handed me a large jar filled with a pink liquid in which lumps of stuff and blobs of white were floating together.

"What's in it?" I asked brightly as she happily unscrewed the cover.

"Potatoes, beef." She answered."I chop up. Cook all day."

I pointed to the white stuff floating around.

"Sour cream," she replied with pride.

I reached over and took the jar full of borscht, and I poured it slowly down the drain of the sink. "Sour cream, tsk, tsk." I turned to her and waved my finger in front of her face. "Sour Cream is not good for Larry's health. He has high blood pressure." I folded my hands over my chest. "Really bad for the heart." I looked her in the eye. "Sudden death." I uttered, and made a slicing motion with my finger across Larry's throat. While she and Larry watched me speechless, I ran water in the sink and rinsed out the jar. I handed it back to Natasha and shook my head. "Sour cream also gives him lower intestinal difficulties." I shook my finger at her."Diarrhea!"

That sent Larry into such a coughing fit I feared he was going to keel over and die in front of us. I turned my back on Larry and said in my most cordial, company voice, "Thanks so much for coming," and I took her by the elbow and walked her to the door, slamming it behind her.

Larry sat down heavily in one of the kitchen chairs and shook his head back and forth. "It's all over between us," he said hoarsely. "I swear it. She's married to her second husband."

I am all sympathy and sweetness. "Larry," I said to him," you don't have to make excuses to me. We're no longer living together. You can see and do what you want." I pointed in the direction of the living room. "Leave the mail all over the floor; throw your jackets wherever you please. It must be so liberating." Larry just continued to shake his head. "I see you even bought yourself a new fish-tank." I got up and set off in the direction of the living room.

Larry rushed ahead of me and planted himself firmly in front of the fish-tank. "Don't even think about it!" he warned me. "I'll have you arrested for assault."

"Cute little buggers," I commented, pointing at the fish. I shoved a pile of mail from the couch onto the floor and sat down.

We stared at each other for a few minutes, unsure how to steer the conversation into neutral territory. I took a couple of deep breaths. I reminded myself that I had come to comfort Larry, not confront him.

"What was it you wanted to tell me about Professor Quinn?"

Larry sat down heavily, next to me. "I thought you might find it interesting that Phillip Quinn is on the Central Park Conservancy. Gives them a chunk of money every year."

Now It was my turn to be disconcerted. "Then he'd know my customer, the President of the Conservancy—Harriet Moskowitz, who knew both Bonita and Kim! And Murphy completely dismissed him as a suspect!"

"This Murphy guy sounds like a jerk to me." Larry grunted, "Stay away from him."

I wondered how much research Larry had been doing on Murphy. A little jealousy was not always a bad thing. As for Quinn—Larry's information was even more important than he might have guessed. Murphy might be wrong about everything—especially the idea that I was the connection between the victims. Maybe it all has to do with Harriet Moskowitz! She knew Kim, Bonita and Quinn. What the connection was between all of them I didn't know, but maybe it would come to light if I looked in the right place. Meanwhile, I struggled to keep my excitement to myself.

Larry searched around in his ratty bathrobe and found a dirty handkerchief. He blew his nose. "I think I have a fever," He said, and stuffed the dirty handkerchief back in his pocket.

We looked into each other's eyes. Two old fighters, circling each other. We looked away from each other for a minute, and then I reached for his hand. Big, fleshy, firm. I saw he was still wearing his wedding band.

"You didn't thank me for the wine." he said.

"What wine?" I asked him

"The wine I sent for your shoe sale."

I shook my head in amazement. So it wasn't Goodie One Shoes. But how did he know about the shoe sale? I certainly never sent him an invitation. Is The Upper West Side really just a village, after all?

"Thanks." I told him, a little sheepishly. "There was no card."

Larry scowled. "I thought you'd remember. Paul Hobbs. Cabernet Sauvignon. Napa Valley. We went there on our twentieth anniversary trip. We drank it at dinner."

I squeezed his hand once and rose from the couch. I was upset by the encounter with Natasha, confused by my feelings for Larry, distressed by this news about Quinn. And confounded by the wine story. In fact, I could hardly wait to escape this whole mess.

I headed towards the foyer. Larry followed a couple of steps behind. "I hope you feel better soon," I told him and walked quickly out the door, closing it firmly behind me.

While I was waiting for the elevator I heard him bellow to the empty air, "Where the fuck did she leave the lox and bagels!"

Chapter 19

The stiletto, a 4 inch needle-thin high heel, appeared in the 1950's. It's not clear whether it originated in Rome or Paris. So sharp were these heels that they were banned from some airplanes and public places where it was feared they could damage the floors.

A dark blue van sped past the cement island on Broadway, wheels churning up the detritus in the gutter. A red Honda station wagon stopped short and breaked nosily in front of the red light. A taxi stopped suddenly to pick up an old lady, and the driver of a Fresh Foods truck behind him cursed loudly.

Murphy puffed on a cigarette and stared out at the traffic. We were sitting on the cement island in the middle of Broadway in front of Emily's Place. Murphy had paid one of his surprise visits. Did not return my phone-calls but suddenly descended upon us like the Gestapo.

I could always tell when he arrived by the subtle change in atmosphere, a shift in the internal weather of the store—the aroma of masculinity. He nodded hello to Merissa and then motioned to me. "Let's go outside," he said, and he took my arm and led me out of the door. His arm was strong and his grip firm. I could even feel the texture of his tweed jacket through the light material of my blouse. Was I a prisoner or a friend? It was hard to tell.

Once outside Murphy loosened his grip. He led me skillfully through the traffic—jay-walking of course. When did a cop ever have to wait for a traffic light? When we were seated on the iron bench on the Island, he took out a cigarette. I had not smelled nicotine on Murphy before. Things must have degenerated.

"I'm so happy to see you," I told him, "I just found out that Professor Quinn is on the Central Park Conservancy." Murphy flicked his ashes to the ground. "Harriet had a special relationship with Kim and Bonita cleaned Harriet's house too so Quinn would have known her. Don't you see, Quinn is the connection between these murders, not me! The way I see it, Quinn was most likely having an affair with both Kim and Harriet, and Bonita found out. He had to kill Kim and Bonita to prevent them telling his rich wife and ruining his life. And that cheap comb with the red threads? He probably had it in the pocket of a sweater or jacket, gave it to Kim sometime before the murder, and then wore the same sweater when he killed Bonita." Murphy blew some smoke through his nose. "There are thirty-five members of the Conservancy Board. Bonita cleaned half a dozen apartments on the Upper West Side. Looks to me Kim had a 'special relationship' with dozens of people you never even heard of."

"Look," he said, "My eyes are blue. So are your sister's. So are Mrs. O'Mara's who lives on Sheridan Avenue in the Bronx." He sighed. "But we are not a family. And this is not Dreiser's American Tragedy. Neither of the women was pregnant and about to spoil his chances to live a wealthy life. Let it go Emily. You're barking up the wrong tree."

I was about to protest when he turned to me suddenly and said, "How well do you know Merissa?"

I watched the smoke from his cigarette spiral out over the traffic. This was a question I had not expected. "I don't understand," I replied. "What kind of question is that? Merissa has worked for me for three years. I see her five days a week. We share a bathroom. We're friends."

Murphy took another puff and then ground out the butt with his shoe. "I mean, before she came to work for you. How much do you know about her past? Did she give you any kind of work history? Any recommendations?"

This was why I do not like cops. You never know where they are coming from. One minute you think you can trust them. You even begin to like them and think they are normal human beings—might even protect you some day even though they were real shits during any protest march I had ever attended. You could be sure they would rather ticket your car than catch the dope addict on the corner but you were willing to forgive them and then—poof! They turned into the Secret Police. I might not know much about Merissa's past but I trusted her more than Murphy the Cop. "Can't really remember much about what she told me. Didn't care then and don't care now."

I stared across the street at the window of Emily's Place. "Seems to me the only reason people have resumes or recommendations is to give the prospective employer some idea of future behavior. I've seen the future and it has been very good."

Murphy reached into his pocket for another cigarette. "Maybe you only saw part of the future. The part about being a conscientious, even dedicated employee."

"That's the part that concerns me the most. The rest of Merissa's life is none of my business."

Murphy took a long drag. "Merissa LaBelle has no history. Invented herself on the spot when she got to New York City and you gave her a job. Real name is Mirabella Brown. Born and raised in Washington D.C. Mom was a druggie. Overdosed when Mirabella was thirteen. There was an older sister. No record of how either of them survived."

I turned away and focused on the pigeons pecking away at an old ice cream cone. So there was no Canada, no Haiti. Just poverty in Washington D.C. Apparently, no education either. No French connection except maybe a tape she bought for herself. Come to think of it, the longer Merissa worked for me the less French I heard her speak. Except for an occasional "*Alors!*" and "*mon petite*" she had never spoken very much. But whatever her pretentions, Merissa had somehow survived. She seemed happy. And she made others happy. Me. Fifi. She had a heart as big as her feet. I didn't care for what Murphy was telling me. If anything, it made me value Merissa even more. "She told me her sister died. There was a child—her niece, Fifi."

Murphy nodded. "Sister was convicted of murdering her common-law husband. Stabbed him five times. She died in jail of a burst appendix. Child and Merissa disappeared. The trail stops when they left Washington D.C."

"Murphy, None of this makes any difference to me. I didn't hire Merissa for her pedigree." Murphy flicked his ashes onto the ground and turned to look at me.

"Merissa wasn't attacked the other night. She lied."

I gasped. "She lied? Why would she lie about something like that?" I got up from the bench and looked down at Murphy. There was something that didn't make any sense here. Murphy was trying to trap me into giving something away. "What makes you think she lied?" I asked. "How could you possibly know she made it up?"

"Because the night she says she was attacked, she was working at St. Anne's Church, feeding the homeless and over-seeing their sleeping arrangements. She slept at the church herself. Didn't go home at all. Didn't leave the church all night." He took another deep drag. "Didn't go anyplace at all until she showed up at Emily's Place later that day."

I sat back down on the bench and rubbed my eyes. "I don't get it.

Why would she lie? What could she possibly gain from making up a lie like that?"

"Ah" said Murphy, grinding out his cigarette on the arm of the bench. "Now you are finally asking the right question."

We stared at each other.

"She told you there was a big guy, big as her grabbed her shoe, right?"

"Yeah. So?"

"Maybe she wants us to believe the shoe murderer was not a little guy with a limp, but actually a big guy with two good feet."

I smiled. "Or maybe there are really two guys; one big and one little."

Murphy nodded. "Yes. She might want us to believe that. Especially since it's possible that the little guy isn't a guy at all."

I popped up from the bench again. This was ridiculous. "So you are thinking the shoe murderer is a woman? She'd have to be a pretty amazing woman to over-power and rape her victims"

Now it was Murphy's turn to pop up from the bench. "Who ever said anything about rape?"

I covered my mouth with my hand. I thought back to the newspaper stories I had read. The women were dressed only in a bra and panties and murdered in some way with a shoe. Did it say they were sexually assaulted? Did it say they were raped? I couldn't remember. But I certainly assumed they had been raped. I'd spent nights crying picturing Kim's brutal attack.

Murphy took my arm and led me back to the bench. "That was one of the details we managed to withhold. There was no semen found on either of these women. Not on their clothes. Not on the shoe." He lifted an eyebrow. "The little guy with the limp could well be a girl." He stared into my eyes. "There's another thing too. We found a foot print in the damp soil around the reservoir. Next to the Cherry trees—right where you told me the 'little guy' with the limp ran off." I held my breath. "And that strange mark we found on your bedroom floor? You were right. It was the outline of the tip of a shoe. It exactly matches the full print we found on the jogging path. It's a strange foot-print. My guys at the lab say it seems to have been made by some specially made orthopedic device—hence those traces of metal we originally found. Must be some kind of bracing mechanism."

"Which proves what?"

"That whoever threw your shoe into the reservoir was present at

Bonita's murder." He paused. "According to the hospital records we saw, Merissa's sister's kid was born with a club foot."

My heart felt like it had stopped beating. Suddenly, it all seemed to make sense. Fifi, Central Park. It was almost more than I could bear.

"Course, we don't know much about the companies who make these shoes. There are dozens, companies all over the world. But, I thought you might be able to help us out. Maybe let us know about any high-class custom shoe companies that might make this sort of thing."

I covered my eyes with my hands. It was all too much for me. I felt as if my whole world had been turned upside down.

Murphy's voice softened. He put his hand on my shoulder. "Are you with me?"

What could I say? All I wanted was to get away from him and find some time to think. "I think I need a drink," I said finally.

"Later." He said. "Right now I need information."

My head began to throb. "But what kind of motive would she have? Fifi liked me. She loved Kim. And she didn't even know Bonita."

Murphy looked off into the traffic. "Jealousy. You liked Fifi but you loved Kim. You also loved your sister, whom Fifi thought she was killing when she killed Bonita."

I shut my eyes and tried to think. Could Murphy be right?

"I'd have to see the print," I said.

"Of course," he responded. "And of course you can't say anything at all to your friend Merissa."

I shook my head. Oh Lord, Did I really have to choose between loyalty to Merissa and loyalty to Murphy? "There must be some explanation... It could still be Quinn. And what about Cheryl and the comb with the red threads?"

Murphy shook his head. "There's never been any real reason to suspect Cheryl. Chances are that comb belonged to Merissa's niece— and she had on a red sweater when she murdered Bonita."

"Let me at least speak to Merissa," I begged him.

Murphy gripped my arm. "You speak to Merissa and you are an accessory to murder. In fact. You may already be an accessory to murder. There is the small matter of concealing a red shoe in your closet. Smearing prints on a cell phone. Moving a dead body. Screwing up the evidence. Who knows what else you might have concealed."

Phony fuck-faced turncoat! I realized I would have to go along for a while. I did not have much choice.

"Show me the foot print,' I said.

When we got to the precinct, there were Denise and Rosa, just as I had last seen them. Rosa at the desk and Denise at the filing cabinet.

When they saw Murphy, they came to attention as if the king had arrived. Rosa vacated her seat and Denise literally ran to fetch him a cup of coffee. The two women fussed around him in a manner that embarrassed me. I felt as if they would be taking off his shoes and giving him a back rub if I hadn't been around.

Rosa recognized me right off. "Hey! Aren't you the lady, lost her wallet? Sorry, we never found it."

Murphy glared at me. "I wouldn't worry about it."

Denise nodded to me. "How's your sister with the bad heart?"

"Fine." I told her. "Fine. In fact she told me she lit a candle for you in church." I would have to remember to tell Shana that Denise had inquired about her health. She'd love it. Memories of that last visit here brought a smile to my face, but deep down I was in complete turmoil. The thought that anyone close to me could have had anything to do with these horrible murders made me want to scream. I could understand Merissa lying to me about her background. She was ashamed. She thought I would not want to have anything to do with someone so low-born. But even that thought burned. How could she have believed I would like her less because of something she had absolutely no control over—her birth and her parentage? And then came the anger. Fierce, red, anger. Talk about biting the hand that feeds you. If that person on the jogging path was her niece and a murderer, Merissa herself was putting my life in danger. Such was my "thank you" for putting food on her table. Yes—and shoes on her feet. I shuddered. And shoes on her niece's feet—or rather—foot. I would nail her and put her niece away for life. But mixed in with my fury was a sadness so deep, I could hardly keep from crying. Friendship, kindness, loyalty—all gone. An illusion. Wishful thinking. And I did not want to stop caring for Merissa. No matter what she had done. She had become a part of my life and I didn't want to give her up.

I sat there and felt like banging my head against the wall. Within a few minutes, the foot print—a heavy white plaster cast—was brought out from a large closet in the back of the office and carefully unwrapped before me on the desk. It took only a minute for me to identify the maker. A small C on its side with a line inside. It was Cicceri and Son, a small Italian company my father had discovered years ago. They made custom shoes. Usually for those with fallen arches. Flat feet. The father was long gone, but the son had taken over. And Merissa had hired them to make a mate for Fifi's Stuart Weitzman's pumps.

I ran my hand over the sole. It was large and extra wide, yet not too different from a regular shoe, narrower in the front than in the back with an indentation that ran the length of the shoe. Some special structure, I guess for extra support. I could picture it. It would be very wide, the sides would be higher than usual but from the front, it could almost look normal. Fifi's shoe. A shoe like that would cost hundreds. Strangely enough though, such a shoe, custom-made, one-of-a-kind, would still be cheaper than the satin pumps from Prada.

I straightened up and shook my head. "Never seen anything like this before," It was the truth—as far as it went.

Murphy sneered. "Come on. You're the shoe expert of the Western World. You're a woman who could identify a shoe size and its maker from fifty yards away." He looked me in the eyes. "Now you're telling me, you don't know anything when it's sitting right in front of you?"

"First of all," I reminded him. "This is not a shoe. This is the cast of a shoe sole. The sole of some orthopedic shoe, left foot." I met his eyes without flinching. "This shoe is most probably made by some surgical supply company. Some medical equipment company. This is not my area of expertise. I deal with fine leathers. Beauty. Delicacy. An art form. This is something else entirely."

Murphy's eyes narrowed. He was disappointed, trying to decide if I was telling the truth.

The real truth was that I didn't know what I was going to say until I said it. Maybe it was stupid, but I just couldn't abandon Merissa. Maybe she could stab me in the back. But I couldn't do it to her. Somewhere in the depths of my soul I still believed in her. I had to give her a chance to explain herself. She was too good to be so bad. I had seen her with Fifi, with Kim. I had seen her with so many people. She really cared about them. And I believed she cared about me. I shook my head. "Sorry," I said to Murphy. "It's just not my thing."

Murphy pointed to the cast. "There's some kind of design on the sole—probably a trademark." He reached for my finger and ran it over the C lying on its side. I shrugged and shook my head. It was easier to lie with motions than with words.

Murphy turned to Rosa and Denise and motioned for them to take away the cast. They came running like two kittens to their bowl of food. Murphy walked me to the door. "It will take me a while," he said. "But we'll trace this trade-mark and we'll find who bought this shoe."

"I know you will," I told him. "I have full confidence in you."

When we reached the door, he turned to me and said, "One more thing I think you ought to know. The sister's kid's deformity was on the left foot."

I swallowed hard. "Yes? "I turned to look at him. "And what does that have to do with anything?"

He chuckled. "The shoe we found with both bodies was a left foot shoe. The shoe that was left in your closet was also a left foot shoe." He opened the door. "It looks like somebody had no need for a pretty left foot shoe."

As soon as I got home, I called Merissa at the store.

Chapter 20

One of the charges against Joan of Arc, that made people believe she was a witch, was that she dressed in men's boots that reached up to her thighs.

Calling Merissa at the store was one thing; what I was going to say to her was another. While the phone rang, I looked around my bedroom. Had that photo of my parents on the bureau always faced towards the window? Hadn't I left my slippers further under the bed after I got dressed this morning? Was that yellow sweater, just back from the cleaner, hanging on the doorknob like that when I left the apartment? I was getting paranoid and I couldn't get over the feeling that "Big Brother" was watching and listening in.

Why not? I had seen enough television to know that cops could do anything and Murphy was no ordinary cop. Of that I was sure. He knew a lot more about everything than he ever let on. He was playing upon me the way Polonius tried to play on Hamlet.

When Merissa finally answered I said, "Listen—don't have much time to chat. That fund-raiser at the church tonight? I won't be able to make it. But I do have a speech I want you to read—and a few gift certificates for shoes that I had specially made. Can you come over and pick them up?"

I heard a sharp intake of breath and then her response. "*Biensur*, Madame. When you want me to come? Store almost empty now."

"Now would be just fine," I told her, and I quickly hung up the phone. I looked up at the ceiling of my bedroom and muttered a short prayer of thanks to whoever might be listening. The world might be completely unreliable but I knew Merissa had to be street-wise enough to realize I couldn't talk over that phone. But where could I talk? Who could I trust? I took a kitchen chair and put it outside in the hallway in front of my apartment door. Then I sat down and waited so I could stop her before she even rang my bell.

I couldn't help feeling my apartment had been violated in some way—I just had this creepy feeling that someone had been in there—and that it also was bugged. I didn't want to give the cops the satisfaction of even hearing me say "Hello" to Merissa. But where I would go with her to be perfectly safe from anyone listening in? I did not have that figured out yet.

Within three minutes Angelina opened her door and stuck out her head. "Dolly," she said to me, "Whatever are you doing out there in the draft?"

Terrific. Problem solved. I could count on Angelina no matter what Murphy thought. I put my finger over my mouth and whispered, "Top Secret!" I motioned for her to come closer and I pointed to the camera Larry had installed and whispered," Big Brother is watching us. Can my friend and I meet in your apartment?"

Angelina took one look at the camera and beamed. "My pleasure," she whispered back, "Did you know I once played Mata Hari at the 23rd St. Theater?" The two of us took turns as look-outs until Merissa arrived. Then we all sat down in Angelina's kitchen.

"Have a cup of tea Dolly," Angelina offered, while Henry fluttered about over-head. Fuchsia-colored kimono with wide-arms flapping, silver bracelets jangling, Angelina embraced Merissa as if she were a long-lost friend.

Merissa was her usual charming self, gliding around the place in a bright yellow shift with a red scarf, admiring Angelina's theatrical souvenirs. Here a signed program from *Fiddler on the Roof*, there a photo of Angelina and Jerome Robbins and a bowtie that once belonged to Frank Sinatra.

Henry hovered over Merissa and seemed fascinated by her hair—combed down and braided in corn rows, close to her scalp. A couple of times he tried to settle on her head and Merissa, laughing, ducked while Angelina muttered, "Naughty Bird, Naughty Bird!" and pursued him around the apartment.

I was glad to have a minute to reflect, and I sat back to survey the scene. It seemed to me there were three birds, fluttering, priming their feathers, showing their colors; one gray, one fuchsia, and Merissa—most colorful of all—chocolate, scarlet and yellow. Circling, admiring, seducing each other with dulcet tones and graceful movements. If only life could be more like this, just people admiring one another, drinking in the sensual sounds and colors and motions around them, like some grand, universal dance.

But right now I needed to have a heart-to-heart, down-and-dirty with Merissa. Our lives depended upon it. I rose from the table and handed Angelina a twenty dollar bill. "I know you hate going out before evening, but could you just pick us up a couple of those chocolate cupcakes from the Cup Cake Cafe on the corner? I know it's one of Henry's favorites too." At the sound of his name—coupled with CupCake Café, Henry squawked "Cup Cake, Cup Cake" and flew about the room.

Angelina wrinkled her nose and reached for her black velvet cape. "If you need me to pick up any arsenic, I know a supplier who keeps his mouth shut," she offered.

"Thanks, I'll let you know."

As soon as the door closed behind her, I turned to Merissa. "Madame Emily" she said. "Some white ladies don't live much better than me. She looked over her shoulder into the bedroom beyond. "Something like this can make a darky feel good about herself."

I was in no mood for Merissa's fooling around. "Come off it, Merissa. I don't need any slave-girl stories today. In fact, I think I've heard enough of your stories to last me a life-time."

Merissa sat down at the kitchen table and stared at me. Maybe she sensed that this would be a new chapter in our relationship.

I could not pull any punches. "Let's start by telling me the truth, for a change," I said. "No more of that bull shit about Haiti and Canada. No more of that French crap. No more Madame Emily. You were born and brought up in Washington D.C."

Merissa shook her head. "How you hear about that? That cop telling you stories? Who you going to believe? That cop never told the truth his whole life."

I reached over and took Merissa's hand. "I'm not interested in where you came from," I told her. "I want to know where you're going—and where your niece is going."

Merissa jerked her hand away and jumped out of her seat."What he say about my niece? What he know about Fifi?"

"Take it easy. He knows you had a sister and that sister had a child. Murphy doesn't know it yet for sure but I just found out that child left a footprint of her custom-made orthopedic shoe next to the body of Bonita."

Merissa sat down heavily on the chair and covered her face with her hands. Neither of us said anything. Then she lifted her face, folded her hands in her lap and took a deep breath and began to talk.

"Fifi. My niece. More like my baby sister. Woman had my sister and me—can't even ever call her Mom—so fried from drugs doesn't know her own kids. Older sister come out too early, too much alcohol in her blood, not even born yet trouble start."

I took Merissa's hand again, and held it tight.

"But she was good to me. Feed me, wash me. That sister only Mom I have. Only thing to love in that whole house, that whole street, that whole city. Me and her.

Then one day, show up with this white dude. He said he French—more like Algerian trash. They move away. Do drugs. Do who know what. Then Big Sister she have a baby. Her man, he don't want no kid around—kid crying, crapping in her pants. He beat her—make her shut up. Then one day Big Sister decide to shut him up instead. She go to jail. I take Fifi.

I hide her from the social worker. Social worker come, look around, shake her white head, leave fast, say place smells. Why she want to spend her time place like this? No way.

Neighbors good to me. Some black people remember how it is to be alone, dirt poor, nothing to eat. They come, bring us food. Missy Katherine, she live next door. She sew us clothes. Teach me to use the sewing machine. Miss Lula, upstairs. She bring me books to read. She teach me; I teach Fifi. But Fifi have something wrong in her head, and her foot. "

She pauses and kicks the side of the table. "Fifi, never even have a name. It only say "Female" on the birth certificate. Her momma too out of it to give her own child a name. I call her Francoise but she too used to Fifi—white dude give her the name of a dog. She never grows up neither. But her body grows up. She get tits and ass. Soon she hanging out with boys when I go to work. I work two jobs to try to get money for an operation for her foot, but it's no good. Never enough money.

"Finally I get enough money, come to New York. Get a real job. Dress good. Talk good. Meet good people."

She squeezed my hand. "Make friends. Good friends."

"But Fifi. She still nowheres. Worse. She finds a man of her own. Strange man. First man ever want her more than one night. She go off with him night, after night. Only one thing wrong. This man love shoes more than Fifi's pussy. This man start buying shoes. Beautiful, expensive shoes. Give them to Fifi to dress up. But Fifi only need one shoe. Right shoe. Left shoe extra.

Pretty soon her man finds something to do with Left shoe. Find another woman. Two pussys, two shoes, one shoe each. Everyone dress up, have fun.

For a while, Fifi play this game. Then one night, game changes.

Man start talking about revenge. He want revenge. Man want to kill one special woman. But first he want to make her suffer. No more fun and games. Man pretend he want sex, but he want blood. He kill Kim with one shoe. Give the other one to Fifi. Now Fifi in real trouble."

I felt terrible listening to Merissa. I could see Merissa with Fifi, clinging to one another in a Washington slum abandoned by everyone. But that was certainly not my fault.

I listened to her story but could I trust Merissa? How did I know that this "Man" even existed? Fifi's mother was a murderer. Sure, she had cause, but she was a murderer all the same. It seemed likely that Fifi could be one too. But then it was possible that Fifi wanted to give me the shoes as a gift, or a warning, but then too Fifi might have participated in the murders—or alone been the killer.

If Murphy was right, I was on the list of victims because of Fifi's jealousy. If Merissa was right, I was on the list of victims because of some crazy man's need for revenge. I got up from the table and bent over Merissa. "What about Fifi stalking me on the jogging path? What was she going to do with that shoe if she caught up with me? How do I know there is any man mixed up in this? The police didn't find semen on either Kim or Bonita."

Merissa leaped up. "What you talking about? No semen? Of course semen. That cop lie to you. Fifi's man get more excited from killing the women, then sleeping with Fifi. After he kill Kim and Bonita, all that man want is to fuck them and kill them. He only need Fifi around to watch. "

"But Merissa, how do I know it's not you who is lying? You lied to me about a tall man attacking you and stealing your shoe. You told me your sister died from TB."

Merrisa covered her eyes again and nodded her head. "Well, yes, the cops, they was getting too close. They lookin for a little guy with a limp. They getting too close to Fifi. They don't never see The Man. He real careful, wear gloves. But he do leave semen. Maybe not in Kim. Kim is an accident. He still fucking Fifi then. But he sure fuck Bonita. He fuck her dead."

It was so awful, I felt I have to believe her. "So then why did Fifi come after me?"

"She don't want to hurt you. She know you and me are friends. She know you good to me. You save me. You save us both. She want to warn you. She want to let you know this man, he wants you. He wants the Shoe Goddess herself—but not for love—for hate, for revenge. He think you killed his sister. He want to fuck you and kill you. She only want to give you the shoe. She give you the other shoes. Put it right through your mail. She give you the red shoe. Sure—I take it and hide it cause I afraid the cops going to connect that shoe with Emily's Place—with Fifi. But after that cop Murphy come, I know they watching Emily's Place already. I bring it back cause I know The Man, he going kill Fifi one day sure if he ain't caught first. She want you to have the shoes so you can catch The Man. When you come after her in the park, Fifi get so scared she throw away the shoe and hide in a tree."

It was all too much for me. I sank back down into the chair. "What about you? You knew who killed Kim. You knew who killed Bonita. You knew who wanted to kill me and who wanted to kill Shana and you did nothing?"

Merissa shuffled her feet. Her eyes rolled this way and that. An animal cornered. Looking for a way out. She took a deep breath. "First I don't know nothing. Fifi have boyfriend. That all I know. I don't know anything till after Kim get killed. Then Fifi get scared. She don't know what to do. I tell The Man I going to turn him in. Tell me he kill Fifi, I say anything to anyone." She shook her head back and forth. "Then I hear about Bonita. I know The Man after Shana. I don't know what to do. I beg The Man. Don't hurt Shana. Don't hurt Emily. No one kill your Sister. He punched me in the face. I think that cop can trace the Man's shoe. Now he got two shoes. Do something with the shoes, 'fore anyone else get hurt. But mostly, I think, I run away with Fifi. Go to Canada. 'Fore I can do anything, Fifi, she move out. He take her with him, so I can't run away with her. I don't know what to do. I look all over for Fifi. Finally Fifi come home. Then I think now I run away with Fifi. Then I save you from The Man. But Fifi. She don't want to go nowhere. She love you. She want to stay right here. She think she can protect you from The Man. She too big for me to carry onto an airplane. What I can do? "

I scowled at Merissa. "You could have done something. Warned me. Sent the police something else."

Merissa bit her lip. "I do warn you. I try to help the police. I want police to catch The Man. "

The Man thought I killed his sister? "Who is this Man you keep talking about. Tell me now!"

Merissa shook her head. "I can't tell nothin' till Fifi safe. Till Fifi far away."

Murphy was right about one thing. I was surely in danger.

And now? What would Merissa do? I knew she'd do anything to save Fifi.

"Murphy will trace that footprint right to Fifi. I told him I had no idea who made the shoe that made that print. I lied to buy you time. But he will find you both, sure as we are sitting here."

Merrisa moved towards the door. "I'm out of here now. Fifi and me are gone. We go to Mexico, South America. We go to Canada. Now she come with me. Don't want to go to jail. We start over again."

I moved quickly and planted myself in front of her, blocking the door. "Listen to me. If you go away, this man will continue to kill people. Fifi will continue to get fucked by worse and worse kinds of men. Fifi needs to be somewhere where she can get some help."

Merissa's whole body shook. "Who help Fifii? No one ever help Fifi but me."

I put my hand on her shoulder. "That's not true. I got her a job, remember? "I also might have been responsible for her love affair with shoes—but I wasn't about to mention that. "Things are different now. I will help Fifi. I will help you both. You can't just walk away and let this man kill innocent women. Sure he said I killed his sister. Made up some wacky reason to kill. But once he started killing, he liked it. He must have known that Bonita wasn't my sister when he got a good look at her. She was Spanish, for God's sake. This man is going to kill again. Innocent women. We've got to help each other."

Merissa started to moan and rock back and forth. "Ain't nobody going to help Merissa and Fifi."

I grabbed her arm again and led her to the kitchen chair. "We don't have much time. Here's what we need to do. Fifi is in big trouble. She is an accessory to murder. You are too. And now, so am I. Murphy told me if I let you know about the footprint I would be an accessory to murder. We are all in this together now."

Merissa bit her lip. "I never wanted..."

"Of course not. But now we are in this, we have to figure out how to get out of it. Here's the thing: If Fifi turns state's evidence..." I didn't really know what this phrase meant but I had heard it dozens of times from Larry." if Fifi agrees to lead Murphy to the real killer, in exchange for a suspended sentence—in exchange for a free pass for you and me—we can all solve our problem—and get rid of the killer."

Merissa scowled. "You mean tell that cop? That cop, he already lie to you about the semen. How you goin' to trust that cop?"

I had been wrestling with that same question myself. Maybe it was Shana who always seemed to think the best of everyone—who had finally convinced me that bad Karma attracts bad Karma, that bad thoughts attract bad luck, but whatever it was, now I had an answer. "So Murphy lied to me. You lied to me. I lied to Murphy. Everyone lies." I bent closer to her. "But you can't lead a life where you never trust anyone. I need you and you need me and Fifi needs us both. We all need Murphy. Why would Murphy lie to us about a light sentence or a free pass? All he wants is to catch a killer. He's got to come back with someone. He would rather have the real killer, but if not, he'd settle for Fifi. If we bring him the real killer, he doesn't need Fifi."

The corners of Merissa's mouth turned down. Her eyes narrowed. Can she do it? Can she trust me and Murphy? Merissa rose slowly from the chair. Her back arched upward and her arms begin to lift towards the ceiling. She unfolds; she unrolls; she reaches upwards like a tree that has been bent and bound to the earth by ties, suddenly released to spring back into its most natural form.

Her face, when she turned to me was grim. No tears for Merissa. She was not a crying kind of gal. Her face had lines and crevices I have never seen before. Etched and carved , they meandered over the surface of her skin. Suddenly she looked much older to me. A different Merissa altogether. And then it passed, the other Merissa with the carved, wooden mask of a face.

Her lips curled back and she straightened her hair. "Hey, Boss Lady. Cheer up. We got to do what we got to do. Call your cop.

Me and Fifi. We in your hands."

I took a bite of my Everything Bagel and glanced at the big clock on the wall of Murray's Bagel Heaven. It was already 2:10pm and nobody had yet shown up for the meeting I had set up.

When I had returned to my apartment I breathed a sigh of relief. I wish that optimism had lasted more than about three minutes, but it didn't. All it took was a phone call to Murphy to bring back the seriousness of my position—our position.

First off I told him I had something real important. Fifi was not the killer but she knew who was. But before I gave him any details, he needed to promise immunity to me, Merissa and Fifi.

His hesitation on the phone was just a tad too long for comfort.

"Sure." He answered. "I'll be right over."

This was not how I wanted to play the game. I might be a woman of a certain age but I was not yet senile. I told him I needed something in writing. A legal document that I could show my lawyer. I would set up a meeting a couple of days from now.

He agreed, a tad too fast, and then he said: "Be sure to bring Fifi and Merissa. I'm not handing out free tickets to a concert. They want a pass, they got to show up."

When I told this to Merissa, she didn't like it at all, but there was not much we could do. Murphy could arrest Merissa and me, and could track down Fifi. It wouldn't take him more than a couple of days to track down that orthopedic shoe. All we could do was play our hand as best we could, even though we didn't hold all the aces. In fact, I had no aces and the cards were marked.

Moshe, a dish towel thrown over his arm, hovered in back of me, "Want some more coffee? Need more cream cheese?" Moshe had been a waiter at Murray's for thirty years. How he managed to raise three kids on what he was making in tips was beyond my comprehension.

Would any of them show up? I wondered. Merissa and Fifi could be half-way to Mexico by now. And I could find myself in jail, as an accessory. And then Murphy came in with a short guy wearing a trench coat. My stomach tightened and I put down my bagel.

Murphy surveyed the minimal crowd and then came over to the table. I looked up at them. The smaller guy looked as if he came from Central Casting. A trench coat. Give me a break. He flashed some kind of badge. I saw hand-cuffs hanging from his belt when he opened his coat.

"Who's your friend," I asked Murphy. "I only reserved a table for four."

He avoided my eyes and looked towards the door.

"Where are your friends?" he shot back, pulling out a chair and motioning for his guy to sit down. "Looks like there's enough chairs to go around. Anyway, him and me, we've already had our lunch."

I wanted desperately to warn Merissa on my cell phone. I got up from the table. "Got to go to the little girl's room."

Murphy put his hand over mine. "Sit down," he said, "You aren't going anyplace."

And then the door opened and Merissa walked in. She looked over at us. For a minute I thought she would bolt. But I guess she was smarter than me. She did not look surprised at all. She glided gracefully to our table, lips painted bright red, Jimmy Choo heels clicking on the linoleum. Every eye turned to see her. In black and white African robes that reached to the floor, she looked like an apparition from *Coming to America*. Merissa sure knew how to steal a scene.

Both men rose. Moshe the waiter rushed to pull out her chair.

"Is this little party for me?" she tilted her head back and smiled at the man in the trench coat.

Murphy said, "Where'd you dig up the African gear? Doesn't suit you at all."

"You makin racial comments, Mr. Copper Man? Don't they teach you nothing about "diversity?"

She nodded in my direction. "Better make a note of that." She shook her head back and forth. "Tsk, Tsk. And I don't see no lawyer either. And nobody read me my rights. Copper man trying to take advantage of poor, ignorant black gal?" She looked around the restaurant and said in a loud voice, "Next thing you know someone going to put their hand on my knee."

Sometimes the things Merissa came out with surprised even me. But I could see where she was going with this. Dressed herself like an African Queen. She would get the case kicked out of court before it even got to the court.

Murphy was not amused. He bent towards her. "Where's Fifi?" Not much for small talk, Murphy the Cop—or intimidation either.

Merissa shrugged. "Where's my immunity papers, Master?" she asked, "And you haven't introduced your friend."

The small man started to rise but Murphy put a hand on his arm. "Just a friend," he said.

He reached into his vest pocket and took out some papers. He handed one sheet to me and one to Merissa.

I was too nervous to read carefully but I saw the words "Immunity" and there was some kind of official seal.

"Remember," I said to Murphy. "I'm still married to a lawyer. This could be entrapment."

"I doubt it," Murphy said. "You called me."

Merissa read hers carefully. When she looked up she said, "Where's the papers for Fifi?"

Murphy shrugged. "No can do. You and Emily get off free. Fifi is a murderer."

Merissa glanced at me. I bit my lip. We had not had a chance to explain. "Fifi ain't no murderer. Don't you cops know anything? How a little gal like that going to overpower a big, strong woman? How a woman any size going to put semen in a woman's pussy?

172

How any of that going to happen?" She sneered at Murphy. "You know Fifi ain't no killer. But she know who is."

Murphy tapped his fingers on the table. "I can't give her immunity. But I can give her something else. We'll figure it out. We can get her a light sentence—psychiatric help."

Merissa looked at him silently for a minute. Then she motioned for the waiter. Moshe came running. "Give me one of those, "she pointed to my Everything Bagel. She picked up her napkin and spread it over her lap. "I got to take your word, is that what you saying? Like today? Did not you promise this lady sitting here three immunity passes?"

"Come off it Merissa. You know better than that. I can only do what I can do."

Moshe arrived with Merissa's bagel and she took a bite. We all watched while she chewed, slowly, carefully. "All right." She said, wiping her lips. "Fifi will lead you to the Man. She tell me we got to set something up." She looked at me. "Man want Boss Lady here. We set up Boss Lady with some shoes and Fifi bring her Man."

Murphy looked from one of us to the other.

I was okay with that. I wanted to get that bastard probably as much as he wanted to get me.

But Murphy did not like it. "Too dangerous. I can't use Emily as bait. We got to think of something else."

Merissa held her ground. "We got to do it this way. Fifi, she can't take the risk. Man could kill her in a minute. Man wants Emily. Fifi got to deliver Emily."

Good Lord, what was I, dead meat? "Wait just one minute," I held up my hand. "I'm cool with this. This is fine. Bring on the Man."

I looked at Murphy. "Just have Murphy here and his friends hiding in the closet."

Murphy snorted. "Emily, Emily. There you go again. Wonder Woman. The Caped Crusader. This man is a serial killer. I can't take the responsibility. "

Sweet. He was willing to put me in jail but not willing to use me for bait. I leaned over the table. "I'll take the responsibility. "I've already signed up to take care of Merissa and Fifi. "I'll sign a waiver, or something. Get you off the hook."

Murphy looked at my half-eaten bagel. "You going to finish that?" he asked.

I shook my head.

He grabbed the bagel and took a bite.

"It's a deal," he said when he stopped chewing. "Try to set something up for tomorrow night." He motioned to Moshe. "Bring everyone a round of these."

"OMMMMM It's Shana," my sister said over the phone.

"Really," I replied, "I thought it was the tooth fairy."

Shana was silent. Uncharacteristically quiet.

"What?"

"You always make fun of me. Ever since we were kids. I'm just a big joke."

I held the phone more tightly. I felt suddenly ashamed. "Not a joke," I told her. "I've always loved you. You must know that."

"I forgive you" Shana said brightly. "It's just your nature like the scorpion who stings the fish who carried him across the river."

I was sure Shana has mixed up the animals here but I decided to say nothing.

"I just wanted to tell you I had a dream about you last night. I know you don't believe in this stuff and you don't believe in me but it's my duty nevertheless to warn you."

I sat down—feeling stung. "Tell me your dream."

"I saw you floating in a sea of gray numbers, gray all over, gray mist, gray water, all gray."

I wanted to tell her that the gray she saw was the gray hair she had given me, but I remained silent. "What does it mean?" I asked her.

"It means something bad might happen to you. You're in danger."

Since I had said nothing to Shana about our plan to trap the shoe murderer with me as bait, I was very moved by her concern for her nasty, condescending sister. "I'll be careful," I promised her.

"Thank you." I hung up.

Somehow, Shana's dream, the memory of Shana's mugging, something seemed to click in my mind. I went to the computer and called up my sales information once again.

The last time I had looked for a man's name. This time I decided to cross check women's names for the Jimmy Choo and Dolce & Gabbana—the brands used in the murders. Everyone who bought a size eight.

I called up the first screen, Jimmy Choo. Everyone who bought a size eight. There were twelve names. I called up the next screen, Dolce & Gabbana, and size eight. There were fourteen names.

I looked at the lists. Only one name appeared twice. Cheryl Smith.

Cheryl the transvestite.

I stared at her name. But Cheryl wore a size ten. Why would she buy a size eight?

And then I remembered. Cheryl and Fifi!

I pictured them that day at Emily's Place as Fifi dove into her arms. The day she climbed ten feet up to the top of the display case to fetch a shoe for Cheryl. The day Harriet Moskowitz offered her a job climbing trees in Central Park.

Cheryl. Of course. I remember the cheap Chinese comb she wore in her hair—her red wig. And Murphy kept rejecting her as a suspect! The only thing still missing was the motive.

Did Cheryl have a sister?

Size eight and size ten. Louise the Loser wore size eight but always stole size ten. Could she have stolen them for her brother—not a boyfriend as I had assumed?

I rushed over to the phone and dialed Murphy's private number.

He picked up on the first ring. "Scared?" he asked me.

"Not at all. Just found out there is a good chance that it's Cheryl the transvestite after all. Remember my hunch about the cheap Chinese comb? Now I've learned Cheryl bought size eight shoes from both designers whose shoes were involved in the murders. And that Fifi herself wears a size eight."

I told him that Louise the Loser wore a size eight but stole size tens. Did she steal them for Cheryl? If so, it all makes sense. Cheryl hates me because of something I did to his sister—I fired her!"

There was silence on the phone. I pictured Murphy puffing hard on a cigarette. "Could be," he said at last, "It's not enough that Cheryl just likes the same designers as the shoe murderer. Did he buy the exact styles that did our ladies in? Do the style numbers match the murder weapons?"

I hesitated. "O.K. smarty pants, "I countered. I can't check the style numbers. I don't have the Evidence any more. You took it all away. Remember?"

Murphy grunted. "Even if the numbers do check out, it's all circumstantial. There might be hundreds all over the planet who have bought those two styles from those two companies in size eight. You told me size eight is the most popular size. And one more thing. How many other pairs of shoes has Cheryl bought from you this year?"

"Hold on," I told Murphy, and ran back to the computer. I typed in Cheryl Smith and looked at the screen. Wow! I hadn't realized that Cheryl was such a good customer. She must have bought twenty pairs of shoes.

I looked more closely. The styles and companies were all over the place. But the sizes were all ten and eight. I went back and told Murphy what I just found out.

"You can't convict a person of murder just because he buys a lot of shoes. I wish we could. All I'd have to do is look at your sales reports and we might be able to solve all the murders in the city." Murphy was quiet again for a few seconds. I pictured him grinding out his cigarette. "Personally, I don't believe in coincidences. Looks to me like you found our man—or woman. But proving this stuff in court is another story altogether. I don't know what Cheryl does for a living, but if she had enough money to buy all those designer shoes, she might have enough money to hire a fancy lawyer. I say go forward as planned. Ok ?"

"Ok." I said, "But do me a favor and find out if Cheryl had a sister."

"I don't know if Cheryl has a sister, but Louise the Loser has a brother." Murphy told me, "And last time I went back to interview him, I noticed he was wearing nail polish."

I stared at the phone. "And when were you planning to give me this information?"

"Emily, all of this is circumstantial. Are you too scared to go forward?"

Murphy knew me well enough now to press the right buttons. No matter how scared I might be, I had no intention of admitting it to Murphy the cop. "See you tomorrow," I said, and I hung up.

Chapter 21

In the fairy tale, Puss in Boots, victims were able to reverse their fortunes by somehow managing to steal and wear the boots of their adversaries.

"Holy Mary, Mother of God, "Murphy said when he opened the closet in my bedroom.

I had done the best I could to clear out some room for him to hide. That was not easy when you owned fifty pairs of shoes and only had two closets. I had ended up putting about a dozen pairs in my oven, and even a few in the bathtub.

The idea was that Murphy would hide in the closet while a couple of his men would watch from across the street. At the crucial moment, Murphy would give them a signal from his cell phone, and they would all burst in and collar the guy.

Of course the success of this depended on a few important elements. First of all, Fifi and the Man had to show. That in itself was very "ify". The more I thought about it, the more I thought that if I was Merissa or Fifi, I would be in Mexico eating tacos and drinking Margaritas. But of course, Fifi wasn't too bright so she might show up. If Merissa let her.

I was cool with the whole idea of being bait back in Murray's Bagel Heaven. As a matter of fact, it seemed kind of exciting. But when I started clearing out my closet, choosing my captive outfit, and working out the details with Murphy, I remembered Shana's dream and I began to wonder. For one thing, here I was, a woman of a certain age, attracted to a cop of a certain age, who was riffling through my underwear drawer helping me choose the proper garments to excite a homicidal pervert.

Murphy fondled a beige satin slip, hesitated, but then tossed it back. He fished out a black lace cammie and rummaged around till he came up with matching bikini panties "Nice." He said, holding it up in front of me "This should do the job."

Embarrassing! Especially since the only thing someone with a shoe fetish really cared about, were the shoes.

But Murphy certainly seemed to be enjoying himself. At least I have some decent underwear. My sex life had not completely stopped.

Then we moved on to the rest of my outfit. It struck me as strange that we were trying to decide between a red sweater and black slacks, or a white, ruffled blouse with a beige skirt—all, of course, to be worn with my black satin stiletto tango shoes—Murphy had picked those out in an instant—in order to capture the interest of a rapist and murderer.

I tried to tell him there was something inconsistent here. I was not supposed to know the killer was coming. So why would I be wearing black satin tango shoes and sexy lace undies alone at 10:00pm at night?

Murphy just shook his head. The killer wouldn't know what I was wearing until he got inside. At that point, all we had to do was keep his excitement up. Whether Murphy had just made this up because he was enjoying himself, or he really did believe it, I would never know.

At any rate, while I pulled open drawers and threw different possibilities on the bed, Murphy roamed around like a German Shepherd, sniffing my perfume bottles, testing the locks on the windows, peering into my cupboards, opening my refrigerator.

I got dressed in the bathroom and pirouetted out. He seemed to approve—a skimpy red sweater that had shrunk in the wash, a short beige skirt and, of course, the shoes.

"Nice shoes," he said.

And I thought I would never wear them again. It was probable if the Shoe Murderer was true to form, he would bring the shoes he wanted me to wear, but this too seemed to make no difference to Murphy. All in all, I felt as if I was dressing up for a Halloween party. Sure took the edge off my worries for a little while at least.

And then Murphy handed me a package wrapped in gold and green striped gift paper. "I almost forgot," he said, "I thought you'd like this."

A gift? *Pour Moi?* This was a pleasant surprise. Maybe danger was an aphrodisiac for Murphy. I thanked him and slowly unwraped it.

There before me in a gold-toned picture frame was the drawing of Kim that the murderer had sent to me and that I had sent to Murphy as evidence.

I felt the tears fill my eyes as Murphy shuffled his feet and looked away. "The lab was finished with it." He explained. And then he looked over at the drawing and said, "Kim was prettier than her picture."

Suddenly it all came together! That sentence rang in my ears and encircled my heart. Charles! Charles the mailman is the killer! "Kim was prettier than her picture!" I repeated. "That's exactly what Charles the mailman said to me at Kim's Memorial!"

I grabbed Murphy's hand.

"What?" he asked me, "What?"

"Charles!" I repeated. "At Kim's Memorial. He said, 'Kim was prettier than her picture!'"

Murphy shook his head. "There were photos of Kim pinned up all over the Chapel. He had met Kim at your shop. Anyone would have said that. What does that prove?"

For me it proved everything. Charles the mailman had delivered the drawing. Charles the mailman had told me Bonita's murderer 'made a mistake' by killing a maid. "Charles wasn't referring to photographs. He would have said, 'Kim was prettier than her photos—or her pictures.' He would have used the plural. But he said 'picture.' He used a singular noun, just as you did. He was referring to this picture—a picture only Kim's most intimate friends, or her murderer would have seen!"

Murphy stared at me for a minute. And then he stared at the picture.

"But what of Cheryl?" he asked me. "You were sure it was Cheryl!" For a moment our eyes locked.

"Let's see who shows up." Murphy said, and he took the drawing from me and put it on the kitchen table facing the door.

We had agreed that Fifi and The Man would ring my bell about 10:00pm. They would make up some reason to buzz me and I would open the door.

Murphy tested his cell, or radio, or whatever that thing was he was wearing on his belt and talked for a minute or two with the guys outside. I hoped they weren't standing under the street lamp in their trench-coats, hoping they wouldn't be noticed. Since I had no window that faced the street, I had no way of knowing what they looked like or where they were.

"Listen now," Murphy put his hand on my shoulder. "We want to catch the guy when he is about to attack you. We don't want any fancy lawyers telling us he just came by to say hello. We want him standing over you with a shoe—maybe he has a knife, or a gun—who knows. Some threatening motion. As soon as that happens, you scream and keep screaming, no matter what happens." He picked up my chin gently until I was looking straight into his blue eyes. "I don't want you taking any unnecessary chances."

"Right." Really now? No chances? In my Tango stiletto's? Who did he think he was kidding?

"I'll buy you a steak dinner after all this is over," he promised me.

I wondered if he had reread Sister Carrie or he was just shooting in the dark. It bothered me that I still could not tell if he had any feelings for me at all, or he was just doing what a cop does.

Murphy bent over and gave me a quick kiss on the forehead. Then he glanced at his watch and settled himself in the closet with the door open.

I sat on the edge of my bed and tried to read. I had chosen Alexander McCall Smith's *NUMBER 1 LADIES DETECTIVE AGENCY*. I liked the way nothing bad ever really happened in those books.

Five minutes after 10:00pm. Ten minutes after 10:00pm. At Fifteen minutes after Murphy got out of the closet and went to the bathroom. Was he about to call off the whole thing? What would happen then? Would he try to stop Merissa and Fifi from leaving the country? Would he arrest me?

Murphy came back into the bedroom like a bullet. "My guys just saw two people coming round the corner. One short and one tall and the little one had a limp."

He ducked into the closet and shut the door hard behind him.

I put down my book and stared at the door.

The buzzer rang. I tried very hard to keep my voice steady."Who is it?"

"Got to...Merissa, she sick," the words were slurred. Since Fifi can't talk, they obviously came from The Man.

"What?" I did not want to make it too easy for them. It was crucial that The Man not suspect that Fifi had set him up.

He repeated it. I waited and then I pressed the buzzer to open the outside door and walked over to my door.

I heard footsteps in the hall and I looked through the monitor Larry had installed. I tried to act as normal as possible, although, I could not remember what normal would be.

Now, I could see both figures. The short one was wearing the hooded sweatshirt I had seen before, but I could see she was a woman. Her light-brown curls framed a sweet, almost angelic, coffee-colored face. Fifi.

The other one was six feet tall with rhinestone glasses, a blonde ponytail, and red gloves. It was Cheryl. Her outfit well coordinated as usual. Chances were good that the red thread found under Bonita's fingernails and in the comb at Kim's place came from her gloves.

What still did not make sense to me was why Cheryl would hate me. Even if I had fired her sister two and one half years ago, I had given her so many great discounts.

I checked to make sure the chain was on and opened the door. I peeked out.

"Fifi! Cheryl!" I said, "What's wrong?"

"Sick. Merissa is sick," Cheryl said. "It's an emergency. We need your help."

I opened the door.

As soon as I undid the chain and opened the door, Cheryl stuck her foot in the door and Fifi ran back out toward the street door.

"Hey!" I got out of my mouth before Cheryl put her gloved hand over it and started pulling me inside.

As soon as I felt that hand go over my mouth I went a little crazy. I started kicking with my stiletto shoes and biting her hand—it was as if my whole body had a mind of its own. The sleeve of her pink blouse moved aside enough for me to see the scratches on her arm.

I held on to the doorway leading into the bedroom and kicked and bit but Cheryl picked me up as if I was a piece of garbage and flung me across the bed. "If you make a sound when I take my hand away, I will cut your throat and slice your face like a salami."

But when she removed her hand, I screamed, "Fuck you!" and was about to throw myself at her when I saw the knife in her hand.

"Fuck you." she said. "That's just what I am going to do."

I must admit that when I first saw the rhinestone glasses and the blonde wig, lopsided now, the ponytail hanging down in front of her nose, I had had an almost overwhelming desire to laugh in her face.

That feeling did not last very long. With the knife in one hand she grabbed my sweater with the other and in one swift movement of the knife, she had cut the sweater down the middle.

I had to wonder if I would be in this position if Cheryl had won the coin toss instead of Harold. "Take off your shoes," she said, her knife making a small arc over her head.

She reached behind her and then dangled a pair of four inch black satin slides, Ralph Lauren, size eight in my face.

I glanced over to the closet. Murphy had told me to scream but I was too scared to scream. Where the hell was Murphy? What was he waiting for? He must have heard our tussling.

I slowly unbuckled one of my shoes. My hand trembled so badly that I could hardly get it off.

All of a sudden, a sneeze—and then a loud pounding from the inside of the closet but the door remained shut. At that moment, I started screaming with all my might.

Whatever was happening in the closet, the instant of distraction allowed me to roll off the bed onto the floor away from my attacker.

Cheryl looked at the closet and suddenly knew something was wrong. But before she could move a muscle, there was a huge commotion at the door of the bedroom and a loud squawking and flutter of wings that could only have come from Henry who lived across the hall.

"Stay just where you are or I will blow your head off!" yelled the unmistakable voice of Angelina Grosso.

I peeked over the top of the bed.

There was Angelina holding what looked like a machine gun.

Cheryl spun around and faced Angelina, her knife held high.

At that moment, I reached down and picked up my tango shoe with its three inch heel. I may be a woman of a certain age but I was not helpless. I hoped my arm was as good as it once was. It was more than a quarter century since I had been a General in Color War at Camp Brookwood. I pushed my arm back the way my friend Sue's big brother had taught me all those years ago and threw the tango with all my might.

It caught Cheryl on the side of her head and she went down, lurching for Angelina. The two of them fell in a heap on the floor, while Henry started dive bombing straight for Cheryl's rhinestone glasses.

At just about this time, Murphy managed to burst through the closet door with his gun drawn.

Squawk! Squawk! Went Henry. Did I mention that he also let loose with some well-placed shit?

"Help! Help! "I screamed with all my might.

"Holy Jesus!" exclaimed Murphy, "A Tommy gun!"

Somewhere in the middle of all this, the two policemen who had been stationed, who knew where, finally burst in. wrestled Cheryl into submission and snapped on some handcuffs.

It was only then that I remembered I was standing in the middle of this crowd in my bra and one stiletto heeled black tango shoe. Whoever said a woman of a certain age could not be the center of attention? Where in hell had I stashed my bathrobe? I ran for the bathroom while the cops did their thing. I hoped they would remember to read Cheryl her rights.

When I emerged, Cheryl was being led out the door by the two assistant cops—in full cop uniform, no less—Cheryl who had lost her wig and glasses in the fray—looked like a real fright. It was habit so I glanced at her shoes and noticed they were Bruno Magli staked heel pumps. A good choice. At least she would not trip over her own high heels when she was carted off to jail.

Murphy and Angelina were sitting on my bed. Henry was perched on Murphy's shoulder with his head tucked under his wing. He had had a hard night's work.

"Where in hell did you ever get your hands on a machine gun?" I asked Angelina.

She threw back her head and laughed. Then she pulled her emerald green kimono with the red hand-painted serpent closed around her bare breasts and picked up the gun from the floor.

She crouched down and aimed her gun at Murphy. "I spent a lot of time in Las Vegas, used to do a couple of shows. Chicago was one." She pulled up her kimono thigh-high. "Used to have a pretty good pair of legs." She lowered the kimono again and looked at me. "Couldn't keep the legs but did keep some of the props."

She handed me the gun. "You know that picture of me and Frank Sinatra?" she said, "I learned a lot from Frankie Boy."

I ran my fingers over the gun. It was made of some light-weight plastic. Up close, it did not look like more than a toy. But from across the room, it worked like a charm.

Murphy shook his head from side to side. How could we both have forgotten about Angelina and Henry?

"I just happened to be going out with my garbage when I saw something strange going on at your door," she explained."

Sure. Right. Like Angelina had not kept a bag of garbage by her door every day for all her years just so she could spy on her neighbors.

"I know you don't usually have visitors at 10:30 at night. Other people in this building? Our friends Peter and Harold?" She rolled her eyes. " But I know Emily here doesn't do much after work that could be fun and games. So I knew something wasn't right." She paused for effect. "And of course, Henry. He always knows when a person is up to no good. Soon as that man comes into the building Henry starts getting upset. He is fluttering all around the apartment, squawking his head off. So I do what any good neighbor would do. I grab my Tommy gun and go to the rescue."

Murphy got up from the bed and adjusted his own gun and holster. "What a pair," He said. "Only in New York City."

"Only on the Upper West Side,' I said, giving Angelina's hand a squeeze.

"Maybe you two could be my special deputies. Do some undercover work. Henry too." At the sound of his name, Henry peeked out at us and flew back to perch on Angelina's shoulder.

Angelina glanced at Murphy and then back at me. She yawned. "Guess Henry and me will be going now." She said. "Glad to be of service."

For a couple of minutes Murphy and I stared at each other. I felt a combination of elation and depletion. Excitement and exhaustion. I never knew they could co-exist.

Then Murphy nodded to me. "I got to go down to the precinct and wrap this thing up," he said. "I could use your other shoe for evidence."

I pulled my robe closer around me and unbuckled the other shoe. I handed it to him and walked him to the door.

"Are you all right?" he asked. He put his arms around me. I wished I had on a prettier bathrobe.

"I'll be fine." I said, my heart beating fast again. Maybe from the closeness of Murphy. Maybe from the closeness of the whole encounter.

"We almost blew it," he said.

I smiled. "What you mean 'we' pale face?" throwing him the line Tonto supposedly said to The Lone Ranger when they were surrounded by hostile Indians. "You're the one who sneezed and got stuck in the closet."

"It was your closet," he threw back. "There's forty years of dust in there. And you should have told me the door sticks."

We clung to each other for a minute. And then Murphy backed away. "I'll be in touch," he said. And he closed the door behind him.

Chapter 22

<small>Archeological evidence shows Egyptian women wore sandals as early as 3500 B.C. that left the foot entirely exposed, a situation they used to their advantage by adorning their feet with jewels.</small>

Phillip Quinn was tall, fair and handsome. Gone today was his tweedy, professorial persona that I had encountered at Kim's. He moved about his living room at 1089 East 85th Street with the relaxed ease of a born aristocrat. He now sat on the dove-colored velvet sofa, feet crossed in his crocodile loafers. His peach short-sleeved shirt had a little alligator on the pocket. Golf clubs rested against a chair in the entry foyer.

That was in stark contrast to Larry, sweaty, his tie at an angle, shirt hanging out of his pants, eyes red from his hay fever, carrying a battered briefcase. And yet, it was Larry who was on the attack.

I stood next to him while he launched our case. After my triumphant encounter with the serial killer, I guess I felt ready for anything. True, Phillip Quinn hadn't murdered my Kim, but he had taken advantage of his position and her helplessness. And he was two-timing his wife besides.

I still shivered when I remembered discovering Bonita's bloody body, but my feelings for Kim had gone much deeper. Call her the child I never had; a symbol of the world's indifference whom I would heroically rescue; a green shoot from an ancient civilization; a dream waiting to be fulfilled. I'm not sure exactly what it was that had made Kim so precious to me, but precious she had been. It might seem a little ghoulish but I carried her ashes around in a little handmade sack I found in Chinatown, that I put inside my purse.

I just couldn't bear the idea that she had lived and died in vain—while Phillip Quinn lived on to pounce on other unsuspecting innocents.

Larry had called me after my unfortunately timed visit to my former home on Central Park West, and tried yet again to apologize. I was adamant, distant, angry, hurt. I hung up on him. For whatever reason, I just couldn't let go of my disappointment in Larry, in my failed marriage. Yes, I was angry at him, but I was angry at myself as well. I was beginning to realize that while he had failed me, I had failed him too. I had not exactly been the happiest companion. I had not made it worth his while to ditch the Big-Assed Babushka. Could not even bring him comfort when he was sick.

My feelings seemed to mellow after I had helped capture the killer—and save Fifi from a life-sentence.

Maybe it was the fact that Fifi had actually shown up—that Merissa had actually been true to her word—that both of them wanted to do the right thing, that finally made me look at my feelings for Larry in a different light. And, I admit it, I had an ulterior motive.

I called him at home one night around 8:00pm when I thought he would be home. He was so surprised to get a call from me I thought he would drop the phone. Told him I had a favor to ask.

There was a silence on the phone.

Maybe he had finally given up on me. I swallowed hard and then sprung my idea. "Here's the thing," I started. "This Phillip Quinn took advantage of a poor immigrant girl who didn't feel as if she had the right to say no. Also, we know he was cheating on his wife. His last girlfriend conveniently disappeared. He is surely guilty of something."

Silence from the other end of the phone.

"Seems to me he owes the world something. There should be such a thing as Cosmic Justice."

"Right." Larry said. "You are beginning to sound like your nutty sister Shana. The only good thing that has come from our separation is that I don't have to see her every Thanksgiving. If you begin to talk about Karma and Past Lives, I promise you I will hang up."

I ignored that and continued. "We don't know if this creep murdered his girlfriend but we do know he will probably continue to abuse his students and his wife. What if we were to confront Mr. Quinn, tell him what we know, and tell him we will go to his wife—his very rich wife who has been supporting him in grand style for the past fifteen years—unless he agrees to set up a Scholarship Fund at the New School for Chinese Immigrants."

For a moment Larry was quiet. All I could hear were chewing sounds. I could picture him eating something really unhealthy like a frozen marshmallow twist. It would be like him to regress to his pre-marital habits.

"That could be called blackmail," he finally answered.

I was ready for this one. "Sure it could be called blackmail. But by whom? Mr. Phillip Quinn, Professor of Art History and Member of the Central Park Conservancy—whose wife sits on the Board of Trustees of the Metropolitcan Museum of Art—is certainly not going to turn himself in. Neither you, nor I nor The New School is going to complain. And the amount we will settle on will hardly be missed."

Larry paused again. Now the sound of ice in a glass. He would be pouring himself a glass of scotch.

"As a lawyer, I could go to jail for something like this."

"I doubt it, we would deny everything. The money would be paid directly to The New School. Who would believe that a prominent lawyer such as yourself would get mixed up in anything like blackmail? Besides, you have no motive. None of the money is going to you."

More silence. At last, Larry said, "You're right. What is my motive? In other words, What's in it for me?"

Was this inevitable? Did Larry ever do anything for nothing?

I sighed. "What do you want?"

"You know what I want. My wife back. I want you to move back into our apartment."

"No deal." I said. "How about we go out next week for dinner?"

Another pause. "You're on."

Guess he could tell I had learned some negotiating skills since I left him.

To give the man credit, though, he did some work. He checked into Quinn's family history and found out Quinn's wife had been left twenty-three million by her father, an oil man from New Mexico. Her mother had been a debutante with a coming-out ball and everything else. Her ancestors had actually been on the Mayflower.

We both felt pretty safe after he looked that up. Didn't think that Mrs. Eudora Quinn, a trustee of half the cultural institutes of New York City, was going to make a fuss over a few thousand dollars a year to a scholarship fund at the New School.

Larry thought it would be best if he contacted Quinn at his office and hinted that he had something important to discuss with him, concerning his Chinese "friend" Kim, and he would prefer to see him at home.

I came along to see the fun.

Quinn did not recognize me as the woman he had encountered at Kim's apartment and at her memorial service. It just goes to show how a woman of a certain age can be invisible to certain kinds of men.

Quinn rang for the maid. He actually had a little bell. And a woman dressed in a maid's outfit, a black uniform with a starched white apron came into the room.

"Will you have something to drink?" he asked after we had introduced ourselves.

"A scotch on the rocks," Larry said.

"I'll take a Perrier."

The maid went out.

"You said you had something important to say to me?"

Larry settled back on his chair. Straight backed, firm. Something one of the Shakers would have made. A chair for delivering bad news if ever I saw one.

"Unfortunately," Larry began, "We know that you had an "irregular," one might say, "unethical and adulterous" relationship with a deceased student named Kim Chang."

Quinn pursed his lips but said nothing.

"Guess you never found that "Chess partner" you were looking for in Kim's apartment building, and had to settle for some sex instead." I blurted out.

Larry threw me a dirty look. Guess my tone was too personal. He reached into his briefcase and took out some papers.

"I have here some statements signed by one "Ma Chew" an elderly Chinese national who lived in the same apartment, where you paid extended visits to a young woman—very young woman—in fact a student—by the name of Kim Chang, and stayed the night."

Wow! I was impressed with that one. Larry had actually gone and interviewed Ma Chew.

Larry shuffled some more papers. "I say very young woman because her birth papers were difficult to trace—somewhere in mainland China—but we have reason to believe she might actually have only been fifteen."

No! I never dreamed my Kim was that young. She had told me she was seventeen. That makes Quinn much more than a low-life. It makes him a sex offender!

Larry looked up from his papers. "Here is a birth certificate obtained by a Missionary Group in Hong Kong where Kim learned English."

Quinn winced at that one. He crossed and uncrossed his legs.

"This is ridiculous! I don't know any Kim. I don't know any Ma Chew. Who are you? Why should I listen to anything you say?" He looked from Larry to me and then back again.

"We're friends of Kim" I said. "Just very special, informed friends."

Larry raised his hand for me to be quiet."We're friends with connections. With the law. With the courts."

Quinn rose from his chair and walked slowly around the room.

"This...Kim..." he said. "There was a student of that name in one of my classes. But I never..."

At that point all conversation stopped because the maid arrived with our drinks.

Larry took a big swallow of his scotch and continued: "Kim is dead now. There is nothing any more that you can do, or not do, to or for Kim"

Quinn went back to his chair. He removed his glasses, blew on them and then polished them with a handkerchief. "How much do you want to keep quiet about this?"

Larry shook his head. "Is this a bribe? I hope we don't have to add the charge of bribery to that of statutory rape and adultery."

Quinn threw up his hands. "Then what do you want? What's your game? Why are you here?"

He looked at his watch. "I have a tennis game with my wife in half an hour."

"I would suggest a better use of your time." Larry said, reaching back into his briefcase.

"My wife and I think that you owe something to people like Kim who will come after her—that in fact, as a Professor at the New School, you have a responsibility to students like Kim—a responsibility so far you have sadly abused."

He smiled at Quinn and then at me. "As it happens, I am a trust and estates lawyer. We can set up quite a nice little charitable trust— a Scholarship Fund for poor Chinese orphans. Asians appreciate education. They are often very good with numbers as well as art. I can even get you a tax break. And I will waive my fee."

We both looked at Phillip Quinn.

He rubbed his chin and stared over our heads out the window onto 85th street.

"I need some time to think," he said at last.

The room was very quiet. After about a minute, Larry said, "Actually, this situation is no longer in your hands."

He looked from me to Quinn and waved his papers. "In fact, the decision is really mine."

He took another swallow of his drink. "If you do not sign these papers, I will inform the proper authorities about the crimes you have committed. On the other hand..." And here he paused for dramatic effect. I did have to give Larry credit for knowing how to hold the attention of his audience. "If you do cooperate, I will be happy to draw up whatever financial arrangements you see fit to benefit the school and its needy students."

Larry pushed the papers he had prepared in front of Phillip Quinn. "I'd advise you to sign these papers. Speak to your own lawyer if you must. You are legally at risk here."

He grabbed my hand and started towards the door of the living room. Before we reached it, Quinn was at our side.

"Please. Please," he said, "sit down. I'll sign your papers. I don't want to speak to my lawyer. There are enough lawyers involved in this already."

Larry moved next to Quinn on the velvet couch and they mumbled legal talk together about percents, payments, and taxes. I stood near the door and wondered if we were really doing the right thing. All I could think of was that cynical phrase: No good deed goes unpunished.

I wondered if I had really helped students who would come after Kim or would they now go to bed with him in fear of losing their scholarship? Did we succeed in scaring Phillip Quinn—or was it really impossible for a leopard to change its spots? And now I was stuck with having dinner with Larry.

And what about me? Here I was trying to help young people, passing judgment about their most intimate relationships and I did not even know how I felt about the man I had lived with for more than twenty years.

Next week would be our twenty fourth anniversary. We were still married. We would celebrate together. I wasn't exactly sure what we would be celebrating. But, as I looked over at Larry's over-weight form, earnestly trying to make sense of a bad proposition—and all for my sake—I found myself thinking that perhaps I would have a good time after all.

When we got outside, I could not help but give Larry a big hug.

"That was great!" I told him. "Where did you get all that information about a birth certificate in Hong Kong?"

Larry smiled and held up his briefcase."Actually, the document I waved in front of him was a certificate of ownership for my new car." And that was the man I had married for better or for worse.

Chapter 23

For centuries the shoe maker's only tool was a pincer, a combination of a gripper and lever that he used for shaping the shoe, aided by his own thumbs and tacks. In a long day, he might be able to complete a few pair of shoes. Now, one automatic toe laster machine can create twelve hundred pairs in one eight hour day.

Murphy sat back on my sofa and loosened his collar. We had finally had that steak dinner. I had broiled a beautiful two inch porterhouse, and served it medium-rare. It cut like a piece of cake. We had baked potatoes with plenty of butter, no green vegetables, and an apple pie with vanilla ice cream.

We both had a Vodka and tonic instead of wine or beer, and old-fashioned seltzer to wash it down.

Simple and satisfying. Comfort food. It was something we both needed.

I served the coffee on the glass coffee table in front of my sofa.

"So in the end I was right about Cheryl and Charles. They were the same person—both guilty, and they both almost killed me."

"Now, now," Murphy corrected me, as he stirred his second cup of coffee. "Let's not exaggerate. Even if I hadn't gotten out of the closet, and Angelina hadn't burst into the apartment, my men would have gotten there in time to save you. Raped, you might have been, but not murdered. And it was me who fingered Charles."

It was true. I was pretty sure about Cheryl but it was Murphy's sentence that illuminated the role of Charles.

I must admit the identity of Charles got to me. The guy was my mailman. Charles Smith. The really polite, quiet, guy you hardly noticed. A man who just became part of the landscape.

Smart.

I shivered. I had suspected José, the guy who delivered the newspapers. I was close but no cigar. José was just too vivid a personality. He stood out.

I made a note to myself to renew my subscription to The New York Times. This mailman, he was as gray as his uniform. I smiled. The gray in Shana's dream. I would have to stop making fun of Shana. The guy was a killer and I couldn't help being annoyed that I had given him free coffee—and who knows how many good deals on designer shoes.

Cheryl-Charles. It made perfect sense. "But wait a minute. I still don't get the motive. Why did he think I killed his sister?"

Murphy smiled. "Charles had a sister—and that sister was Louise the Loser. After you fired Louise, it seems she had so much trouble finding another job, she left the city. Had a friend in Boston, who promised to help her find a job.

"Then one day, she gets run over by a bus."

He chuckled. "It seems Louise could never do anything right. But Charles was really fond of her. So he blamed you for killing her."

At least Murphy had gotten that right. Charles-Cheryl wanted to hurt me with every murder.

"Course Merissa probably knew her better than you. Cheryl was one of her best customers."

I winced. Merissa had had to go down to the station a couple of times and sign some papers, and so did I, but Murphy had kept his word and she was back at work a couple of days after Charles' capture.

Fifi was in jail. Everyone was afraid she would run, even Merissa, so there was no bail. She would either be sent to some half-way house, or psychiatric ward where she could get some help, or spend a few months in jail and be sent home in Merissa's custody.

In the meantime, Merissa had some fences she would have to mend. With me.

I could forgive her trying to save Fifi. I could forgive her concealing whatever she felt she needed to conceal for their safety. But the fact remained that Merissa's complicity had led to the murder of Bonita—with Shana and me as the ultimate targets. And how long would she have let it go on if Murphy hadn't found that footprint?

So at Emily's Place we avoided each other, barely speaking. On the other hand, they both could have gone to Mexico and thrown me to the wolves. In the end Merissa did not desert me. I would have to let time soothe our wounds.

But there were still things that didn't make any sense to me. Particularly after I realized that the killer was my mailman. "But why did he need Fifi to set me up? He had the key to our apartment building. All he had to do would be to ring my bell in his uniform and tell me he had a special delivery. I would have opened the door."

Murphy cocked his head and chuckled. "Human nature. It's all about human nature. Every killer has his 'normal' side. Seems he never committed a crime in uniform. Told us he never wanted to 'bring dishonor' on the uniform. Seems he took the adage 'Clothes make the man' very seriously. When he was Charles, he was too timid to do anything violent. But Cheryl was capable of anything. Almost as if he had a split personality."

There was a lot of truth in the concept of the banality of evil. Outside of the fact that the guy was a cold-blooded pervert killer, he was probably as polite and hard-working as anyone I knew.

"And one more thing I can tell you I bet you didn't know—Goodie One Shoes? That was Charles and Cheryl too."

I shivered. All that horror that could be traced to love of shoes. Louise stole shoes for him. I fired her for stealing. That started the engine of revenge. Cheryl-Charles got turned on by women wearing one shoe—and Fifi loved getting the extra shoe.

For the first time I wondered about my own role in this. Was I as guilty as a drug-dealer, feeding the dangerous habits and appetites of my customers?

Murphy reached for my hand and pulled me down on the sofa next to him. Our thighs touched. Nice. I had not been this close to a man for some time. Three months to be exact, when I had had a very short fling with Marvin Weiss—one night—a friend of a friend who turned out to be a real jerk.

I had obsessed for about an hour over what I would wear for tonight's dinner. I did not want to look too dressed up and scare him off. On the other hand, I did not want to look frumpy. It was bad enough he had seen me in my ratty L.L.Bean bathrobe.

I had rejected my see-through lilac blouse and navy slacks, and finally put on a knee length black A-line skirt and short-sleeve red tee shirt—without an evil eye.

Choosing the shoes took another hour. I finally put on a black sling-back sandal with open toe and two inch clear plastic heel. I may be a woman of a certain age but my legs were still good. I had not jogged all those years for nothing.

I smiled up at Murphy and snuggled a little closer. I liked the clean, scrubbed smell of him. I liked him.

Did he return any of these feelings? It was hard to tell. Sometimes I thought Yes, and sometimes I thought No. I was brought up at a time when a woman waited for the man to make the first move. I could drop some hints. I could create an opportunity like tonight, but I was not about to grab him and kiss him.

Besides, I wanted a man who wanted me. I wanted to be wooed. I did not have enough time or energy to waste on someone who was not really interested in me. In the essential Emily.

But, having finally gotten free of one man, did I really want to be tied up with another? And he had a daughter—a complication as dangerous as a mine field—or as transformative as any spiritual awakening Shana might have dreamed of.

I was really getting ahead of myself here. I would need to take things one step at a time and see what developed.

So where did Murphy stand on all this? That remained to be seen.

He patted the sofa on the other side of him.

"What do you call this color?" he asked me.

I didn't take much more than my books and my shoes from my apartment on Central Park West and I didn't have much money for furniture. I ended up buying my sofa from one of the AIDS thrift shops. It only cost me fifty bucks. But I had it reupholstered for two hundred. Still. These days, that was a deal. I had found a remnant of some gorgeous gray, green, blue, beige color that was no color I had ever seen before.

"I call it 'taupe,'" I told him.

He nodded. "Very high class for a basement apartment."

"It's not a basement. It's a garden apartment."

He smiled. "I would say that any apartment where you look up at the sidewalk is a basement."

I certainly did not feel like arguing with him. But he surely was not trying to add to the mood. I wondered what he was getting at.

"You don't have to live here. You're still married to that rich lawyer guy aren't you?"

So that was where he was going. I wondered if he was jealous. "I'm not living with him; I'm not sleeping with him, and I'm not taking any money from him. I would say to call us "married" is a mere technicality."

He rubbed his chin. "Some people would say what God brought together no one can pull apart."

This was a surprise. Since when was Murphy a good Catholic? Maybe he was looking for excuses to let me down softly.

"Don't tell me you believe in that stuff?" I asked him.

"I'm not sure what I believe any more," he answered.

I squeezed his hand. "Me neither. How about a brandy?"

For a moment we looked at each other. It seemed to me that this was going to be the moment of truth. He was either going to look at his watch and tell me he had to be going—or he would tell me he wanted a brandy and would probably stay the night.

It was at that moment, his cell phone rang.

He fumbled in his pocket and fished it out. He flipped it open. "Yeah. Right! I got it. I'll be there. Give me twenty minutes."

He looked at his watch, and rubbed his hand over his eyes. He rose from the sofa. "I'm afraid I've got to be going. This is what life is like with a cop."

I got up and walked him to the door. "Life is like a lot of things. I'm willing to take what comes, day by day."

"Looks to me like life is going day by day. I got another murder to see to. A man this time. No shoes."

At the door he paused and lifted my chin so our eyes met.

"You're a fascinating woman," he said. "And you cook a mean steak. I'll be in touch."

I wondered if he was telling the truth.

Roslyn Siegel, Ph.D. was born in Brooklyn, close enough to Ebbets Field to see the glow of the stadium lights from her bedroom and she has lived most of her adult life on the Upper West Side of Manhattan.

She has a B.A .from Barnard College with English as her major (a minor in art History) an M.A. in English from New York University, and a Ph.D. in English, from City University.

While in graduate school, obtaining her degrees and teaching part-time at Hunter College; Brooklyn College, New York University and the New School for Social Research, Siegel met, married and helped support a medical student who eventually became a psychiatrist with an office on the Upper West Side. They settled into an apartment in a pre-war building on Central Park West and raised two children: a son Randy and daughter Janine.

During this period, a part-time stint as the Editor of the now defunct, New York State Craftsmen's Newsletter, put her in touch with many of the most important craftspeople working in the 80's and 90's, including the galleries and museums featuring their work. Connections with the artists themselves, and the Museum Directors of The American Folk Art Museum and the Museum of Contemporary Crafts ultimately led her to write many feature articles on the contemporary craft movement for the New York Times, and a book, *DECORATING WITH TILES*, Simon & Schuster. Her articles on art and design also appeared in New York Magazine, The Village Voice, Cosmopolitan Magazine and other periodicals.

Eventually abandoning academia for the world of publishing, Siegel occasionally wrote articles in various magazines, including Publisher's Weekly and The New York Times where many of her short book reviews have appeared. She has also written an art book for children, published in coordination with the American Folk Art Museum and illustrated by works from their collection, CRITTERS A to Z.

Roz Siegel has held Senior Editorial positions at Simon & Schuster, Crown, The Literary Guild Book Club, and Consumer Reports. She has worked as a freelance writer, editor and literary agent, and is currently employed as Director of Acquisitions for a reprint publisher in New York City, MJF Books.

Always interested in crafts and design, Siegel was a serious amateur potter in the 80's and about ten years ago began studying gold-smithing. Recently she was commissioned by the President of Barnard, Debora Spar, to create a commemorative brooch, based on the logo of their newest building, The Diana Center.

Roslyn Siegel still lives with her husband of 48 years, Lloyd Siegel, M.D., in an apartment on the Upper West Side. For many years she has happily jogged around the reservoir in Central Park where some of the action in her novel takes place.

She is the proud grandmother of five: Hallie, Evan, Willa, Josh and Eli.

Goodie One Shoes is her first published novel. Her father never owned a shoe store.